HUMANS, BEING

June 2015

Clunk.

There was something in that clunk, something definitive. It wasn't a slam or a bash, or even a thud; just a deadpan clunk; the death knell of Vic's marriage. A fifteen-year relationship, ten years of marriage, boiled down to one carefully closed door. Their relationship had been lurching from one disaster to another. It had never quite recovered from the unfortunate incident with a bridesmaid at Kathleen's wedding. They'd stuck at it out of a sense of duty; staying together for Elis. 'Working at their relationship,' the people at *Relate* called it. But, deep down, they both knew the only work needed was demolition.

During the long sleepless, sexless nights, Vic had imagined this moment. He'd longed for the ecstasy of release, of getting away from the web of misery. A smile crossed Vic's face as he thought of the possibilities: new women, all the sport he wanted to watch, leaving the toilet seat up, bacon sandwiches for breakfast, lunch and dinner; the true taste of freedom.

Vic stared at the cricket on the screen. He knew exactly what Kylie would say: 'What are you doing wasting your life watching that rubbish?'

He looked at his watch. It was dinnertime. Was he hungry? Not really but Elis would be. Vic opened the fridge, looked at the bacon and smiled. He took out a pepper, mushrooms and other vegetables. He'd make a veggie sauce, Kylie's favourite. A long time ago, before they were married, he'd put Worcestershire Sauce in the recipe, forgetting it wasn't suitable for vegetarians. Faced with the dilemma of throwing the food away, or lying to his vegetarian girlfriend, he'd decided to keep his gob shut and watched guiltily as Kylie cleared her plate. He'd put a few shakes of Lea and Perrins in today, just because he could.

As he chopped the veg, he imagined Kylie behind him. 'Don't slice the onions so thick. Hey, you know I like the mushrooms chunky.' He wouldn't miss her nagging.

HUMANS, BEING

GARETH DAVIES

Cinnamon Press
:: small miracles from distinctive voices ::

Published by Cinnamon Press, Meirion House, Tanygrisiau, Blaenau
Ffestiniog, Gwynedd, LL41 3SU

www.cinnamonpress.com

The right of Gareth Davies to be identified as author of this work has been
asserted by him in accordance with the Copyright, Designs and Patent Act,
1988. © 2019 Gareth Davies.

ISBN 978-1-78864-051-0

Designed and typeset in Garamond by Cinnamon Press. Cover design by
Adam Craig. Cover image: Craig Whitehead/Unsplash.

Cinnamon Press is represented by Inpress and by the Welsh Books Council
in Wales. Printed in Poland.

The publisher acknowledges the support of the Welsh Books Council.

Acknowledgements

Thank you to Tim Rhys and Michelle Angharad Pashley for their patience,
Nikki for coming up with the title and those who believed in me and
encourage me to keep going.

Soon the sauce was bubbling away. He stood the spaghetti in the saucepan. 'Ten minutes, El,' he shouted.

He opened the drawer and saw the *Star Wars* Light Sabre chopsticks that Kylie had bought him. Jesus, he'd opened that drawer a hundred times and not noticed them but, now she was gone, they jumped out at him. He held them next to his chest, fighting the tears and feeling the knot tie a little tighter in his stomach. She was gone.

'Stop being daft,' he told himself, 'ridiculous things, stupid bloody films.' But knowing that lopsided smile would never be for him again, knowing he'd never get to kiss those cheeks, or touch those breasts, and knowing he'd never taste her veggie curry again, was making his heart crack like toffee. He'd thought of her as the last piece in his jigsaw but, with her gone, it was like the whole puzzle had broken. He had to put it back together, knowing that even when it was complete there would always be a piece missing.

Elis loved those chopsticks, although he didn't have a clue how to use them. How would he cope when he found out Mum wasn't just spending a few days at Nana's?

Vic put the chopsticks back and slammed the drawer. Despite the knot in his stomach, the smell of the sauce was reminding him he *was* hungry and the pasta must be ready.

He stood there looking at the pasta slumped in the water. Half of it soggy and cooked, the other half keeping its head above water like an inexperienced swimmer; still as hard as when he'd got it out of the packet.

'Fuck it.'

'You okay, Dad?'

Vic wiped his nose and saw Elis standing in the kitchen doorway, iPad in hand, a concerned look on his young face.

'Yeah, I just messed up the spaghetti; it's gonna be another ten minutes.'

'Cool, more Minecraft,' Elis said. 'Don't worry, Dad. It's only pasta.'

'Yes, El, it's only pasta,' Vic said, turning away just before a tear leaked.

January 2016

Vic looked out over the audience and wondered what the fuck he was doing there. Out of the sixty or so people in the club, about ten were laughing, there were some smiles, but mostly stony faces. The office gossip or the girlfriend's tonsils seemed far more entertaining. At least they were bored, not abusive. He had no energy to deal with hecklers tonight. Knowing his luck, the hecklers would be funnier than he was.

'You could track my relationship with my wife by the size of our beds. We started with a single bed in my old flat and that was plenty big enough for what we needed. Then, when we moved in together, we got a double. It was only a small double but still it felt huge and we used every inch of it. Then, when we bought a place, we bought a king-size. Oh, how I loved that king-size; lots of room to play, experiment and have fun. Look, I've got a photo of it in my wallet. On second thoughts, perhaps I shouldn't show you that.'

Why didn't they laugh at that? That usually got at least a titter.

'I began to wonder what was going on when she suggested single duvets. She used to wrap herself up in it like a caterpillar in a cocoon. It was impenetrable. It was a chastity duvet.'

Nothing.

Bastards!

He pressed on. 'I knew the relationship was in trouble when she insisted on buying a super king-sized bed…'

He looked out at the audience. He hated every single one of them. He took a deep breath and ploughed on. 'It was massive. We were basically sleeping in different postcodes. She could have had a lover in her half and I'd never have known.'

Still no laughter.

'She claimed it was because our son used to come into our bed at night but, when she put the barbed wire down the middle, I began to get the message, it was time to go.'

Three people laughed.

He got the message. Time to go.

'You've been a wonderful audience.' He left the stage to a lukewarm round of applause.

'How was your show last night?' Mia asked.

'Bloody awful, barely a cackle,' Vic said. I don't know why I bother.'

The lunchtime trade was thinning out, leaving the place empty apart from Vic, Mia and the hard core freelancers using the trendy café as office space. Vic stirred his coffee.

'Maybe I should give it up. it plays havoc with my social life. When am I supposed to meet anyone? I've got Elis all week and then work all weekend. It's impossible.' Vic looked at his best friend with that hapless look that he'd perfected. He took a mouthful of coffee.

'You're lucky. You've got the weekends to yourself. Poor Kylie has no weekends. She's looking after Elis.'

'But I'm working.'

'Surely women are throwing themselves at you at gigs.' Mia toyed with her phone.

'I wish.'

Mia's phone buzzed. She looked at it and flipped it over.

'Well okay, how about the mums on the school run? There must be a few desperate housewives there.'

'It's mostly men who drop their kids off.'

'Really? Any nice ones?' Mia tucked a strand of hair behind her ear and smiled.

'Haven't you got Stan?'

Mia looked at her phone again.

'God knows what's going on there,' she said. 'It's been two days since he was last in touch. I don't know if I miss him or if I should report him missing.'

'I don't know why you're still with him.'

'He's lovely.' She hesitated. 'When he's lovely.'

'And a dickhead when he's not.'

Mia nodded. 'But he's all I've got and I don't wanna turn out like you.' She bit the skin on her little finger.

'Charming.' Vic scooped some foam out of his cup.

'Well look at you, moping around, feeling sorry for yourself. You'll never get a woman looking like that.'

'I'm not moping.'

'Could have fooled me. Smile more. Stop waiting for something to happen.' Mia turned the phone over and over on the table.

'Are you expecting a call?'

'Sorry, just force of habit.' Mia, put her phone down.

'Hey—' Vic looked at his watch. 'I better go, I've got to get back to Bristol tonight. Wish me luck.'

'Good luck.'

Mia watched Vic leave the café and turned her phone over. Three messages. She smiled. She began to type out a reply, then hesitated. Her little finger rested on her lip. If she pressed Send, there was no going back; the frogs would be out of the box and, even if she did manage to get them all back in, she'd never be able to clean up the mess. But if she deleted the message, she'd be stuck in the box with the frogs forever. What the hell? Surely frogs couldn't make that much mess, could they?

It'd only taken twenty minutes but felt more like three hours. Mia had been watching the door like a cat ready to pounce. Each time someone walked in, she either cursed them for not being Andy or decided it was a sign she should stop being silly and cancel it. Each minute that passed was another chance to end this foolishness. But she didn't move. Why hadn't she told Vic about Andy? She told him everything about Stan; all the ins and outs, all the broken promises and make-up sex. So why not about Andy? Was it because she was ashamed? No, it was because there was nothing to tell. She was meeting a colleague for coffee, that's all. It was completely innocent and if she told herself that enough times, maybe she'd believe it.

'Hello Mia.'

Mia had abandoned her vigil for less than a minute and that was when Andy walked in. At least she hadn't been staring at the door like one of those love-sick teenagers in her class. She looked at Andy's boyish grin and smiled. The butterflies flitting in her stomach suggested this meeting wasn't innocent.

'What can I get you?' he asked.

'Oolong tea for me, please.' Jesus, where did that come from? She'd never drunk oolong in her life.

'Oolong, ooh, there's posh,' said Andy, with a smile.

She smiled back and watched him as he sauntered over to the counter, completely at ease with himself.

This could be fun, Mia thought.

'Fancy coming back to mine? I've got a lovely bottle of wine.' Andy said, when the drinks were done.

'No, I've got work to do,' Mia said.

'Fine, I'll have to drink it myself.'

'Okay but just wine. No funny business.'

Do you have a cleaner?' Mia said, looking around Andy's flat.

'No, why?' Andy held out a glass of wine.

'Thanks. I've been to single men's flats before and yours is suspiciously clean.'

'Okay, you caught me.' Andy stepped in closer. Mia knew what the look in Andy's eyes meant. She'd let him kiss her but nothing more.

Andy's tongue explored her mouth. 'Let's go through to the bedroom,' he suggested.

Mia nodded but promised herself she wouldn't let this go too far, she'd keep her knickers on and her legs crossed.

Mia listened to Andy panting next to her. She stroked his hairy chest. He cwtched her closer. She looked at the condom and thought how funny they looked after use.

Her phone buzzed. *Now*, she thought, *typical*. She sat up and reached for her bag and looked at the screen.

'I'd better go,' she said.

'Stan?'

'No, it's my son. Wondering where I am.' She swung her legs out of bed.

'Let's do this again.' Andy kissed her bare back. 'Soon.'

As she drove home she wondered what Andy was up to. He didn't seem to care that she was with Stan. Was that weird? Maybe it was a macho thing. Maybe he thought he could win her. She sighed. Never mind what Andy was up to, what was *she* up to?

It was beginning to rain as Vic left the club. It had been another hit and miss night. The routine about Kylie not having a shadow had gone down well but the bed material was getting worse. He put his head down and crossed the road.

'Hey!'

Vic looked around and saw a young woman across the street. Assuming she was a prostitute, he kept walking.

'Vic,' she called out.

The young woman was smiling and heading towards him.

'I loved your set. It was hilarious. I thought I'd say hello.'

This wasn't happening, this didn't happen, not to Vic. It might happen to other comedians but not to him. The rain became more intense.

'Thank you,' he said.

'I wondered if you'd like to go for a drink?'

The woman was older than he'd first thought but pretty, really pretty.

'What, now?' He looked at his watch. His first instinct was to say no, go home and watch YouTube videos. But he remembered Mia's words. *Don't wait for things to happen.* Vic softened his voice. 'Yeah, I'd like that.'

The pub would have been completely empty if it hadn't been for the old timer at the end of the bar, drinking himself to an early grave. They took a seat in a booth at the back. Vic smiled, sipped his sparkling water and picked up a beer mat from the table.

'Did you really cook only half the spaghetti?' Toni asked.

Vic nodded. 'Yep.' He tapped the mat on the table.

Toni laughed a little too enthusiastically and touched Vic's arm.

Vic looked at her. She reminded him of someone. He couldn't place who.

'Why don't you have a beer?' she asked.

'I'm driving.'

'I live just around the corner and the kids are with their dad. You could sleep at mine.'

Vic could guess she wasn't expecting to do too much sleeping. He couldn't remember a woman making the first move, ever. He had to pick up Elis tomorrow and he didn't have his toothbrush or interdental sticks. One night without them would play havoc with his gums. God, sometimes he needed go into a dark room and have a word with himself. He was being offered sex and he was worrying about his gums.

'Great,' he said, 'I'm gasping for a beer.' He pointed at her empty glass. 'Same again?'

She nodded.

While Vic was having a pee, he took the opportunity to get some supplies. He looked at the machine. Jesus Christ! Three pounds for two condoms, what kind of price was that? He had no choice; he put the coins into the slot.

'Hey, calm down, tiger,' Toni said, interrupting their kiss. 'We've got all night.'

Vic moved away. He felt his face flush.

'Don't stop!' she said, pulling him back. 'Just no need to do everything all at once.'

They kissed again and this time Vic tried not to rush things. *Slowly, slowly,* he repeated to himself. He moved his hands with more purpose, taking time to explore her body over her clothes. He nuzzled her neck, the way Kylie used to like, but didn't get much response. So he gave up and went back to her lips. She started undoing his shirt and running her hands through his chest hair.

'I'm going to take a shower,' she said, wriggling her ample arse as she made her way towards the sitting room door.

A shower? Why was she going to have a shower? Vic was just about ready to do the deed and she was off to have a shower. Did she expect him to have one, too? Was this her way of saying she didn't trust his personal hygiene?

Vic looked around. There were children's pyjama bottoms and toys all over the floor. He guessed Toni's kids must be about the same age as Elis; maybe they could have play dates. Maybe he was getting ahead of himself. He picked up a copy of *OK!* magazine and thumbed through it.

'Come up,' Toni shouted. 'There's a towel on the rack and shower gel in the cubicle.' So, she did want him to shower.

Clean and naked, Vic wandered into the master bedroom and put his new purchase on the bedside table. He smiled at Toni, who was lying naked on the bed. It wasn't what he expected. Released from her clothes, she didn't look as shapely as she had when dressed; she seemed to have spread like melting butter. He forced a smile; it was too late to back out. He lay down. Her skin was soft and damp, tender to the touch. She moaned as he stroked her; she was more sensitive that he remembered Kylie ever being. She turned him on his back and started to kiss his chest, moving down to his stomach. He expected her to stop there but she didn't. He closed his eyes and relaxed, enjoying this surprising turn of events. A few minutes later Toni was straddling him. He sat up and eased her away.

'What's wrong?' Toni said.

'Condom,' Vic replied.

'No need,' she said, pulling him back towards her.

'I'd prefer it.'

'It's fine, I'm on the pill.'

Vic was tempted but moved her away and reached for the contraceptives.

Toni rolled her eyes.

*

Vic lay awake, staring at the ceiling and listening to Toni's snore. Had he enjoyed that? It was sex; everyone enjoyed sex, didn't they? She'd seemed to. She'd certainly made a load of noise and had shaken like an earthquake before collapsing back onto the bed and falling asleep. But Vic wasn't so sure. It was different. With Kylie it had become safe, a choreographed routine to be performed once a month. But Toni was a wilder beast. Vic hadn't felt in control. He'd still been trying to make love to Kylie but she wasn't here. He felt limp and dirty. He couldn't wait to get back into his car, drive home, have a shower and wash the experience off. But he couldn't go now. For one, he was still over the legal limit and, two, it would be rude, wouldn't it? He pulled at the duvet and tried to get some sleep.

The rain wasn't heavy, just persistent. The windscreen wipers made a steady rhythm. The morning had been a nightmare. Toni had given him an overly milky cup of tea and made it abundantly clear he'd overstayed his welcome. Vic left his business card on the table, like it had been an audition. He didn't expect a call back; he hadn't passed the test. Vic tapped the steering wheel in time with the windscreen wipers and started singing an old Transvision Vamp song.

Why was he singing that? It must have been ten years since he'd last heard it. Then it dawned on him. He smiled. That's who Toni looked like. Wendy James. Not the Wendy James of 1988 when he'd had an almighty crush on her. But how Wendy James might look now, melted butter and all. Not a bad reintroduction to the world of sex.

'Damn,' he exclaimed, slapping the steering wheel. He'd left the unused condom on the bedside table, one pound fifty up in smoke.

Vic picked up some toys scattered around the room and put them in Elis's toy corner. His son seemed to be dealing with the new circumstances better than him. It probably still felt like an adventure, living with his dad in the new flat Monday to Thursday and going to his mum's for the weekend. For the first time in ages, Vic had read to him that evening. After Elis had dropped off, he watched him quietly. Watching that innocent face sleeping was Vic's favourite time of the day, a time when he thought he might like another child.

Vic poured himself a glass of wine and sat on the sofa. Maybe he was starting to get used to the new circumstances, too. He opened his laptop, stared at the screen, trying to remember the ideas he'd had during the day for some new material. Nothing. Maybe thirty minutes of cyber-slacking would get the creative juices flowing. He opened Facebook.

'No way, no fucking way,' he exclaimed. 'No fucking way.' He stood up and walked around the room, his hand on his forehead. He couldn't believe it. It couldn't be true. He circled the room and went back to the computer to check he hadn't imagined it. He hadn't. He felt sick. He took a mouthful of wine but it tasted bitter on his tongue. He paced the room again. He could feel tears welling in his eyes.

According to Facebook, Kylie was 'in a relationship' with Natalie. Natalie, the bridesmaid from Kathleen and Alfie's wedding. The one he'd been flirting with all night. Kylie had got the right hump with him. Stormed off in a huff, she had. He hadn't done anything, not even kissed her, so he'd always thought Kylie's reaction was over the top and now he knew why; she'd been angry with Natalie, not him.

He took another gulp of wine. He'd known the two of them were friends, he'd even known Kylie had moved in there when she'd walked out on him, but she'd told him Nat had a spare room. He'd assumed Kylie and Elis were sharing; obviously, that wasn't the case. He looked at the photos of the two of them. How hadn't he seen it before? It was so obvious, the holding hands, the smiles. Christ, they were all over each other. It had all looked so innocent when he'd believed it was but now, now he saw it in a whole new light and innocent it wasn't.

Fifteen years and she didn't even have the decency to tell him to his face. Did everybody else know? Did Elis know? Of course he bloody did. Vic shook his head.

He slammed the lid of his computer down, dragged his hand across his eyes and went to get himself a new glass; whisky was the only answer, whisky and music. Surrounding himself with the Housemartins, Bronski Beat and Duran Duran always put a smile on his face; that and half a bottle of whisky.

'Come on, Eileen, blah blah blah blah.' Did anyone know the words?

A movement, a flash of redness broke into Vic's reminisces.

'Dad?'

Vic looked round to see Elis standing there in his Spiderman pyjamas, with his pink pig dangling by the leg.

'Oh, Sorry Elish, did I wake you?' Vic staggered to his feet and scooped up his son. 'Come on, let'sh get you back to bed.'

'Dad, are you okay?' Elis looked quizzically at Vic as they lay next to each other in Elis's small bed.

'I'm fine, El,' he sniffed.

'It'll be all right, Dad.'

Elis was asleep in no time. Vic got up, did his teeth and went back to lie down next to his son. The luminous stars on the ceiling blurred in his vision.

Vic watched Debbie come back from the toilet. He couldn't believe he'd let Mia talk him into a blind date, but, after the disaster of Toni and the shock of finding out about Kylie, it had been decided he needed to be back in the game. Mia had said Debbie was pretty in a kind of 1980s way and she was. She looked like Sheena Easton in her pre-Prince days. But why on earth had she agreed to this date? She had her arms crossed firmly and if she'd sighed once, she'd sighed a million times. She kept reminding him she was missing *Coronation Street* for this.

'Want another drink?' Debbie asked. Vic knew he should say no. Make up some excuse about an early start in the morning. Say something, anything, to get him out of there.

'Go on then,' he said.

The bell for last orders. Vic felt it was signalling the end of a bruising boxing match, a bout Vic had lost on points. He'd spent the last hour speaking to her head, the side of her face, and her chin, but never to her eyes. At last, he could go home.

'Your place or mine?' Debbie said.

'What?'

'Well, Mike's got the kids. I thought you might like to come back.'

This was crazy, she'd barely managed a smile all night and now she wanted sex. Is this what being middle-aged and single was all about? Get your kicks while the kids were with the ex? Company for company's sake? It was cheap, it was demeaning. He didn't really like this woman; there was no way he was going to shag her.

'Yours,' he said.

They barely spoke on the short walk to Debbie's.

'I'll just take a shower,' Debbie said, as soon as she closed the front door. 'Make yourself comfortable.'

Debbie came down in her dressing gown. 'There's a towel in the bathroom for you. I'll be waiting.' She smiled for the first time that evening; it transformed her face.

Did all forty-something women have a shower before sex? Vic pondered as he washed his bits. If so, why? He remembered the thrill of undressing women when he was younger. Remembered half-clothed sex, up against the bedroom door or on the stairs, or even in the lane before they'd reached the house; all this showering was washing away part of the excitement. As he was drying himself, he realised Kylie had started having showers before sex, too. She hadn't in the beginning. It had started after Elis was born. There must be a reason behind it.

Like Toni's, Debbie's body was nothing like he'd imagined it to be. How did women manage to look so different clothed and naked? Who knew? Did he look different in clothes to out of them?

Debbie was more submissive than Toni; she bordered on lazy. Vic decided to cut the foreplay. He reached for a condom.

'No need,' Debbie said.

Twenty years ago, if Vic had suggested unprotected sex, the girls would have kicked him out of bed and called him an irresponsible bastard. These days, the female of the species was encouraging it. Did they want to get pregnant and trap him? Did they like playing an STD version of Russian roulette? Another wonder of the modern world.

'I prefer it,' he said, knowing condoms helped him last a little longer. In fact he was indebted to the prophylactic for making him a much better lover than he otherwise would be.

She rolled her eyes. 'Whatever.'

'You'd better go,' Debbie said. That was brutal, he'd only just removed the condom. 'Mike's bringing the kids over early. I'll call you a taxi.'

Vic was only too happy to escape. Best to leave before it was back to awkward conversations and uncomfortable silences. Funny how showering made it easier to get dressed. There were no socks on radiators and T-shirts thrown over backs of chairs; his clothes were in a neat pile. He listened to Debbie drone down the phone and then they waited in silence for the cab. They said the goodbyes of people who knew they would never see each other again.

Well, Mia, I tried, Vic thought, as the taxi sped through the rain, *but I don't think I'll trust another one of your blind dates.*

Vic looked around the café. There were two hipsters spread across his usual spot. He took a seat by the window and waited for Mia. Vic saw her walking towards the café and smiled to himself; she always made him smile. She pushed open the café door, waved at Vic and made her way towards the counter.

'How did it go with Debbie last week?'

'Weird,' Vic said.

'Weird how?'

'Thought the date was going horribly, then ended up in bed.

Is that how it works?'

'Hmm, not usually. But you got a shag out of it.'

'Yeah, I suppose. Talking of shags, have you seen how expensive condoms are?' Vic took a mouthful of his latte, giving himself a foam moustache.

'Not recently. I don't buy them.' Mia pointed to her top lip: 'Foam Mo.'

Vic wiped the milk away. 'Thanks. You use them though?'

'Yes of course. Well, *he* does,' Mia said. 'I haven't got the hang of femidoms yet. So, how much are they?'

'Three pounds for two in the pub vending machine, not much cheaper in Boots; a tenner for twelve. That's nearly a pound a go.'

'Lucky you're not getting any action, then,' Mia said. 'You're saving a fortune.'

'It doesn't work like that though, does it. Even if you're not getting any action, you've still got to buy the bloody things, just in case.' Vic poured more sugar into his coffee.

'Why don't you bulk buy?'

'I've thought about that, and it is cheaper. But it's bad luck.'

'Bad luck? Why?' Mia shifted her seat to let a woman with a double-buggy squeeze by.

'They'd mock me, wouldn't they? They'd sit there in my drawer, laughing at me. You thought you could get through twenty condoms? Foolish man. Our expiry date is three years away. Think you can use us before then? No chance.' Vic laughed.

Mia didn't. 'Are you trying out new material on me?'

'Yeah and it obviously needs work.'

'It's too long winded but it's got potential,' Mia said. 'Maybe that's why Stan doesn't want to shag me. He's saving money on johnnies.'

'Things still dodgy?' Vic asked.

Mia nodded. She bit her finger. 'I don't get it. It's great when I see him, but he's reluctant to see me. It's barely once a week. A woman has needs you know.'

'I think we're too available,' Vic said.

'Charming!'

'No, not you. We, us. Twenty-first Century, middle-aged people. We all chat to each other on text and Facebook and on the phone, so why bother getting together?'

'Especially when he has the rugby to watch and the darts to play and his mates to drink with. I'm just an afterthought. Something to do at the full-time whistle.'

'Not good.' Vic shook his head.

'It isn't. He makes me feel second-rate,' Mia said. 'Jesus. I don't need a man to do that for me. I can do it myself.'

'I still think you should ditch him, Mia. There's got to be someone else out there for you. What about that Andy bloke you're always talking about?'

Mia felt her face flush as she recalled the previous night with Andy. She bent her head. 'He's a sap.'

'Shame, you could do with some excitement.' Vic looked at his watch, 'I'd better go, meeting Ash for a pint tonight.'

'What, Lily is letting him out?'

'I know.'

'Off you go, I'm going to do a bit of work,' Mia said. 'You boys have fun.'

She watched Vic cross the road and disappear into the car park. Jesus, how did he know about Andy? Had she been talking about him without realising it? Why didn't she tell Vic about him? She didn't know what to tell him, that's why? What was Andy? Her bit on the side? A new boyfriend? A Stan replacement? She liked Andy; he was caring, considerate, but a bit shifty. He wasn't the dependable rock she'd got used to with Stan.

Mia paid the bill and headed out to the street. Her phone buzzed in her handbag. She'd texted Stan earlier, to see if he was free, but Andy usually texted the day after sex; he was nice like that. Who would she prefer it to be? That was the billion-dollar question. It'd be good to know Stan was still interested but a text from Andy would make her feel warm and fuzzy. It might be from her son, or from the bank. The moment of truth.

It was from Stan. He did have time for her, would wonders never cease?

Stan certainly didn't have a cleaner. Mia moved a pair of jeans from the sofa and sat down. Stan appeared with two plates. An action movie and a chilli: Stan's idea of a romantic night. It was true, he made the best chilli in town and Mia didn't mind the odd action movie now and then, but it hardly got the pulses racing.

Mia put her empty plate on the table and poured herself a glass of wine. She watched Stan balance his beer glass on his belly.

'Who's he?' she pointed to the new characters on the screen.

'Sssh, watch the film and you'll find out.'

'But I don't understand how he managed to get hold of the codes.'

'Sssh,' Stan repeated.

Her phone lit up, she checked it, turned the phone face down on the arm of the sofa and sighed. She'd just been to the toilet, so she'd need to wait at least half an hour before she could read the message.

'Who was that from?' Stan said, not taking his eyes off the screen.

'Oh, just my bank,' Mia replied.

Stan grunted.

They watched a superhero throw a villain across the screen. The villain got up and came stamping back.

'I'm thirsty,' Mia said. 'Will you get me a glass of water, please?'

'You've got wine there,' Stan said.

'But I want water.'

'Get it yourself.'

'Stan?'

Stan let out an exaggerated sigh and pressed the Pause button, leaving a villain suspended in mid-air. As soon as he'd stomped out, Mia turned her phone over and found herself looking at the picture of Andy's cock. She'd been hoping for something a little more romantic, but at least he was thinking about her.

'Don't forget the ice,' she called as she typed a reply. 'And can you bring the Pringles?'

She clicked the phone button, darkening the screen just as Stan returned.

'There you are, Your Majesty,' he said, handing her the water and the crisps. 'Anything else I can get you? A pillow? A duvet?' He sat down and pressed Play.

Mia curled up into him. 'Thank you, my prince,' she said and kissed him on the cheek.

February 2016

Ash and Vic sat in pub, nursing pints of Guinness. A Depeche Mode song played on the juke box and both men attempted to sing along.

'So, have you shacked up with Mia yet?' Ash asked, taking a mouthful of beer.

'Certainly not.'

'Come on, she's crazy about you. I've seen the way she looks at you.'

'Bullshit. She's got Stan and she's always trying to set me up with other people. Not exactly the actions of someone who's crazy about me, is it?'

'You mark my words,' Ash said, 'if you clicked your fingers, she'd come running and, in my humble opinion, you're in denial because you like her too.'

'Since when did you become Denise bloody Robertson?'

'Ha ha. Are you working this weekend?'

'Yeah but here, so no overnighters.'

'I'd come and see you but we're going to a dinner party Saturday night, over at Jo's. Such fun.'

'Sounds wonderful.' Vic said. 'Hey, as I'm in town, fancy going to the rugby on Saturday?'

Ash looked down and sucked air in through his teeth. 'Hmm, not sure. I promised Lily I'd go to IKEA. I'll see what I can do.'

Vic knew that was a no. 'Want another pint?' he said, pointing at the two, almost, empty glasses.

'Go on then but it better be my last.'

Before the divorce, Vic hadn't minded going home at ten p.m. *Before* the divorce, he used to get invited to dinner parties. Now, going home at ten felt lame and the invitations had stopped. Not that Vic particularly wanted to go to a dinner party but it would be nice to be asked. He smiled at the barmaid, who smiled back as she put the beers on the bar. One day, he'd build up the courage to ask her out but she'd probably say no, after all, she had to be about half his age.

Vic didn't make it to the rugby. As predicted, Ash had not been able to escape traipsing around IKEA, looking for bathroom furniture, and Vic couldn't face going on his own. Of course, he wished he'd gone but it was too late. He thought about Ash's world; he'd be at that dinner party now. Vic used to hate them, especially when the other guests found out what he did for a living. 'Tell us a joke,' they'd say and they'd never laugh. The joke was on him: being single disqualified you from such things. Vic wondered if Kylie and Nat got the invite, instead.

'Have you played Bristol recently?' Colin Eagle, a fellow comedian, woke Vic from his thoughts. 'Last time I was there, I ended up going back to this lovely lass's flat. She was gorgeous. Remember Wendy James? Transvision Vamp? She looked like her. Not in her prime, obviously, but still. And she was a right little goer. We did it three times and once in the morning as well. And, she made me a cracking fry-up before I left.'

Vic felt his insides tie in a knot.

'You mean, Toni?' asked Wally. 'Yep, I've had her. Gorgeous arse on her.' He outlined the curves with his hands.

Vic looked at Wally with disgust. He was a sleazy, sexist comedian with routines straight out of 1972. He could understand Toni enjoying Colin but Wally? Really?

Vic's mind drifted again. He'd thought he was special but she was obviously working her way through all the comedians on the circuit. And what was all this about three or four times and breakfast in the morning? For Vic, it had been once and a quick cup of tea before being shovelled out of the door.

'Talking of cracking figures, have you seen the barmaid in here?' Wally said, curving his hands over his chest. 'What I'd give to get my head in between those, eh, Vic?'

'I'm sure she's a lovely girl,' Vic said.

'Who cares?' Wally said. 'As long as she's a goer.'

Wally and Colin laughed.

Vic looked down at his phone.

'Ooh, look at you. Who died and made you a feminist?' Wally made like he was holding a handbag. 'Are you jealous that I didn't notice your knockers?'

'No, I just… Oh, it doesn't matter.'

Wally sucked in his abdomen. 'Talk of the devil. Alright darling. I'm free after the gig if you fancy some fun.'

'Can I get you gentlemen any drinks?'

Colin and Wally ordered beers, Vic, a sparkling water.

The barmaid smiled at Vic before leaving.

Vic inclined his head.

'You jammy bugger, I think you're in there, son,' Wally said

'No accounting for taste,' Colin said.

'Leave it,' Vic said.

Out front, the compere had warmed the crowd up, Colin had gone down a storm and the MC was just beginning to introduce Vic. He stood, took a deep breath and made his way to the stage.

'What's the deal with date nights?'

Silence.

'Is anyone here on a date night?'

A few people murmured.

'For those of you who don't know, a date night is what couples do when their relationship starts to become boring. They have a night out together. Isn't that right, sir?' He pointed towards a man who was sitting with a woman on the front row.

The man scowled at him.

Vic's words tumbled out of his mouth without much thought. This must have been the thirtieth time he'd done this material. He used to love it but the words felt bitter on his tongue. Writing a routine about Kylie had seemed like such a good idea. He thought he would find it cathartic but it was doing the opposite. He was living in the past, reminding himself every night of what he was trying to forget. He'd go back home, or back to a sterile hotel, and feel miserable.

He ploughed on. 'My wife and I did it; it was her idea. She said all we did was sit in front of the television screen, grazing, barely talking to each other. So, what did we do for our date night? We went to the cinema. Spent thirty quid on a baby sitter, twenty quid on tickets and popcorn, and ten quid on parking, just so we could sit in front of a screen, grazing, barely talking to each other.'

Nothing. Not even a polite giggle. The smug bastards.

He had three minutes left in his set. He contemplated wrapping it up early. Would anyone notice? The manager would and he was already glaring at him from the back.

Vic snapped. 'Look at you lot. I fucking hate the lot of you. You're exactly what I'm talking about. You're a bunch of idiots. Go out on a date and come to a comedy club. Anything's better than talking to each other. Even listening to me!'

Vic was shaking now. Being off script was exciting. He hadn't got any laughs but his usual stuff wasn't going down any better and at least this was fun.

'So, next time you guys go out, why not go to somewhere where you can talk? Let me recommend a marriage guidance counsellor. My name's Vic Bead. Thank you very much. Good night.'

Vic stood by the bar watching Wally take all the laughs.

'He's a pig, isn't he?'

Vic looked around to see the barmaid standing behind him.

'I couldn't possibly comment,' Vic said.

'Well I can,' she said, 'and I want to slap him. He's not funny either.'

'No comment,' Vic smiled.

'You were feisty tonight,' the barmaid said. 'Not like you.'

Vic was glad to see she was smiling. He shrugged.

'I'm Amanda.'

'I'm Vic.'

'I know.'

This was the moment. The moment when he should ask her to go for a drink. He thought of Ash and how easily the words would slip off his tongue. He thought about Mia's words. He worried, that was the problem. He thought too much. What if she said no? What if she laughed in his face? What if she called him a sexist? A barmaid should have the right to work without being pestered by men. What if she was flirting with him? She was flirting with him, wasn't she? Or was she just being friendly?

'Fancy a drink after you finish?' He'd said it and he wanted to crawl into a hole.

'I'd love one,' Amanda said. 'I thought you'd never ask.'

'I'm sorry the place is such a mess,' said Vic, dashing round picking up T-shirts and toys.

'Don't worry,' Amanda said. 'I didn't come here to judge the cleanliness. I came here to get dirty.'

Vic smiled, put his arms around Amanda's waist and planted a kiss on her lips.

They manoeuvred themselves through rooms, still locked together at the lips, finally collapsing together on the bed.

They'd been kissing for a while and clothes were being shed. This was more like the good old days, no mention of showers or soap.

He thought too soon. Midway through removal of her bra, Amanda said, 'Can I have a shower?'

'Now?'

'Come with me.'

Vic didn't want to but what could he say? Had these women read something in *Cosmo* that said sex was better after a wash? For Vic, it made no difference; it didn't affect his performance. Maybe he should write a routine about it.

'Don't worry,' Amanda said to him, 'It's a compliment.'

Vic stared at the ceiling.

'I'd rather it was over in a flash. Better than you grinding on and on.' She laughed and kissed his cheek.

Vic continued to stare at the ceiling.

'It happens,' Amanda said and kissed him again. 'He'll be up again in no time, you'll see. And meanwhile you've got other tools at your disposal.'

But it never did get up again and Vic didn't sleep well that night. He'd finished quickly before, so that hadn't been a surprise, but he'd always bounced straight back up. This time he'd come in seconds but didn't come back and nothing Amanda had done could raise an encore. She'd teased him, saying it was just resting, but he knew full well it wasn't resting. It was kaput.

When had this happened? When had he only been able to perform once a night? For the last eight years with Kylie, he'd hardly had to use it more than twice a month, twice a night was unheard of. So, at some point in the last eight years, something had changed. Maybe he was running out of erections. A question flashed through his mind: When was the last time he'd had morning glory? He always used to wake up with a toy to play with but these days, nothing. When did they stop? Vic didn't like it; he didn't like it at all. This was mortality in the flesh. A brief moment of hope flashed in his head as he imagined new material for a routine but, God, what was funny about a limp bloody penis? Nothing. Not to him anyway.

The Cimbali machine hissed angrily as the hipster barista made Vic's latte. Mia was ready with a twenty pound note.

'Isn't it my turn?' Vic said.

Mia shrugged.

When the drinks were ready, they took them to a free table at the back of the café. 'How was your gig last week?' Mia said.

'Not great but it picked up a bit at the end.'

'Do tell.'

'Lovely little lass called Amanda, works behind the bar at the club. Looks a bit like Sonia, remember her?'

'Sonia?'

'Liverpudlian pop princess from the eighties.'

Mia nodded. 'You're a sly one. Are you going to see her again?'

'I dunno. I doubt it.'

'Why not?'

'I feel like a kid in a sweet shop at the moment. There's so much choice. I want to try everything. I can't get stuck with the sherbet fountains because there are gobstobbers and dib dabs and love hearts and…'

'Okay, I get the picture.' Mia said. 'Talking of which, look, I saw this and thought of you,' Mia said, showing Vic an advert on her phone.

'Two hundred condoms for fifty quid. Now that is a bargain.'

'That's what I thought, so…'

Vic's face darkened. 'But sadly, it'd be pointless buying two hundred condoms.'

'Why? I thought your love life had picked up. You're bound to get through them before the use by date.'

'It's not that, it's just…' Vic picked up a spoon and put it down again.

'What?'

'It's just, well, I'm beginning to wonder if my erections are finite. You know, if, one day, I'll run out.' Vic looked down at his coffee.

'What the fuck are you talking about?'

'Men eventually have difficulty getting it up. The penis just gives up. It's reached its designated number of erections.'

'That's ridiculous.'

'Is it?' said Vic, as he stirred his coffee. 'What if I only have, let's say, a hundred left?'

'Why a hundred?' Mia scooped some froth into her mouth.

'Any number, really. What if men are given a ration when they're born of, say ten thousand and so, now, I only have a few remaining.'

'Are you having difficulties?'

'No, certainly not. No but, well, let's just say, I've noticed a difference.' He took a mouthful of coffee and leaned in closer. 'When I was younger, I used to have more erections than I knew what to do with. I would even have a contingency, you know, um…' Vic searched for the right word— 'fiddle.'

'You mean a wank?'

'Ssssh, can you say it any louder? But yes, one of them before my girlfriend showed up to ensure I lasted longer when we did it.'

'Really?'

'Yeah, I thought all men did. And it was never a problem, because I knew I could get it up three, four, five times a night. But now, I don't dare play with it up to three or four days before seeing a woman, just in case I've used up my erection quota for the week.'

'Are you being serious?'

'Yes. They've become rare commodities. If I'd known this was going to happen, I wouldn't have wasted so many as a boy.'

'Hang on, are you trying a new routine on me again?'

'No, I'm being serious,' Vic said. 'There's no way I can I buy two hundred condoms, because I'm not sure I have two hundred erections left.'

'So, you're telling me you've given up masturbating, hung up your tissues and cancelled your subscription to YouPorn?'

'God no, of course not. They're the highlight of my week. But I must be careful about when I do it. I've got to plan them in advance.

'You're crazy. Hey, want another coffee? Help me celebrate.'

'Celebrate what?'

'Get the coffees and I'll tell you.'

Vic ordered the coffees and checked his phone. He didn't know what he was hoping for but he was disappointed it hadn't arrived. The barista smiled as she put the coffees on a tray.

'Cheers,' Vic said and returned to the table. He plonked the tray down.

'That was quick,' sad Mia.

'Come on, what are we celebrating?'

'Today is my Divorceavesary.'

'Your what?'

'Divorceavesary. Six years since we signed the papers.'

'Bloody hell, has it been six years already?'

'Yep. And tomorrow is Eddie's sixth wedding anniversary.'

'Christ, I suppose it must be. I'd forgotten he got married straight away.'

'Yes, well, he did; the bastard.'

'Are you doing anything to celebrate this, what was it, divorceavesary?'

'No, except dance on his grave.'

'He's not dead.'

'Shame.'

'Do you ever see him?'

'No, thank god. Even Sid sees him for what he is. He still goes twice a month, bless him. More out of duty, I think, and when they need a babysitter or he needs a new computer game.'

'Six years is a long time. Maybe it's time to…'

'To what?'

'Well, I was thinking about what you said, about you and Stan? One way to keep tracks on him would be to move in with him.'

'No way.'

'Why not?' said Vic, taking a sip of coffee. 'You've been seeing him for, what? Five years?'

'Because I'd end up being his housemaid. I have enough problems picking up after a 16-year-old. But also because it wouldn't be fair on Sid, having another man around the house. It's better like this.' Mia looked at her phone. 'Shit, I better go.'

'Where are you off to?'

'Sid's with his dad, so, I'm gonna have me some Saturday afternoon fun.'

'Things okay with you and Stan then?'

'Yes,' she said. Vic didn't notice that she didn't look at him.

'Great, see you soon.'

It wasn't Stan Mia was having her fun with, it was Andy. His flat was always warm, the sheets were always clean and his love making always eager but, despite feeling satisfied, Mia felt slightly unfulfilled. She listened to his voice through his chest. He was rambling on about something; she enjoyed the sounds more than the words. She touched his face and smiled. She was thinking about the men in her life. There was Stan, masculine and arrogant, Andy, tender and patient and Vic, eloquent and humorous. Vic? How did Vic get in there?

*

31

Vic's alarm clock hadn't woken him. What had roused him was the hardest, stiffest erection he could remember.

'Well, look who's back,' he mumbled to himself and started to gently stroke it. 'Get you,' he said, admiring it under the covers. 'Let's have some fun, shall we?'

It nodded its consent.

Vic looked around to make sure he had tissues close at hand and set to work. Sometimes, he thought masturbation was better than sex. In fact, most times he did. He mentally ticked off the advantages: he knew exactly how to satisfy himself, he didn't have to talk to himself afterwards and there was no pressure to satisfy others.

The bedroom door banged open. 'Dad!'

Vic's hands shot out from under the covers and he sat bolt upright. The blood drained from his face.

'Elis?' He pulled his knees up under the duvet, hiding the tent pole. His son ran and jumped at the bed, Vic moved his body just in time as Elis cuddled into his dad and tried to climb under the duvet. He put his hands by his side blocking entry.

'You can't come in until you say the magic words,' he said.

'Cricket bats,' Elis said.

Vic slid one hand under the duvet and tried to grab hold of his pyjama-bottoms.

'It changed this morning.'

'Why?'

'Security measures.'

Elis giggled. 'Footballs.'

'Nope.'

'Cristiano Ronaldo.'

'Nope.'

'What is it then?'

'It's whatever is written on my bedroom door.'

'There's nothing on your bedroom door.'

'Isn't there? Go check.'

Elis leapt off the bed and ran to the door. Vic yanked his trousers up as Elis came scampering back.

'There's nothing there.'

'So, what's the password?'

Elis squeezed his eyes shut. 'Nothing?'

Vic threw back the duvet. 'Clever boy—in you get.'

'Shall we go for ice cream?' Vic said, later that day.

He watched a smile appear on his son's face. He missed not having Elis at the weekend when they could do stuff together. Half-terms treats were always fun, especially on grey miserable days like today.

'What's Cristiano Ronaldo's favourite flavour, Dad?'

'Um…' Vic scratched his chin. 'Caterpillar.'

'Don't be silly, Dad.'

'No, these footballers have all sorts. I read he likes caterpillar ice cream and Gareth Bale loves grasshopper.'

Elis's eyes widened. 'Really?'

'Yes, it's a delicacy.'

Elis frowned and rolled his eyes. 'Dad!'

'Okay, I confess: I'm messing with you.'

'I know. Natalie says Ronaldo likes mint choc-chip ice cream.'

Vic's jaw tightened. 'She's wrong. I read somewhere it's choco.'

Vic opened the door to the ice cream parlour and stopped in his tracks. Mia was there with a man who was spooning ice cream into her mouth. The man wasn't Stan.

'Choco what?' Elis asked.

'Choco-late, of course,' Vic said, turning and grabbing Elis's hand. 'But, I tell you what, let's go to Baskin Robbins, that's Messi's favourite.'

'Okay,' Elis shrugged.

They sat in Baskin Robbins licking their ice creams in silence. Vic could feel his stomach tying in knots. He was angry at the world. Angry at bloody Natalie and her Ronaldo knowledge, angry at Elis for getting sticky fingers, angry at Mia for God's know what. Why hadn't she told him and why did he feel jealous? Was Ash right? No! He didn't fancy Mia. She was his friend; he'd known her years. She was a mate, wasn't she? Of course she was.

He felt odd because she hadn't told him. Yes, that was it. Nothing more.

'Look Dad, I made this in school last week.'

Vic took the piece of paper from Elis's hand. In Elis's scrawling handwriting it said, 'My Hero,' and under that ten-year-old's tribute to his father. Tears welled in Vic's eyes. He hugged his son. The proudest dad in the world.

After dropping Elis off at his mum's, Vic sat alone in a café, nursing a coffee. Kylie had insisted on having Elis for half of half-term and Vic couldn't face going back to an empty flat. He was trying to work but the woman sat next to him was distracting him. She looked a little like Cyndi Lauper, with her haze of red hair and piercing green eyes. She was concentrating on an array of papers and books strewn across the table and, as she reached for her coffee, she looked up at Vic and smiled. Smiling took years off her. With the curl of a lip, she went from a stern-faced, late-thirties woman to a fresh-faced teenager with a twinkle in her eye.

'Hi,' Vic said. He never did this kind of thing. Usually if he was caught looking at a woman like that, he'd blush and look away and escape as soon as possible. But there was something about this vision in front of him that gave him strength.

'Hello,' the woman said.

'Studying?'

'Well done.' She looked back down at her notepad.

Bugger, thought Vic. 'I'm Vic,' he said.

'Hi, I'm Cariad.'

'Cariad,' he repeated. 'Beautiful.'

'Thanks.' Cariad went back to her books.

Vic closed his eyes and sighed. What right did he have to disturb this woman? She was just trying to study. *Unwanted advances* was the buzzword. Vic tutted when he read about those MPs but here he was, pestering a woman. But how do you know if advances are unwanted? If society discouraged women from asking men out, men had to make advances. It stood to reason that some of them would be welcome and some unwelcome.

'I'm sick of this bloody essay.' Cariad said. 'I'll buy you a coffee, if you keep me company for five minutes.'

Vic smiled. 'No, I'll get it. What will it be?'

'A flat white.'

Vic's smile was broader than the Severn Bridge. He'd not only spent twenty minutes chatting with the best-looking woman in the world, he'd managed to get a date for Thursday night. Dreams did come true.

For a Thursday night, the wine bar was buzzing. Vic had done a short set at a pub across the road and had arranged to meet Cariad for a drink. He looked around for the shock of red hair. There she was, in the corner, with a glass of white wine on the table in front of her.

'Hi, I'm sorry I'm late.'

'That's fine. How was the show?'

'Yeah, could have been better. Can I get you another?'

'No thanks, I'm fine for now.'

Vic returned from the bar with a glass of red and sat opposite Cariad. 'Cheers.'

'Cheers,' she said.

They chatted about this and that and, as Viv watched her laughing, a strange feeling came over him.

It wasn't love, nothing quite as deep. He liked her. That sounded daft; he liked other women too. But this was proper liking. There needed to be a new word; 'loke', somewhere between love and like.

Cariad flicked her long red hair and took a sip of wine. She was saying something about her last job. Vic stared into her green eyes.

'What?' she said.

'What do you mean, what?' said Vic.

'You're staring. It looked like you were going to launch into a speech about baby names or something equally weird,' she said.

Vic wasn't a big fan of playing games but he knew that if there was one thing a woman didn't like, it was a man acting too keen.

'Me? God no. I was just thinking how nice you looked.' He hated the words as soon as they left his mouth. They were true but they sounded desperate. 'So, you were telling me about why you left your last job.'

Cariad's sing song voice enchanted Vic. He loved the way her face changed as she talked. How animated she was. How her green eyes, so grey when serious, were filled with light and mischief when her luscious lips broke into a smile.

Cariad's laughter broke into Vic's thoughts and, without a clue why, he too began to laugh.

'I'm just nipping to the loo before we go,' she said.

'Go?' Vic looked at his watch, Jesus, it was nearly eleven. He watched her walk through the bar. Everything about her was perfect. Okay, she was possibly too slim to be healthy but she wore it well, with just enough curvature to keep him interested.

Vic watched the other men watch her, as she made her way back towards their table, and felt a sense of pride that she was with him, then felt guilty that he'd felt proud, then felt proud again when she sat down and smiled at him. The situation called for bravery.

'Do you want to come back to mine?'

Cariad looked down at her wine, picked up her glass and cleared her throat.

'I've got an early start in the morning, maybe next time.'

Outside the bar, she pecked him on the cheek and headed towards a taxi. Vic sighed and wondered how a wonderful evening had crashed and burned so quickly.

Despite the threat of rain, Vic decided to walk home. He hoped the fresh, damp air would do him good. As he walked, he replayed the night's events; how had he misread the signs? He checked his phone. No messages. *Fine*, he thought, *I'll send her one*. No, it was too soon, or was it? Maybe she was waiting for a message from him. Yes, she was sitting in the taxi right now, staring at her blank phone wondering why Vic hadn't contacted her. A simple, thanks for the lovely evening, wouldn't hurt, would it?

He typed out the words, pressed Send and immediately regretted it.

March 2016

Vic looked at his phone. Five days since the wonderful disastrous date with Cariad and still not a peep. He put his mobile back in his pocket and put some bleach into the trolley. Food shopping with Elis was the highlight of Vic's week. He loved watching his son stride around the supermarket as if he owned the place. And Vic got plenty of smiles from the women there, too. A single dad with a child in tow seemed to be a natural aphrodisiac.

'What's that?' Vic looked at the packet of toilet paper Elis was about to put in the trolley.

'It's what we use at home,' Elis said.

'We don't use that.'

'I meant at *home* home.' Elis said.

Vic took a deep breath. 'Well, at *our* home we use this one, don't we?'

Elis crossed his arms in the way only Elis could. 'Natalie says it makes you cleaner.'

Natalie can kiss my arse, Vic thought. 'Toilet paper's all the same, El.'

'Natalie says it's worth the few extra pennies.'

Yes and she can afford the few extra pennies, Vic thought to himself. Two incomes, half a kid, Natalie's flat. They had a fraction of the overheads Vic had, of course they could afford posh bloody toilet paper. 'Well, we can make do with our usual paper,' he said.

Elis shrugged.

Vic looked at him. That shrug. It was one of Kylie's favourite gestures and Elis had perfected it. '*Home* home' echoed through his mind. '*Home* home'. What did that make where Vic lived? For a split second he felt like leaving Elis there. The people from his '*home* home' could come to collect him. He returned the posh toilet paper to the shelf and, from that moment on, all Vic's attempts to engage his son in conversation were met with grunts.

*

'Hello, is there anybody there?' Mia said, tapping the side of Vic's coffee cup with her spoon.

'What?'

'You were miles away.'

'Sorry. I've been trying to think about how to make my place more homely for Elis.'

'Why?'

'He calls Kylie's place '*home* home'. I guess mine lacks a woman's touch.'

'But that could be a good thing, a man cave.'

'I'm not that much of a man, though.'

'True.' Mia smiled. 'Let me think about it. How are you and your women?'

'My women? You make it sound like I've got a harem.' Vic played with the sugar shaker, trying to tease out the granules one by one.

'Well, am I wrong?' Mia smiled.

Vic put his arms out wide, protesting his innocence. 'There's only Debbie.'

'And Amanda and that, what was her name, Tori?'

'Toni, and they were just one-night things.'

'Poor Debbie.' Mia shook her head. 'I wish I'd never set you two up, now.'

'And why's that?

'You're stringing her along.'

'Am I? I'd say I'd been nothing but honest with her. I've made no promises.'

Mia spluttered. 'You're telling me you've actually had *that* conversation?'

'Kind of. I've told her I'm just getting over a divorce and I'm not looking for another wife.'

Mia shook her head.

'What's that shake for? She's said the same.'

'Be careful, Vic.'

'About what?'

'Does she know about your other women?' said Mia, staring at Vic.

Vic concentrated on his coffee.

Mia continued to fix Vic with her gaze.

'No, of course not.' he said eventually.

'Why don't you tell her?'

'It's none of her business.'

Mia stirred some sugar into her coffee. 'And how would she feel if she found out?'

'I don't know, do I?'

'Yes, you do and that's why you haven't told her. She'd be devastated and you know it. Be careful, Vic,' Mia repeated. 'Us women often say one thing and think another. We'll hang on in there, hoping you change your mind.'

Vic looked at his coffee and then at Mia. 'Like you're doing with Stan, you mean?'

Mia's laugh was cold. She hadn't told Vic about Andy and she felt guiltier as each day passed. Vic was right, she was waiting for Stan to change but was it fair to be having a bit on the side at the same time? And why hadn't she told Vic? She knew the answer to that, really. She didn't want her best friend to judge her.

'And Cariad?'

Vic picked up his phone, twirled it around and put it down again.

'So?'

Vic shrugged. 'It's a mystery. It seemed to go okay. We had a good laugh. I thought there was chemistry.' Vic took a mouthful of coffee and wiped his top lip.

'And?'

'So, I asked her back to mine and...'

'And she blew you out?'

Vic nodded. 'She said she had an early start.'

Mia sighed.

'Bad?' Vic asked.

'Not good. It's not quite *let's be friends* but it's up there.'

'Shit, no wonder she hasn't replied to my texts.'

'Texts? Plural?'

'Only two.'

'Okay, that's not so bad. When was the first message?'

'That evening, just a quick message.'

'What did you write?'

Vic read from his phone. 'Nice night, shall we do it again?'

Mia shook her head.

'Not cool?'

'Very uncool. Never text on the same night. Put your phone away, turn it off.'

'We'd been chatting all week on text. I thought I was being nice and…'

'And women like nice, do they? And the second message?'

Vic looked down, his face turning red. 'It was two days later.'

'Better, not quite so needy. Nothing back? No reply?'

'Nothing, zilch, nada.'

'You've been parked,' Mia said.

'Parked? What's that?'

'Well, it's one down from the friend zone. Think of an old car left on the drive, it's there if you need it but, basically, you know you'll never use it again.'

'Parked?' Vic repeated. 'Great. So, she's left me on the top floor of a deserted multi-storey car park. The floor that's out in the open, where leaves and burger cartons collect on my windscreen and around my tyres. After several lonely months, the police will tow me away and the people at the wreckers' yard will find the unrecognisable corpse of our relationship.'

'Erring on the dramatic side but yes, something like that,' Mia told him.

'So, what do I do now?'

'Nothing you can do. Once you've been parked, the ball's not in your court. She's the one with the keys.'

'You're mixing your metaphors.' Vic said with a sigh. He scooped the last of his latte foam into his mouth.

Mia left the café and headed into the supermarket. She wandered around the aisle thinking of Vic and his women. That boy was

41

going to get himself into trouble if he wasn't careful. Mind you, she was one to talk.

'You're So Vain' was playing over the tannoy and Mia resolved to walk into any party she went to as if she was walking onto a yacht. She practised as she walked down the aisle, but remembered walking onto a boat was usually a hazardous affair, so decided it might be better if she walked into a party like she was walking into a party. She picked up a bottle of white wine, looked at the label and decided it would do.

Was that Andy in the queue for the check out? It looked like him. It was him. She was about to say hi when she froze. Oh fuck, right in front of him was Stan. She stared at them. Stan, short and squat and confident; Andy taller, slimmer, muscular, but somehow effeminate when compared to Stan. She knew she should hide, linger in the frozen food aisle until both her lovers left the store. But she was mesmerised by the pair of them, perfect strangers, completely unaware they were connected by her. Her heart was beating fast but she wasn't scared.

Andy bent down and put something on the conveyor belt. Condoms. Mia watched as Stan said something to Andy. Something about the condoms? Maybe something about getting lucky, maybe asking who the lucky woman was. *It's me, Stan*, she wanted to yell, *I'm his lucky woman*. She felt her face redden.

Stan was being served. He turned to look at the conveyor and then around the shop. Mia backed out of view and bumped straight into an old woman

'Be careful where you're going young lady,' the woman said.

'Sorry, madam,' Mia said, swinging her trolley around and heading towards the safety of the feminine produce aisle, giggling to herself.

Monday's were always weird. The 'come down' day after the highs and lows of performing over the weekend. This one was especially weird, because Vic was performing again tonight. Normally, he could take a day off but, today, it was new material and he needed to familiarise himself with his set. Sick to death of the four walls of the flat, he decided to go and buy milk and sit in a café, rehearsing until it was time to get Elis.

The supermarket was quiet. He made his way directly to the dairy aisle.

'Hey, Vic, how are you?' Vic looked around and found Louise standing behind him. Was she Sally's mum, or little Macy's mum? He knew he'd seen her chatting to Kylie a few times.

'I'm fine, thank you,' Vic said, picking up the milk and putting it in his basket. 'How are you?'

'Better, now I've seen you.' She looked him up and down. 'Such a shame about you and Kylie.'

'*C'est la vie,*' Vic said.

Louise put a hand on his arm. 'None of us could understand how Kylie could leave a catch like you.'

'Well, I'm not such a saint,' Vic said.

'Listen, I've got a free hour, shall we get a coffee?'

Vic looked down at Louise's hand, still resting on his arm. He didn't want coffee with a gossipy mum; he had to rehearse.

'I live just around the corner, why don't we have coffee there?' said Louise, giving Vic's arm a gentle tug.

'Okay, why not?'

As soon as her front door closed, Louise lunged at him, kissing him with a passion.

Was there a rule that you shouldn't sleep with your ex's friends? If so, Vic was about to break it. He hadn't started it but he wasn't about to stop it, either. He held her face in his hands and used his fingers to massage her neck. She moaned and raised one foot up off the floor.

'Let's have a shower,' she said, as she came up for air. Vic rolled his eyes. He'd just had one.

Oral sex. This was another thing his comedian colleagues claimed never happened and, he had to admit, it had rarely happened with Kylie. But he was with his fourth girl since the divorce and all of them had relished the snack put in front of them. He hadn't asked for it. They'd all offered it, free of charge, and seemed to enjoy it. Kylie had treated oral sex like the ironing;

something that had to be done but something she'd rather get someone in to do, if she could.

Maybe it was something to do with having a shower. You wouldn't put an unwashed carrot in your mouth. But a clean, fresh one was often very inviting. Anyway, Vic wasn't complaining; He just lay back and enjoyed it.

There's something delicious about that post-coital state in the middle of the afternoon. The sounds of the suburbs drifting across two sweaty bodies.

'You're good,' Louise said.

'You did all the work,' he said.

'I couldn't have done it without you.' She smiled and kissed him. 'We better get going, unless we want to leave our kids hanging around the school gates. Can you help me strip the bed?' she said. 'I'll need to wash these before Dave gets home.'

Dave. Of course, Louise was married to Dave. Vic saw him occasionally at various kiddies' parties. They'd discussed football together, and cars, and the best way to get to Swanage. Should he feel guilty? He shook his head, as he pulled the duvet out of its cover. Four women since the divorce, one married, one had a comedian collection, one was a one-night stand and one who used him as glorified masturbation—what was the world coming to?

As Vic drove to the school to get his son, 'Kids of America' came on the radio. That was it. Vic had been wracking his brains wondering who Louise looked like. It was Kim Wilde.

Elis was waiting by the school gates with Louise's daughter, Sally. Vic called him over and saw Louise just in front of him. She winked. Vic hoped Elis didn't see it.

'Any homework, Elis?' Vic asked, as they drove home.

'I've got to read ten pages of my book.'

'Great, you can read it to Mia, she's coming to look after you for an hour tonight.'

'Cool.'

*

44

Vic was back at the very open mic gig where he'd first performed, all those years ago. It hadn't changed much. Many of the old faces were there, still hoping they'd get to move up a level. Open mics were the first step on the ladder; if you were lucky you'd get a couple of paid gigs, an agent and get on to the next rung, only coming back down to test drive new material. Vic had been lucky quickly and he knew there were others here who thought he didn't deserve it. He hadn't wanted to come back but his agent had insisted he try out his new stuff before he did it in the clubs. There were about twenty-five or so punters. About half were probably wannabe comedians.

'What was the first record you ever bought? Can you remember?' Vic asked a few people in the front row.

No response.

Vic ploughed on. 'I know, I hate that question, too. The person who asks it is either some precocious music lover who was way too cool for playschool, or…'

The hoped-for laugh didn't come.

'… or someone who's just found out their first purchase happens to be really cool. But it's a lottery, isn't it? I was six when I first spent my pocket money on a seven-inch piece of vinyl. I can see you are impressed. Don't be. Six: at that age, I had no idea the future me would be cursing six-year-old me for making a bad choice. I had no idea that decision would live with me for the rest of my life. If I had, I might have put more thought into it. Why do people judge me now on my six-year-old music taste? People don't expect the first book you ever read to be Tolstoy, or your first bar of chocolate to be eighty percent cocoa with chilli chips, so why should my first record be David fucking Bowie?'

A few people tittered.

Vic rushed on. 'No one takes you aside and gives you a little chat. I was completely unaware, as I was looking through the top forty clutching my pound, that the decision would either set me on the path to being in with the in-crowd, or set me up for a life-time of ridicule. God, when I look back now, I can see how my life could have been different. What if I'd chosen Ian Dury,

Blondie, Sham 69 or Elvis Costello, how great would that have been? Blue Oyster Cult's 'Don't Fear the Reaper' and Patti Smith, 'Because the Night', were both in the charts that week. Christ, I could be up there with Steve Lamaq. But no, I spent my pound on something not very cool at all.'

'What was it?' someone shouted right on cue.

'The Smurfs, 'Where are you all coming from?' Vic shot back.

The audience laughed just enough to give Vic a degree of hope. But he knew it was more of a rant than a routine.

The precocious music lover he was slagging off in the routine was Natalie. The idea for the routine had come to him when Elis had bought home a mix CD that the witch had given him. It was, apparently, all the music she'd been listening to when she was Elis's age. It was full of the most pretentious bollocks you could imagine. The Smiths, Magazine, The Cocteau Twins, Joy Division, early REM and, of course, David bloody Bowie. There was no way Natalie was listening to that when she was ten. Where was the fun? Where was Wham or Haircut One Hundred? Vic knew that the CD wasn't for Elis, it was a coded message to him showing him how bloody great Natalie was. What a free spirit she was. But Elis adored it. Of course he did, Natalie could do no wrong. For Elis, it was like having your cool aunt come to stay, forever. Vic had tried to introduce Elis to the wonders of Erasure and The Communards but Elis had dismissed them, telling Vic that Natalie thought they were naff. So Vic had a choice, play the bloody CD in the car everywhere they went, or risk upsetting his son and, given that Vic felt like he was losing Elis already, they played the CD in the car everywhere they went.

April 2016

For reasons that Vic couldn't work out, Debbie had become a regular fixture in his life. At the start, they'd kept up the pretence of going for a drink or meal before the sex but, soon, they just met at one of their houses on nights when the children were with their ex-spouses. Vic continued to roll his eyes at Debs' insistence on showering and Debs continued to roll her eyes at Vic's insistence on using condoms but they each tolerated the other's needs, just about.

Vic was sat up in bed sipping his wine with Debbie curled up beside him. Neither spoke; they rarely did. She was the one person in his life who he knew least about. They weren't friends on Facebook, or Twitter, or WhatsApp. After she left his flat tonight, he wouldn't know where she was going, or what she did, until the next time they met. Did she have other lovers? Would he care if she did? Did she tell her friends about him? If so, did she say what he was? Friend? Lover? Handyman? What did she think about him? She devoured him with relish when they were together. Their lovemaking had come on leaps and bounds since that uninspiring first time but the rest of it remained a mystery.

'I'd better go,' she said, stretching out like a kitten.

Vic watched her as she called a taxi. This will be the last time, he decided. Next week, I'll say I'm busy and then I'll find a way to finish it.

'See you next week?' Debbie said.

Vic smiled. 'If Kylie will take Elis, then yes,' he said.

'Okay, let me know.' She kissed his cheek and was gone.

Vic drained his wine and checked his phone. He had a message from Mia. Did he fancy a coffee tomorrow? He texted back a yes and went into the kitchen to see if there was any more wine.

*

The coffee machine hissed and spluttered a thick dark liquid trickled into two cups.

'I feel sorry for you women,' Vic said, picking up his latte.

Mia frowned. 'Is this an actual statement, or are you trying out another one of your routines?'

'No, I've just been thinking about things and, well, I've come to the conclusion that women get a tough time of it.'

'And you've only just realised this, have you?'

'Do you remember when Boy George claimed he'd prefer a cup of tea to sex.'

Mia shook her head. 'What's Boy George got to do with it?'

'Bear with me. In some interview with *The Sun* or *The Mirror*, back in about 1984, he said he preferred tea to sex. I remember kids talking about it in school. Back then, I thought he was mad but I don't know, maybe he had a point.'

'You're saying you prefer tea to sex?' exclaimed Mia.

'No, well, yeah, I think that's exactly what I'm saying.'

'I don't get you. When Kylie left you, you were moaning about not getting any and that you wanted to be like a kid in a sweet shop. Now you're getting it regularly, you're saying you'd rather have tea. Are you for real?'

'It's just, well, I don't really enjoy it anymore.'

'Maybe you're doing it wrong.'

Vic raised his eyebrows. 'Hah, yeah right. And that's the point, Mia.'

'What's the point?'

'I'm simply going through the motions and, not wanting to boast…'

Mia rolled her eyes

'… there hasn't been any complaints.'

'So, what's the problem?'

Vic took a deep breath. 'When I was in my twenties, I was keen as mustard, eager to please, hard as nails and as clumsy as the Chuckle Brothers. I fumbled and rummaged my way around women's bodies, lucky not to break a few ribs in the process. For me, caress meant knead, nibble meant bite, and take your time meant give it another twenty seconds. I think I was onto my second girlfriend before I knew what a clitoris was and onto my third or fourth before I accurately located it. I was full of good intentions but I was utterly clueless.'

'Yes, that all sounds about right,' Mia said. 'But, what's your point?'

'The point is, these days I know what I'm doing.'

'Or maybe women have become better actors.'

'Very funny. The thing is I can't be bothered. Remember that song, 'Lazy Lover', by The Supernaturals?'

Mia shrugged.

'You know—' Vic sang the chorus. 'Well, the title says it all and that's me: more interested in doing something else, instead.'

'Charming,' Mia said.

'I know and the thing is, you women are at your sexual peak in your late thirties, whereas men, by that time, are over the hill and descending fast. So, what do women do? Do they choose a man their own age whose libido is deflating like a punctured lilo, or do they try and find a twenty year-old who has the sexual ability of a bull in a china-shop?'

'You're such a romantic. I hope all men aren't like you.'

'How's sex with Stan?'

'Rare.'

'I rest my case.' Vic sat up straight.

Mia looked at her phone and turned it over. There were two messages, one from Stan one from Andy. She took a deep breath. 'Vic, I've got something to tell you.' God, why did she feel like she was breaking up with him?

'You've got a new man.' Vic said.

Mia started. 'How did you know?'

'I saw some bloke spooning ice cream into your gob the other day.'

'So delicately put.'

'So, who is he?'

'Andy.'

'Ah, the famous 'I'm-not-interested-in-Andy' Andy.' Vic did air quotes. 'And what about Stan? Is that over?'

Mia shook her head and looked down.

'You little minx,' Vic said and smiled.

'You don't think it's bad?'

'It's your life, and I'm hardly one to talk, am I?'

Mia got into her car, put the key in the ignition but didn't turn it. She leant back and closed her eyes. As she sat there she ran through the conversation she'd had with Vic. He'd called her a minx. A minx. He'd smiled at her. He'd been understanding. He didn't use any of the awful terms she'd feared he might have resorted to. She'd been so scared about telling him but he'd just shrugged and got on with life, like it was no biggie. She'd been using terms like slut and whore about herself; Vic had used minx. He didn't say what she was doing was wrong. She decided to be more like Vic. Then decided that was probably not the best idea. She started the car and checked her phone again. Another message from Andy, asking her to bring wine.

Clutching the bottle of wine, Mia rang Andy's doorbell. He kissed her passionately and led her straight through to the bedroom. Vic may have been right about Stan but he was only half-right about Andy, he had all the moves and he was able to perform them at any time, in any place. She glanced at the bedside cabinet. She smiled and then frowned. Something wasn't right. It was something about the condoms. Something not good, she realised. The box was only half full. She hadn't seen him since she'd watched him buying a new box in the supermarket. That could only mean one thing: he had another lover. Could there be any other logical explanation? Maybe a friend needed some protection in a hurry? Do men borrow condoms from each other? Do men use condoms for a posh wank? Could he have put some condoms in his jacket pocket in case they ever ended up at her place. Or was it evidence that Andy had other women, or... or... maybe he had other men?

Mia became aware of Andy grunting on top of her. She dug

her nails into his back and groaned to speed up the process. Eventually, he rolled off and cuddled her to him. She lay there in the darkness, wishing she could escape. She tried to forget about it. But she couldn't.

'I should go home,' she said.

'Stay,' Andy said, 'I was just about to open that bottle of wine.'

But Mia was already pulling her clothes on.

Vic enjoyed the warmer days and longer evenings. It meant he could take Elis to the park after school and give him some fresh air.

This was a bonus evening. Kylie had asked if Vic could pick Elis up from school as she had to work late. Vic was only too glad to oblige and happy to be out of the house. He'd spent the day trying to work yesterday's leaking libido conversation into a workable routine. It wasn't working.

Elis marched around the playground with two little girls in tow. He was their Superman and they were his Lois Lanes. The little scamp was better with women than Vic. Vic was whistling a random tune. He rocked back and forth, his hands in his jeans pockets.

'Hi. You're Elis's dad, aren't you?'

Vic turned to see a woman who looked like either Pepsi or Shirlie from Wham. Vic never knew which one was which.

'I am,' he said.

'Hi. I'm Annie, Amy's mum.' Annie pointed to one of the small girls trailing in Elis's wake. 'I think she's got a crush on your boy. It's Elis this and Elis that at home.'

'He's a bit of a lady's man,' Vic said. 'I guess having two mums helps.'

'I guess so,' Annie said, 'but he's lucky to have you, too. I wish Amy had more of a male influence. Her dad's very part-time.'

Over the last few months, Vic had noticed that women mentioned their marital status very early on in conversations. He wasn't sure if they did this subconsciously but he had the impression that it was a sign. 'My boyfriend this...' equalled red light, or, 'My ex that...' equalled amber. 'Her dad's very part-time', was a new one on him. So, how to respond?

'Has anyone ever told you that you look like either Pepsi or Shirlie from Wham?' he blurted.

'Who? I thought Wham was just George Michael and that other fella.'

'Andrew Ridgeley,' Vic said, glancing at Annie and realising she was significantly younger than him. 'Pepsi and Shirlie were the backing singers. You look like one of them.'

'Oh, right. Which one?'

'I never knew which one was which.' Vic brought up a photo of them on his phone. 'Guess,' he said.

'I don't think I look like either of them. But, if I had to guess, then that one.' She pointed at Pepsi.

'Natalie!' Elis screamed.

Vic looked away from Annie and saw Elis running towards his ex-wife's lover. Their hug cut like a cheese wire around Vic's oesophagus.

'Look,' he heard Elis say.

Vic couldn't see what Elis was showing her. It didn't matter what it was. What mattered was Elis hadn't showed it to him. Natalie came over towards Vic and Annie, her hand on Elis's head.

'Hey, pumpkin, go and say goodbye to your friends.'

The cheese wire tightened. *Pumpkin*—? Elis had strictly forbidden Vic from using any pet name, especially out of the house. Even 'El' was frowned upon. How the fuck could Natalie get away with calling him pumpkin?

'Hi, Vic.' Natalie smiled at him. 'Kylie's still at work, is it okay if I take Elis home, just this once?'

Vic returned her smile through gritted teeth. If he said no, Elis would hate him. If he said yes, it would be the tip of the iceberg; soon the rules he made with Kylie when they'd agreed on custody would be out of the window and Vic would be handing Elis over to the devil woman every time.

'No problem. Tell Kylie I'll call her later, regarding homework and things.'

'You can tell me,' said Natalie.

'I'll call Kylie.' Vic watched them natter away as they left and then turned back to Annie. 'I'd better go, a childless man around a playground is frowned upon.'

'Aren't you forgetting this?' Annie held out Vic's phone.

'Oh yeah, thanks. Bye.'

'And Vic…'

Vic looked back.

'I put my number in your contacts, under 'Amy's mum'. My parents will look after Amy most nights. Call me.'

By the time he got home, Vic already had three missed calls from Kylie. He put the kettle on, made a cup of tea and called her back.

'So, he's got to take photos of things from history.' Vic paced his living room as he always did when on the phone to Kylie.

'Vic, you could have told Natalie this.'

Vic took a sip of tea. 'I'd rather discuss our son with you. If you don't mind.'

'You make her feel like a nobody, you know.'

Vic bit his tongue. There were so many answers to that and none of them were good.

'I just think we need to set boundaries, okay?'

'It's homework, hardly a matter of life or death.'

Vic sighed.

'Oh and I know it's not his birthday but we'd like to get him a PlayStation.'

Vic nearly spat out a mouthful of tea all over the phone. 'We said no video games until he was eleven and we said presents only at birthday and Christmas.'

'I know but Natalie says they're educational. We've got to move with the times, Vic.'

'You've both obviously made your minds up, so what's the point?'

He ended the call and poured himself a glass of wine.

'Natalie says they're educational, Natalie says they're educational, bloody shit-face Natalie…' he muttered.

He didn't mind Elis getting a PlayStation, that wasn't the issue, but Vic couldn't afford something of equal thrill value. Vic's flat would become even more inferior. It already lacked the correct toilet pape, and, now, it would also lack a games console. Vic would be the parent without a clue what the latest games were. His son was not only growing up, he was also growing away.

Vic scrutinised Mia. 'I'll buy these.' He gestured towards the barista. 'You find a seat.'

Vic carried his drink to the table. 'Yours is coming. Are you okay? You look terrible.'

'Oh, that's nice," Mia replied. 'Some of us have to work, you know. We can't afford to lounge around all day, drinking coffee.'

'Oh, dear, what's rattled your cage?' Vic smiled.

'Sorry. Bit of a stressful day.'

The barista called out. She made to move to get her drink.

'I'll get it,' Vic said, jumping up to fetch her latte plus a handful of sugar sachets. 'I thought you might need some energy,' he said. 'So, why the bad day?'

'We've been doing peer observations.' Mia sighed, emptying three sachets into her drink.

'What's them when they're at home?'

'I sit in on my colleague's classes and they sit in on mine.' Mia stirred the drink.

'Sounds like a nightmare. I hate it when I see other comics watching me.'

'Oh, it's not too bad. The main problem is it takes up all your free lessons.' Mia took a gulp of coffee. 'Plus, it's excruciatingly boring and *then* we have to discuss the lessons with each other.'

'And, is it beneficial?'

Mia shrugged. 'I suppose. You usually find out that you're not as shit as you thought you were, and that the kids are all bastards, and that we all have the same problems. So, you could say it's cathartic.'

Vic thought about that for a minute. 'I wish they had such things for sex.'

'Did you just say what I think you just said?'

'Depends what you thought I said.'

'Very funny. You're not being serious, are you?'

'About having sex peer observation? Deadly serious.'

'Bloody hell, Vic. That's… that's odd, to say the least.' Mia shook her head as she tried to scoop foam from her coffee cup.

'I've been thinking about the conversation we had the other day.'

'Which one?'

'About preferring tea to sex.'

'Ah, that gem.'

'Maybe I'm doing it wrong. I've learnt everything I know about sex from the schoolyard and second-rate comedians. Would you say they're the most reliable sources of knowledge?'

'Not exactly, no.'

Vic rubbed his temples. 'What if there is something more to it? Something I'm missing and that's why I don't enjoy it.'

'More to it? What could be more? It's innate, isn't it? Not sure there's much you can do wrong.'

'What if there are techniques that I don't know about?'

'You're crazy,' said Mia, shoving her coffee cup aside.

'I'm not. I was trying to write a routine about handshakes…'

'You've lost me. What have handshakes got to do with sex?'

Vic sat back in his seat. 'You can never experience your own handshake, so you never know if you have a nice firm grip or a limp one, and that got me thinking about kisses. You can never know if you are a good kisser, because you can never kiss yourself. And that led me to sex.'

'Ah, at last, proof that the male brain is always a mere three steps away from sex.'

'Anyway, that's why your peer observation idea sounds great.'

'My idea? It's not my bloody idea.'

'It's still a good idea.'

'You might get arrested.'

'So, any better ideas?'

'I'm not the one who needs ideas.'

'Oh, I know,' Vic exclaimed. 'A feedback form.'

Mia's eyes sparked. 'You're saying you'd want women to give you feedback on your performance? Give me a break, I've seen what you're like when you get a bad review in *The Echo*.'

'Hmm, good point.'

'The thing about sex,' Mia said, leaning in a little closer, 'is that it's a negotiated settlement. It's not about how other men do it, or how other women do it, it's about how you do it with the person you're with.'

Vic leaned forward and rested his elbows on the table. 'Go on.'

'Have you ever been with someone new and somehow it felt wrong?'

Vic nodded.

'That's because you're still making love to your previous partner; doing what she liked and not what the person you're with likes. You're making love to the wrong person.'

'Bloody hell, I hope I got her consent.'

'I'm trying to be serious but if you...'

'Sorry, carry on.'

'Okay, basically, I think your problem is not being in a regular relationship and so it's all unfulfilling.'

'I'm seeing Debbie regularly.'

'And how's the sex with her?'

'Terrible at the start, not at all bad now.'

'It's such a shame you don't like her.'

'I know.' Vic looked at his watch. 'Shit, I'd better go.'

'Where are you off tonight?'

'Tonight and tomorrow in Reading. Want to beat the traffic.'

'Have a good one.'

'Who here likes hot chocolate?' Vic looked out at the audience, a few people nodded. 'Yeah, we all do, right? We all like a nice hot chocolate on a cold day. I mean, I don't need to have one every day but, on those icy cold winter days, or maybe after Bonfire Night, it's a lovely, warming treat. Anyone out there a real fan?'

A lady in the front row raised her hand.

'How many types of hot chocolate can you think of?

'Um one, maybe two.'

'There's a café near where I live that sells, wait for it, thirty different types of hot chocolate. Thirty! That's a different type of hot chocolate every day for a month. Thirty different types of hot chocolate. It's staggering. I can think of three: hot chocolate, hot chocolate with cream, hot chocolate without cream. Oh, no, that's only two. So, someone has come up with twenty-eight more types. The question is, why? Surely, there are better things to do than reinvent something that's good enough as it is. My ex-wife used to take ten minutes deciding whether to have the whipped cream or not—can you imagine what her decision-making process would be like with these twenty-eight extra options? We'd be standing there all week.'

Vic was rewarded with a ripple of laughter. But he knew there were too many words.

'We're sold this idea that choice is a good thing but I'm not so sure. I think choice is what causes a sense of ennui, a feeling of regret. We've all heard of plate envy, right? That never existed twenty years ago. Why? Because there was less choice.

'Modern society has disappointment etched into its soul and it's all because of the preponderance of choice. We can't have it all but we want it all. So, imagine, I order the white chocolate with whipped cream and almonds. Great. Then, when it arrives, I can't help thinking I might have been better off with the dark chocolate and chilli espresso, or whatever other nonsense the person sitting opposite me is drinking. So, instead of enjoying what I have, I'm sitting there, sipping my white chocolate with whipped cream, mourning the lost opportunity of the dark chocolate and chilli espresso.'

The routine lacked a killer punchline. The laughter was more polite than raucous. But it was better than stony silence.

Back at the hotel, Vic looked at his Facebook fan page. One message. His face lit up. Only one but it was better than none and zero had been his average over the last few weeks. He clicked on it.

> *» Loved your set tonight Vic. Best comedy I've seen in ages. Hope to catch you in Birmingham. Tina xxx*

Vic smiled. He had a fan. And a keen one, too; he didn't even know when he was playing Birmingham. He clicked on Tina's name. Bleach blonde hair, an angry smile, but nice enough; there was something of the Debbie Harry about her. He wracked his brain to think if he could remember seeing her in the crowd.

He clicked Reply.

> *» Thanks, hopefully see you in Brum.*

Vic checked his phone; no messages. He thought about Googling his name but, the last time he'd done that, it had taken him several whiskies to recover from the vitriolic reviews. He flicked on the TV and surfed the channels; nothing caught his eye. He clicked the kettle on, decided it was too late for tea and clicked it off.

Laying on the bed, he checked his phone again. Nothing. Unlike a sane person, he hadn't given up hope of a reply from Cariad but the thing that upset him the most was there was no message from Elis. There used to be a sweet little good night from him each night when he was at Kylie's but, these days, they were becoming less frequent. It was too late to send a text to Mia, so he flicked back through the channels, trying to find something, anything, he could fall asleep to.

Two hours later, he was still wide awake, staring at the ceiling, listening to three grown men having a drunken argument in the corridor outside his hotel room.

'Whose fucking idea was it to come to Reading?' one voice said.

A second voice yelled, 'Yours, you twat. It was your fucking idea. There's a great comedy club you said.'

A third voice. 'Great club, but the comedy was shite. That second guy on, Jesus, how bad?'

'Hot fucking chocolate, who cares?'

Vic tried to cover his head with a pillow but it was no use, he heard every ugly word. He'd like to hear them try to entertain a room of drunken pricks.

He got up and banged on his door. 'Shut the fuck up!'

Three doors slammed, and silence was restored.

Flopping back onto the bed, Vic checked his phone.

Another message on his fan page, from Tina Long.

> *Thank you so much for replying to me, you made my day. Will definitely see you in Brum. Looking forward to it already.*

Vic could remember when pubs shut at two on a Sunday. Thank god they didn't anymore. He'd called Ash on the way back from Reading, more in hope than anything else. But, amazingly, Lily and the kids had gone shopping, leaving Ash at a loose end and thirsty. They sat at their usual table, near the bar.

'Hey,' Vic exclaimed, 'you're not going to believe this but I've got a fan.'

'You? A fan? Ha, ha, deaf and blind, is she?' Ash laughed to himself and took a swig of beer.

'No.'

'So, had a sense of humour failure, then.'

'Fuck off, Ash. She obviously understands good comedy. She's cute too,' said Vic, holding up his phone.

'Wow, she *is* cute. You sure she's not mixing you up with someone else—give it here.' Scanning through Tina's messages, Ash looked up and frowned. 'Bloody hell, Vic, I'd be careful mate, she sounds like a stalker.'

'Don't be stupid. She's just keen.'

Vic took his phone back and re-read the messages. Was Ash right? No, surely not. He could always turn a positive into a negative. She was just someone who enjoyed his comedy. Nothing to worry about.

'So, will you?' Ash asked.

'Will I what?'

'Go there.'

'You've got a way with words Ash.' Vic smiled. 'I don't know, we'll see.'

'I would,' Ash said.

'Thanks for your input. I'll bear that in mind.' Vic nodded. 'Hey, did I tell you Mia has a new bloke?'

'She's finally left that loser Stan?'

'Not exactly.'

'Ooh, gossip.'

'Yeah, she's started a thing with some bloke she works with. Friends with benefits, I guess.'

'You sound jealous. Are you jealous?'

'Jealous? Why would I be jealous? I've told you there's nothing between me and Mia. There never has been.' Vic took a swig of beer and stared straight at Ash.

Ash smiled at him.

'For fuck sake, I spend as much time with you, and I don't want to fuck you.'

'I'm not Mia.'

'I know that, the point is, I spend just as much time with you, *as a friend*, as I do with Mia, *as a friend*, and so, no, I'm not bloody jealous, alright?'

'So, that's clear then,' said Ash. 'You're jealous.'

Vic took a swig of beer. 'Oh, fuck off. You going to the rugby on Saturday?'

'Aren't we playing Friday this week?

Vic sighed, he knew what was coming next. 'No, it's a Saturday kick-off.'

'Sorry, I think it is my turn to take Elliot to a party,' said Ash.

And there it was. This week's excuse.

'Why don't you ask Lily if she'll swap?'

'I'll see what I can do,' Ash said.

Vic knew exactly what that meant.

May 2016

'How did it go with Annie?' asked Mia, putting her coffee on the table and wiping froth from her fingers with a paper napkin.

'Fizzled out.'

'Oh, I'm sorry. I thought you were sweet on her.'

'I wasn't the problem.' Vic scratched his chin. 'We went out three times and she seemed quite keen, but she didn't want to get, you know, physical.'

'She didn't want to fuck you straight away, so you stopped seeing her? Typical.'

'No, it wasn't like that, it's just…'

'You really are an idiot.'

'Why? She said no, I respected that.'

Mia shook her head.

'Surely, that makes me a good guy?' Vic said.

'Have you never seen a woman order dessert?'

'What's that got to do with it?'

'No, I couldn't possibly… Oh I might just have a little look at the menu…' Mia mimed picking up a menu then putting it down. 'No, I won't… But the *creme brûlée* looks so tempting.' She picked up the imaginary menu again. 'Are you ready to order madam? How big is the *creme brûlée*? About so big madam. Oh, I'll just have a little one, then.' Mia smiled. 'Recognise that?'

Vic frowned.

'You were the *creme brûlée*.'

'I was the what?

'Vic, not every women jumps into bed on the first date. Jesus, if she went out with you three times, listening to your boring stories, it says to me that she was biding her time, making sure you weren't just after one thing.'

Vic let out a sigh and brought his hands down on the table, making a stray spoon tinkle.

'Take me and Andy for example. On our first date, he asked me to go back to his and I said, No. And I meant it but I knew if he asked me asked again I'd say yes. He did ask and I said yes; it was a qualified yes, just wine; No funny stuff, I said. I reckon it took him thirty minutes to get my clothes off, once we got to his. We never did drink much wine. Obviously, Annie has a bit more self-control than me. But she was playing the same game.'

'Why did you say no in the first place?'

'I dunno. I'm old fashioned, I suppose.'

'Old fashioned?'

'Yes. I worry about what my friends think. What the neighbours would think. And what Andy might think. We're programmed by society to behave in a certain way. So, we say no but we don't mean definitely no. We mean, do your mating dance for me.'

Vic shook his head.

'I go through that little charade with almost every man I sleep with,' Mia said.

'But what if he thinks your no means no?'

'He won't, cos they're not idiots like you.'

'So, how do I know if no does mean no.'

'It's a different type of no. If I'm not interested in a man, I use one of these lines: I've just started seeing someone else; It's not you it's me; Let's be friends. What did Cariad say to you— Let's see how it goes?'

'Thanks for reminding me,' Vic said.

'That's a hard no. A definite. What Annie gave you was a soft no. Poor girl. She's probably sitting at home wondering what she did wrong.'

'I'll text her now,' said Vic, reaching for his phone. 'What should I say?'

'It depends. How long since you last saw her?'

'Two weeks.'

'You can't text her now.'

'Why not?'

'She'll think you've been dating someone else and it hasn't worked out. That she's your back up.'

'Fucking hell! Why can't we just say what we mean?'

'Because that, my friend, would make everything too easy.'

They both drank their coffee in silence.

'So, how's your love life?' Vic asked.

'A disaster,' Mia said.

'Why?'

'I think Andy has other lovers.'

'Oh, why?'

'I saw him buying condoms the other day but, when I went around to his place, the box was already open.'

'That doesn't mean he's having an affair.'

'It raises the chances. And another thing—his phone pings constantly when we're together. Who's texting him? Is he flirting on WhatsApp? Or flicking through Tinder? Is that wrong for a man who has a lover? How far does sexting have to go before it's considered being unfaithful?'

Mia stared at her empty coffee cup.

Vic glanced at her before staring down at his own coffee. He adjusted his seat. Looked up again. 'It's like I was saying before; we're all too available.'

'I know, there's so much choice. He's got Tinder on his phone. I asked him about it. He says it's just a bit of fun. But I bet if one of those twenty-something bimbos made him an offer, he wouldn't refuse.' Mia slammed her spoon down on the table. 'He's meant to be my bloke and he's on a dating site.'

'Well, he's not your only bloke.'

'At least I'm honest. He says I'm the only one. But I'm not, am I?'

'Your evidence is circumstantial.'

'Trust me, I know,' said Mia. They sat in silence for a moment. 'Anyway, are you gigging this weekend?'

'Yeah. I've got a Friday-Saturday up in Birmingham, trying to see if I can get a Sunday in, somewhere on the way back to Cardiff.'

'Cool you're busy these days.'

'I know, as the act gets worse, I get more bookings.'

'Reverse Sod's Law.'

'Something like that.'

*

Vic had twenty minutes to tidy up Elis's room before he had to head out. He picked up the books and placed them on the shelf. He turned his attention to the bed. He knew he should change the sheets but he didn't have time. So, he simply plumped up the pillow and shook out the duvet. He sunk onto the bed and looked around his son's room. It was so different from when he was a kid. Back then it was all models and Lego but, these days, Elis did all his building on the iPad.

He sighed and checked his watch. 'Damn,' he exclaimed, 'I'm going to be late.'

Pushing himself up from the bed, a reflection caught his eye. Something tucked down beside the bed. He fished it out. It was a sandwich bag, neatly folded quilted toilet-roll sheets inside. He stroked it. It did feel soft but really? Was Andrex Soft such bad toilet paper that Elis had to bring his own quilted paper? When had his son become so fussy about his toilet paper? Did Kylie and Natalie pack him off with other stuff when he left theirs on a Sunday evening? Vic snatched open the cupboards and the wardrobe. He flung books off the shelf and lifted the mattress, looking for other 'home' comforts. He didn't find any.

'Where do you hide them, you little...'

He realised what he was about to call his son and sat down on the bed. He wasn't very good at this. He couldn't compete with Elis's two mothers. Perhaps Elis should live with them full time. Then he could have all the quilted toilet tissue he needed. He couldn't imagine life without Elis but maybe it would be better for the boy.

Running his hands through his hair, he began to clear the mess he'd made. Forty minutes later than planned, he threw a kit bag onto the back seat of the car, put the address of the hotel into his satnav and set off.

The three minutes before going on stage were always the worst. He always thought he needed the toilet, needed a drink, had forgotten his lines. Today was terrible. The drive had been stressful. The toilet paper issue filled his thoughts until Worcester, when he'd hit roadworks followed, later, by rush hour around Birmingham. On top of that somewhere out in the audience was a woman who wanted to do naughty things to him. He took a deep breath and rolled his neck, tried to shake out the tension in his shoulders.

'Ladies and Gentlemen, make some noise for the wonderful, Vic Bead…'

'So, some of my friends have started doing that hundred days of happiness thing again on their Facebook feeds. Have any of you done that?' Vic was about halfway through his set. He shielded his eyes and attempted to look out into the audience.

'If you don't know it, it's where you post a photo every day, of something that makes you happy. Apparently, it's meant to improve your mental health but, for me, it's the most depressing thing I've ever seen.'

A few people tittered.

'People have posted pictures of glasses of wine, their mothers, and letters from the tax office. They've told stories about smiles from strangers in the street, or eating sweet corn. I swear to God, one of my friends took a photo of his feet and said how nice it was to change into flip flops. Fucking hell, if that's what's making people happy then we need to revisit happiness.'

More laughter. Vic smiled as he peered into the audience again. Was Tina there? She'd said she'd be there.

'But what really depresses me is the implication that no one is having sex. Either that or they're having really, really bad sex.'

He paused. No laughter came. He pressed on. 'If I had sex, any sex—' he could hear Mia's voice in his mind berating him for using cheap sympathy fuck tricks but he didn't care— 'then, that would be the first thing I'd write about. Not that anyone would believe me.'

He heard a feminine giggle. Was that Tina?

'But no one's writing about having mind-blowing orgasms or even fake orgasms. Does this mean they're not having sex? Surely, sex should stand out more than say, having a slice of honey cake, or watching your favourite cat video on YouTube, or changing into flip flops.'

There was a constant rumble of laughter. Enough to keep Vic's spirits up. Vic began pacing the stage. He stopped and glared at the audience.

'But think about it. Imagine you're the partner of someone doing the hundred days of happy and you *are* having sex. How would you feel, after you've humped away for at least six minutes, getting them to the brink of an orgasm, and you don't even warrant a mention? You're lying there, smoking your post-coital ciggie, thinking that performance should make it onto their hundred days of happiness, but when you check Facebook later, all your partner has put up is a photo of an odd shaped carrot.'

Vic stood at the bar, sipping his beer as he watched one of the other acts. He could feel a smile growing. His set had gone well. His new material had actually worked; well, up to a point. This wasn't the case for the guy currently on stage. He was dying on his arse. Vic usually wanted his colleagues to succeed but, recently, it had been Vic making the other comics look good, so, it was nice that it was someone else's turn.

'Hi.'

Vic turned around to see Tina. She was shorter than he'd imagined but she looked just like her profile picture.

'You were hilarious tonight,' she said with a smile. 'Let me buy you a drink.'

Vic thought 'hilarious' was a slight exaggeration but he wasn't going to argue. 'Most kind. I'll have a lager please.'

'New stuff today?'

'It depends. How many times have you seen me?'

'Three times. I've driven up from Reading today to see you.'

'Really? Where're you staying?'

'Nowhere. I'm driving home tonight, then driving back up tomorrow to see you again.'

Driving all that way back home only to repeat the drive the following day should perhaps have rung an alarm bell in Vic's head.

'That's ridiculous,' he said. 'I've got a hotel room. Why don't you stay?'

Tina's face lit up like a Chinese lantern. 'I'd love to,' she said, and squeezed Vic's arm.

'Who's Mia?' Tina said.

'She's my best friend, why?' Vic said, wandering from the bathroom with a toothbrush in his hand. 'Oi, what are you doing with my phone?'

'Sorry, it buzzed.'

'Still.'

'I said sorry.' Tina smiled.

'Hand it over—thank you,' he said, as he made his way back into the bathroom.

'What did she want?' Tina asked.

None of your god damn business, Vic thought. 'Just to see how the gig went,' he said.

'Does she always text you after a gig?'

'Sometimes.'

'Interesting.' Tina bit her lip. 'So, she's your best friend? Isn't that odd? Having a woman as a best friend?'

'I never think about it.'

'Were you ever, you know, lovers?'

'Nope,' Vic said.

'And you don't fancy her?'

'Nope.'

'So, there's nothing between you?'

'She's got a bloke.' Christ, they'd only just met and he was getting the third degree.

'I'm going to brush my teeth now.' Tina slipped off the bed and stomped into the bathroom.

Vic typed a message to Mia and locked his phone.

Tina was back, phone in her hand.

'She's pretty.'

'Who is?'

'Mia.' Tina turned her phone round. Mia's Facebook page stared back at him.

'How did you find her?'

'I searched your profile.'

'Oh.' Vic scratched his chin. 'Do you always stalk people via Facebook?'

'I'm not stalking, I'm just interested in you. Anyway, she's beautiful.'

'Aye, she's lovely,' Vic agreed.

'Can we stop talking about her?' Tina said.

'It wasn't... Yes of course, fine by me,' he said.

'Good. Hey, do you always wear that outfit on stage?'

'Yeah mostly, why?'

'No reason, I just think you'd look better in jeans and a shirt, more relaxed.' She got into bed with a look in her eye that made Vic shudder. She didn't want to do it again, did she? Vic just wanted to sleep but that look in her eye suggested Tina wasn't going to take no for an answer.

The sex had been a frantic first time around, Tina trying to do the complete Karma Sutra in one go. Second time was better but it still felt like their bodies didn't quite fit together.

'Did you like that?' Tina said, once she'd got her breath back.

'Of course,' Vic lied. He couldn't tell her it'd felt like putting the wrong piece into a jigsaw.

'What was your favourite bit?'

'Sorry? My what?'

'Your favourite bit.'

'I liked it all.'

'Good,' she said and kissed him on the cheek. 'It was the best ever!' She put her head on his chest and hugged him.

If that was the best ever, she must have been getting some fairly lousy sex, Vic thought. He attempted to roll Tina onto her side but she clung to him like a limpet.

He listened to her breathing turn to snoring and wished he was alone. Why did people sing about waking up next to lovers? It was nonsense. You spend half the night fighting over the duvet and then wake up to their smelly breath and bed hair. There was the possibility of a routine in that but no doubt it'd already been done. He sighed, untangled himself from Tina's embrace, rolled over and tried to sleep.

Vic had seen Tina twice since the first night. On both occasions, the sex was manic and, on both occasions, she'd quizzed him about Mia. It was as if she was cross-checking his answers with ones previously given. Trying to catch him out. Today, Tina was having a text rant because he'd mentioned he was waiting in a café for Mia.

Vic was halfway through his second coffee when Mia came into the café. He stood up.

'What do you want?'

'Latte?'

'Skinny?'

'No, obese.'

Vic smiled. 'You sit down, I'll bring it over.'

'You know, all the women I date hate you.' Vic said as he put the coffee on the table.

'That's charming, that is.' Mia said.

'Oh, it's nothing personal. In their minds, you're not a person, you're a concept.'

'A concept? Even more charming. Go on, keep digging.'

'It's the *Harry Met Sally* thing,' Vic said.

'I hate that fucking film.'

'I do, too, but it's everyone's point of reference for a male-female platonic relationship. The whole premise is that men and women can just be friends but, because Hollywood has no balls, it has a soppy romantic ending where the two hook up. Debbie's been asking me what the deal is between us and I've just texted Tina telling her I was seeing you and she's into one of those there's-nothing-wrong sulks.'

Mia shook her head. 'Why on earth did you tell her?'

'She asked me, why should I lie?'

'What did she say?'

'Her exact words were,' Vic read from the screen, '*Why don't you just marry Mia?*'

'Ouch.' Mia's eyes widened

'It's nonsense, isn't it? If I said I was seeing Ash, she wouldn't ask me if I'm going to marry him but, because you haven't got a dick, I can't keep my hands off you.'

'Why didn't Kylie mind?'

'Well, cos we didn't see each other that often back then, I suppose. What does Stan think about us?'

'I told him you're gay.'

'What?'

'Well, not exactly, but you were with Kylie, so he didn't mind. Then, when she left you for a woman, I might have suggested that it'd been a marriage of convenience on both sides. He bought it.'

'And Andy?'

'I don't think he cares.' Mia looked wistful. 'He knows about you, he knows about Stan, he just doesn't mind. He likes to have the good times without the hassle. I could have a different man every week and he wouldn't mind. It might even turn him on.'

'Bloody hell.' Vic stirred the remains of his coffee. 'And do you still think he has other women?'

Mia looked at the ceiling. 'I'm pretty sure he does. I try not to think about it.'

'The world's screwed. We're fed this idea of normality— normal life, normal sex life, normal family—but we're all freaks, aren't we? No one I know conforms to the idea of a monogamous, nuclear family.'

'Except Ash.'

'Well, yes, but *is* he? We don't know what goes on behind closed doors.'

'I'm normal too,' Mia smiled.

'Oh yes, because having two men is completely normal.'

Mia threw a sugar sachet at him. 'Tell your bloody women, I'd never marry you in a month of Sundays.'

*

Vic left Mia and headed for the school.

'How was computer club, El?'

'Great, we're learning how to make our own app.'

'Wow. When I was your age we just had chess club.'

'That's cos you're ancient.'

'I had a pet dinosaur, though. Fancy an ice cream?'

Elis nodded so hard Vic thought his head might come loose.

'Come on then, what do you fancy?'

Ice cream was Vic weapon of choice these days. Kylie had been a vegetarian for years and was moving towards veganism, so Vic knew he was the only one capable of satisfying the boy's need for full-fat dairy products.

They sat at the table, Vic with his small tub of chocolate ice cream, Elis with his technicolored sundae.

'That's one big ice cream,' Elis said.

'I bet you don't get that with your mum,' Vic said. He hated the words as soon as they were out of his mouth.

'Sometimes Nat takes me for ice cream.'

Vic hated the reply even more.

'Are you just going to stare at it?' Vic said.

'Can we take a photo?' Elis asked.

'Smile.' Vic clicked and turned the phone around to show Elis.

'Send it to mum,' Elis said.

Send it to mum, for fuck's sake. Kylie never sent photos when Elis was with his mother.

'Okay.' He smiled.

He watched his son shovel ice cream into his mouth, around his mouth and onto the table.

'Good?'

Elis nodded.

They sat in silence, eating their ice creams. Until the phone pinged on the table.

'What did she say?' Elis asked.

'She said you're a little scamp,' Vic lied.

Elis smiled.

Vic typed a reply.

» I'll feed the kid what I like.

'Hey, Dad, I reached level four of *Lego Worlds.*'

'Wow,' Vic said. He sat and listened to words he understood, but concepts he didn't, as Elis told him all about the different computerised Lego worlds. Computerised Lego, who would have thought? At least it didn't hurt when you trod on it.

'Elis, are you up?'

Vic continued to put out the breakfast things, checking the door every few minutes.

'Elis, I won't tell you again.'

Silence.

'Elis.'

Finally, Vic heard movement. He looked at his watch.

'Elis, breakfast is ready.'

A zombie in stripped pyjamas walked past Vic and took his place at the table.

'Elis! Put the iPad down and get dressed, now!'

'But you said breakfast…'

'Go and put your uniform on.' Vic grabbed Elis's school bag. 'Do you need PE kit today?' he called.

There was no response He stuffed the lunch box in the bag and took out a crumpled piece of paper—a letter from the school. He scanned through it. A Roald Dahl costume needed for tomorrow. Thank god it wasn't for today. A tough ask but not impossible. Elis shambled back in to the room, his shirt untucked, his eyes glued to the iPad.

'Elis, why didn't you tell me about this?'

Elis shrugged.

'Put the bloody iPad down and eat your cereal, it's getting cold.'

Elis groaned.

Vic snatched the iPad away.

'Dad, I was playing with that.'

'What do you want to go as? The Fox, the Peach? Matilda?'

'Can I eat this in there?'

'No—no television before school.'

'Nat lets me.'

Vic watched his son spoon cornflakes into his mouth. 'Elis, I asked you a question. What character do you want to go as?'

'Don't care,' Elis said.

'Bloody Matilda it is then,' Vic mumbled under his breath. 'Now, c'mon get your shoes on and do your teeth.'

Elis moved towards his iPad.

'I said, shoes and teeth.'

They sat in silence all the way to school.

'See you later,' Vic said.

Elis shrugged.

Vic watched Elis from the car, as he crossed the playground. How had this happened? Vic had turned into his own mother. So many negatives. So many commands. Don't do this, don't do that. This wasn't how Vic had planned it; he was going to be the cool, easy going dad but he'd turned into a dragon. Of course, Kyle and Nat only had Elis on the weekends when there was no school to get to, no homework to do. No wonder he preferred their place, with the soft toilet tissue. Maybe it would be better if they had him on a school day for a week or so.

Vic checked his phone; three messages from Tina, none from Cariad. He scrolled through his contacts and hit the green button.

'Hi Vic, what's up? Elis okay?'

'Yeah, he's fine. Listen, something's come up, would you be able to take Elis full-time for a couple of weeks?'

'We'd love to. When?'

'If you pick him up from school on Friday as planned and then keep him for the next two weeks, if possible. I've got a few last-minute gigs on the other side of the country.'

'Don't you worry, he'll be fine with us.'

Vic put the phone down and started the car. The rain battered the windscreen. He closed his eyes and rested his head on the steering wheel. He took a deep breath. He was no good at lying but that had been easier than he'd imagined. Too easy, in some respects. Of course, Kylie would jump at the chance to have Elis.

June 2016

Just as Vic stepped out of the shower, the doorbell rang. He pulled on his bathrobe and went through to answer it.

'Tina, hi,' Vic said. 'I was just getting ready for a gig.'

'I know, I've got a ticket. I thought I'd pop in and surprise you.'

'That's, um, nice. Yes, come in.' Vic turned and walked back into the living room.

'No kiss,' Tina said, still standing at the threshold.

'Sorry.' Vic went back and gave her a quick kiss. She yanked him towards her for more.

Vic frowned as the kiss continued. Had he even given Tina his address?

'Want a quick cup of tea?' he said, as he pulled away.

'I was hoping we'd have time for something a little hotter.' Tina smiled and tried to get her hand inside his dressing gown.

'Let's leave it till after the show, eh?'

'You don't seem too pleased to see me.'

'Oh, I am,' Vic said. 'But I get antsy before a show, especially if I'm trying out new material.'

'I can go, let you get ready.'

'No, don't be silly. Sit down, I'll put the kettle on.'

Vic brought two mugs into the living room and placed them on the coffee table. Tina was looking at a photo of Kylie and Elis on the bookshelf. 'Kylie?' she asked.

'Yeah,' Vic said, wondering how Tina knew her name.

'You don't think it's odd?' Tina looked at him. 'Having a photo of your ex-wife.'

'That's my son photo, she's his mother and this is his home.'

Tina mooched around the place, checking out the CDs, picking up photographs and peering at his books. She opened a drawer and closed it again.

'Do you still love her?'

Vic scratched his cheek. 'Who?'

'Kylie.' Tina stared at Vic. 'You do, don't you?' Tina headed for the door. 'I was stupid to come.'

'Tina,' Vic said but it was no good, she'd gone.

Tina hadn't replied to a text and wasn't answering calls. He heard the MC calling his name. Would she be out there? She had a ticket. He took a deep breath and walked on stage. The lights were bright. He squinted but could only make out vague shapes.

'So, the girl I'm with at the moment is pretty kinky, trouble is, I'm not. She said, have you ever had sex in a strange place? Yes, I said, I had sex in Leicester once.'

A small round of laughter.

'There was this one time when we role played. She dressed as a whore and went to sit in a bar. I dressed as a businessman. The trouble was I was running late. By the time I got to the bar, she was already leaving, with another punter. I should have been upset but the money came in handy. We tried it again and all was going well until she wanted me to, you know, go down there, below the equator. I said, when I visit real prostitutes, they don't expect me to satisfy them; that didn't go down well. We finally did it but it wasn't very good. Still, maybe I shouldn't have asked for my money back. Ladies and Gentlemen,' Vic put the microphone back in the holder. 'I've been Vic Bead, good night.'

He did a little bow and left the stage to a good round of applause. His set hadn't been perfect but he seemed to be getting better.

Backstage he took a sip of beer and checked his phone. He had a message from Tina.

» I'm in the bar if you want to say sorry.

'If *I* want to say sorry,' Vic mumbled to himself, but he grabbed his jacket and headed out to the bar.

'Still wearing a suit on stage?' Tina said by way of greeting.

'Yeah, I like it,' Vic replied.

'Well, if you like it, I suppose that's all that matters, but I think you'd look better in jeans and a T-shirt."

'Look, I'm sorry about earlier.' Vic knew his lines. 'I told you,

I'm a bit meh before the show.'

'That's okay, I should have called.'

Vic kissed her and ordered fresh drinks.

'I didn't really like the new stuff,' Tina said.

'Oh, really, why not?'

'Too laddish.'

'It got the laughs, though,' Vic said.

'Is that all you care about, cheap laughs?'

'I'm a comedian.'

'I suppose. I didn't like you talking about me like that. I'm not kinky.'

'You? It wasn't about you.'

'Well, I'm the girl you're seeing, aren't I? Or is there someone else.'

'It's comedy, Tina. Fiction. Not everything is true.'

Tina crossed her arms. 'Another thing,' she said, 'you need to be punchier. The Leicester joke is funny but the wording's wrong.'

'Is that a fact?'

'It is.'

'Well, thank you for your expert analysis, I'll bear it in mind.' Vic took a mouthful of beer and turned his attention to the stage.

'Can we go?' Tina said. She crossed her arms and looked down at the floor.

Vic kept staring at the stage. 'I really wanted to see one of the other acts.'

Tina sighed. 'Whatever.'

'Okay, let's go. I can watch them tomorrow.'

Oh, damn, Vic thought, *I forgot to buy milk, it's midnight, oh well too late now. I'll have to have toast in the morning. I also need to get my other suit from the dry cleaners. Why did I pay for a twenty-four-hour service if I was going to leave it there for a week? I need it for Sunday though. I wonder if the TV people will be there. Thank god Jerry's dropped out; second choice is better than nothing. Good exposure and a nice little earner too. Maybe I can get a bike for Elis. Ash's friend, Danny, sells second-hand bikes, I wonder if he can get a good deal. What are cool bikes these days? Nothing beats a BMX.*

'Vic? Vic? Can we swap positions? I'm getting tired.' Tina climbed off him and lay on her back.

'What? Oh, yes,' he said and put his arm around her.

'Come on, then.' Tina looked at him.

'I thought you said you wanted to stop.'

'No, just a different position.'

'Oh, yes, right, I see.' Vic climbed on top of Tina.

'That's good,' Tina said. 'Do you like it?'

'It's lovely,' Vic answered, as he once again lost himself in his thoughts.

Next morning, Tina was up with the lark. Vic hoped she'd announce she was heading off early.

'What do you want to do today?' she said. 'Neil's got Jacob, so I'm free all day.'

'I don't know. I was going to do some work, and I need to collect my dry cleaning.'

'Why don't we go into town and get some brunch? I'll jump in the shower.'

What women did in the bathroom for the seven minutes they were in there, before they turned the shower on, was a mystery. He went into the bathroom, turned the water on and got in. But with women, there was always seven minutes of near silence. Were they meditating? Stretching? Doing that mindfulness thing? Did they critique their face and body in the mirror? Perhaps the lighting made them look more attractive, who knew?

Vic lay in bed, waiting for the water to start before typing out a message and pressing Send.

'Shit, shit, shit,' he said. He'd sent it to Tina, not Mia.

He read the message.

>> *Not sure if we can meet today. Tina's here.*

>> *I'll see if I can get rid and let you know.*

It wasn't great, not great at all. He was up the creek and the

paddle was long gone. There was nothing he could do. Nothing.
Unless…

The water of the shower was still running. Vic guessed he
had about three minutes. Her bag was on the table, he peaked in
and saw the phone sitting there. It was a chance. He looked at
the closed bathroom door. Time was ticking, ticking. He stared
at the screen. Passcode, what was her bloody passcode?

150576

The phone buzzed its rejection. He flicked the side button
to silence it. Okay, not her birthday. How about the first 6 digits
of her phone number

741271

Another no. The water was still flowing. What if? What if?

271073

The screen dissolved open. The water stopped.

Messages.

Delete.

Screen lock.

Drop the phone.

Run back to bed.

Crunch, the bathroom door opened.

'I love your shower,' Tina said, rubbing her hair with a towel.
'Are you alright?'

'Yes, why?'

'You're sweating.'

'It's seeing your delicious body.'

Vic pulled her towards him.

'Not now, I've just had a shower.'

Vic sat on the sofa and wondered when he'd last showered. He'd
had one before the charity gig on Sunday. Today was Thursday,
so that was four days. Good going. He raised his arm, sniffed
and peered down at his boxer shorts; they weren't looking their
best. Alexander Armstrong said goodbye on behalf of Richard
Osman and himself and then the *Pointless* theme music began to

play. The next episode started. Vic sighed. When the highlight of your day was yet another episode of archived *Pointless*, the pointlessness of your day was highlighted. He picked up four mugs and three plates and took them into the kitchen. He barely recognised the grey, hirsute man he saw in the reflection in the kettle.

'I really should go out,' he said to himself, as he poured water on to another tea bag. 'If only to buy tea.' Vic took his mug back to the sofa and settled down for another edition of the quiz show.

His phone buzzed. It would be Tina again. She'd asked him if she could come down and visit and he'd said no. His phone was still steaming from her onslaught.

'Tuvalu,' he said in answer to a question on the quiz and then pumped his fist when he found out it was right. Another set of credits rolled and Vic pressed Pause. He lay back on his sofa and closed his eyes. He wasn't a completely hopeless case, he could still think clearly enough to know he should pull himself together, but he didn't have the energy or will to act on that thought.

'At least have a shower, then see how you feel,' he said, as he hauled himself up and headed for the bathroom. 'And maybe get rid of the beard.'

Still in his dressing gown but feeling refreshed, Vic picked up his phone. Three missed calls and seventeen text messages. Sixteen from Tina, one from Mia. He opened the one from Mia.

» Fancy a coffee?

Yes, he did. A coffee would be just right.

Mia was already in the café when Vic arrived. He ordered a flat white and joined her.

They chatted about this and that. Vic told Mia about the message mix up. 'I was in a panic. I had to delete the message.'

'I don't blame you.' Mia smiled.

'She's using my birthday as her passcode.' Vic said, stirring his coffee.

'So?'

'Well, isn't that a bit odd?'

'How long have you been together?'

'About a month.'

'A bit creepy.'

'Exactly. What's your passcode?'

'I'm not telling you that.'

'I bet it's not Stan's birthday, is it? Or Andy's, come to that.'

'No, I'm not that sick.'

'And you've been together much longer. I rest my case. And another thing, she criticised my routine. What gives her the right to tell me how to do comedy?'

'What did she say?'

'She said I was too wordy.'

'She might have a point, Vic.'

'Oh, don't you start. Suddenly, everyone's an expert on comedy.'

'She's just trying to help.'

'I don't need help.'

'Look—' Mia tapped the table with her spoon. 'I accept that she's moving quickly on all fronts. But you should be flattered. She's obviously crazy about you. It's good Vic.'

Vic groaned. 'I don't want her to be crazy about me. And, anyway, I think this one is just plain crazy. She turned up at my house uninvited. I'm not even sure I'd given her my address.'

'God, Vic, listen to yourself. What do you actually want?'

'She's already planning our future. I can barely deal with the here and now. It's the main difference between men and women. Men live in the present but women live next week, next month, next year, next decade, next…'

'That's bullshit. It's not men, it's just you, Vic. You're scared of commitment.'

'I'm not scared of it. I've been there. Don't want to go back again.'

'Bloody hell, Vic. Not long ago you were complaining that you didn't have anyone, now you're complaining that you do.'

'What am I going to do? She should be my perfect woman. She's got a lovely figure. She dresses like she stepped out of my imagination. She's intelligent. She likes my comedy, mostly, but somehow we don't click.'

'Leave her.'

'I don't want to leave her. I just don't want it so full-on.'

'So, stay with her but let her know how you feel.'

'That's easier said than done.'

'Give me strength.'

'It's me that needs strength. What do I do?'

Mia picked up a napkin and tore off the edges.

'What's up with you?' Vic asked.

'What if… what if monogamy is an outdated concept?' Mia looked at Vic, her eyes wide.

'Go on,' he said.

'Well, you were talking about normality the other day and it got me thinking. What if we're not meant to be with just one person? What if we need a range of people to satisfy our needs?' Mia tucked her hair behind her ear and smiled.

Vic nodded. 'It's a thought.'

'So, explain to me why I feel so guilty about having both Andy and Stan. There's Andy: loving and caring, great lover but somehow, I dunno, something's missing, he's detached. And then there's Stan: a complete bastard, lousy in bed, if he ever gets into bed, but he's Stan. Neither gives me exactly what I want but, together, I get what I need.'

She crunched the shredded napkin into a tight ball.

'It's like I want Stan to impregnate me and Andy to bring the kid up.' Mia bit the skin from beneath her thumb nail. 'If I ditched Andy, I would be trying to turn Stan into Andy. I'd get pissed off when he was out watching rugby or playing darts. Remember how annoyed I used to get with him before Andy came on the scene? Believe it or not, our relationship is much better now.'

'I've often thought that Kylie and I would still be together if we'd had affairs. I mean, we were perfect for each other, in so many ways, but then the sex ran out and that caused us to drift apart. I miss her. She was my best friend and, now, we hardly talk.'

'Could you have dealt with the jealousy? If you'd known she was out with Derek or Dave or Natalie or Laura, would you have been okay with it?'

Vic glanced around the café. 'Probably not and that's the problem. We're programmed by society to feel guilt and jealousy. The whole world demands 'normal' relationships. One man and one woman. Whatever the reasons—political, societal, religious or health—it doesn't matter: monogamy has become the accepted norm. It's been perpetuated by years of soppy love songs, soap opera plots and even legislation.'

'Vic?'

'Yeah.'

'You're mansplaining.'

'Sorry.' Vic's face began to redden. 'It's just I've been thinking this as well. I'd have hated it if she'd lied to me but I would have hated to know she was out shagging while I was home, looking after Elis.'

'That's it, that's why I feel so shit. It feels so clandestine, so sleazy. I have to make sure Stan doesn't find out about Andy. I'm playing a seedy little game. And I can't tell anyone but you. I bet society would say I was a slut for having two blokes but why? Having two blokes works for me, does that mean I'm wrong?'

'Who gives a shit what society thinks? Whatever makes you happy, go with it.'

'But I can't do that openly, so I have to live a lie and I hate that.'

They drank coffee and peered at each other across the cup rims.

'Do you think they suspect?' Vic asked.

'I don't think Stan does and, I told you, Andy knows about Stan already. He's cool about it.'

'Perhaps he's a post-jealousy man.'

'Or perhaps he's a cynical bastard who just sees an easy relationship. He gets the sex but never has to visit my parents.'

'Or deal with you when you're sick,' Vic said. 'Do you remember, just before she left me, Kylie had that stomach bug. Both ends, really nasty.'

Mia held her hand up. 'Yes, thank you, I remember.'

'Anyway, I think she'd already started her tryst with Natalie by then. So, Natalie was getting the fun while I was clearing up the mess.'

'Charming. No, the real reason is he thinks he can shag around.'

'Still suspect him?'

'Yes but I've got no proof. I bet if I told him I was leaving Stan, Andy would run a mile.'

'Or maybe not. He might think you're special. He could be secretly waiting for you to do just that.'

'Ha, right,' Mia exclaimed.

'And Stan?' Vic asked.

'What?'

'Do you think he has a lover?'

'I dunno. I sometimes think he has. I mean, how can a man have such little interest in sex? He must be getting it somewhere.'

'Or perhaps he agrees with me and Boy George.'

'Whatever, he'd still fly off the handle if he found out about me and Andy.'

'Complicated territory,' Vic said.

Mia walked away from the café with a spring in her step. The more she talked to Vic about her situation, the better she felt. She realised she had nothing to be guilty about. She was giving them what they wanted without demanding what they didn't want. She was providing a service; she should be proud. And who cared if Andy was putting it about, as long as he was there when she wanted him?

'Hello, Ms. Strong.'

Mia stared at the young man in front of her and frowned.

'It's Harry, Harry Edwards. I did my teaching practice at your school last year.'

'Oh, Harry. Hi, how are you?'

'I'm good.'

'Are you still teaching?'

'Yep, I've got a job at St David's.'

'Ouch,' Mia said.

'It's not as bad as its reputation.'

'Sorry. Good for you.'

'Do you,' Harry paused, 'have time for a coffee?'

'Well…' Mia looked at her watch. 'I've just had…'

'Oh, Okay, no problem, I, well, I…' Harry's face and neck reddened.

'Go on, then, but I don't have long.'

Harry smiled and walked beside Mia, as she retraced her steps back to the café she'd just left. Harry insisted on buying the drinks. Mia went for oolong tea.

'So, I walk into the class and they all had their tops open,' Harry said, 'the boys and the girls. I didn't know where to look.'

'No way, what did you do?'

'I ran out of the classroom and got the head of year but, by the time we got back, they were sitting there like model students.'

Mia laughed and reached across to pat Harry's arm.

'It's not funny,'

'Sorry. I'm laughing with you. Perhaps we should all wear cameras, like policemen do.'

'It's hard, isn't it?' Harry said.

'You'll get the hang of it.' Mia smiled at him and patted his arm again. 'The first year is always the hardest. Look, I've got to go. Maybe we could do this again?'

Harry face lit up. He got his phone out and Mia reeled off her number.

By the middle of the following week, Vic was back on his feet. His weekend gigs had gone well and he'd gone to a barber for a Turkish shave. He hurried along the path and checked his watch; he'd only be a couple of minutes late. His phone rang. He looked at the screen—Kylie. *I don't have time for this*, he thought. He let it ring a few more times before sliding his thumb across the screen.

'Hi, Kylie,'

'Dad, it's Elis.'

'Elis, great to hear your voice. Everything okay?'

'Dad, Dad, I got an award today. I'm class star of the month.'

'Wow, that's brilliant, El. Well done. I'll pick you up on Sunday morning, we'll go to Frankie and Benny's to celebrate but don't tell your mother.'

'Our secret, Dad.'

'Good boy. See you Sunday.'

'Miss you, Dad.'

'Miss you, too, El,' said Vic, as he pushed open the door of the pub, relieved to see Ash had already got him a pint.

'So, you've just been sitting in your boxers for two weeks?' Ash asked.

'No, just the first five days.'

'Do any writing?'

Vic shook his head. 'Not the first week and this week just bits and pieces.'

'Watch any box sets?'

'Nope, just old episodes of *Pointless*.'

'Man, you're a lucky bugger,' Ash said. 'I'd love to be able to do that.'

'I thought you were going to bollock me.'

'Bollock you, why? It sounds bliss. The perfect holiday. Ten days without the kids, without Lily, without the school run. Wanna swap places?'

'Don't give me that,' Vic said. 'You've got the perfect life.'

'Grass is always greener, mate.' Ash took a mouthful of beer. 'Nah, you're right, I wouldn't change it for the world but, sometimes, I do envy you.'

'You envy me? A man who's spent five out of the last ten days in his boxers? Of course you do.'

'I do man, I tell you. You've got a cool job, you've got a wonderful son, you've got great friends, loads of women chasing you, god knows why and, then, when it all gets you down, you can close the door and be alone. Best of all worlds. I've haven't had time for myself longer than the time it takes for me to take a dump since Mollster was born.'

'Oh shit,' Vic said.

'What?'

'It's Cariad.' Vic nodded in the direction of three women, as he sank down into his chair. 'I told you about her.'

'Cariad? Cariad? Rings a bell. Which one was that?'

'Say her name louder, why don't you? The one who parked me. One date. I was crazy about her but she didn't return my calls.'

'Ah... Go and say hello.'

'I can't.'

'Go on, you know you want to.' Ash smiled, moving out of the way so Vic couldn't hide behind him.

'You bastard. She's seen me.'

'Hi, Vic, long time no see,' Cariad said.

'Hi, I'm Ash.' Ash stuck out his hand.

'Nice to meet you, Ash. So, Vic, what you been up to?'

'Oh, you know, this and that. Getting a few more gigs.'

'We should get together again, sometime,' Cariad said.

Ash nudged Vic under the table.

Vic nodded.

Cariad smiled. 'I'll call you.'

'Vic would love that,' Ash said.

Vic watched Cariad as she made her way back towards her friends. He whirled on Ash. 'What the fuck was that? I thought you were my friend.'

'Looks like she wants to drive you again,' Ash said.

July 2016

Vic had either died and gone to hell, or was sitting in Frankie and Benny's. He looked at the prices; how could Iceland sell the same crap for a fifth of the cost? But Elis had a smile like it was the start of the summer holidays and, judging by the noise, it was popular with most of his peers too.

'How have you got onion in your hair?' Vic said, wiping the remains of the hot dog from Elis's clothes and face.

'Hey, Dad, I've got this for you,' said Elis, thrusting an envelope into Vic's hand. 'I told Mrs. Clarke you were a comedian and they asked if you'd come in and talk to my class and the other Year Six class, too.'

'About what?'

'About your job, Dad,' said Elis, raising his eyes towards the ceiling. 'We've had lots of people come in, a firefighter, a nurse, a vet.'

'Won't I embarrass you?'

'No way, Dad. It'll be cool.' Elis spooned ice cream into his mouth. A big splodge landed on his jeans.

Vic smiled. 'Okay,' he said. 'I'll see if I can arrange it. Now, go to the toilets and clean yourself up.'

Elis jumped up and ran to the toilets. Vic felt a smile cross his face. Talk to his class, bloody hell, he thought.

When Mia arrived at the café on Monday afternoon, Vic saw the mischievous glint in her eye straight away.

'What's up with you?'

'You are never gonna guess what I'm doing tonight,' Mia said, taking a mouthful of coffee.

'Go on.'

Mia turned her phone around.

'Who's that?'

'Harry,' Mia smiled.

'And who the hell is Harry?'

'I'm going on a date with him this evening.'

'Mia, he's about twelve.'

'He's twenty-four.'

'Still years younger than you.' Vic started counting on his fingers but gave up.

'He's gorgeous, isn't he?'

'Well, yes. If you're a priest.' Vic laughed.

'He's not a child, he's a fully-grown man. You're just jealous.'

'Of what? I don't want to sleep with twenty-four-year-old boys,' Vic said.

'No but you wouldn't say no to a twenty-four-year-old woman, would you?'

Vic smiled. 'So, where's he taking you, the youth club, the soft-play area?'

'Shut up, Vic.'

They drank coffee.

'Hey, you'll never guess who I saw the other day?'

Mia put her fingers on her temples and stared at Vic. 'No, you'll have to tell me.'

'Cariad.'

'Oh, and?'

'She said she'd call me, but nothing.'

'Like I said, parked.'

'Why did she say she'd call me, then?'

'To keep you interested.'

'Women!'

Mia's phone pinged.

'Look at that.' Mia turned her phone around.

'What the fuck's that?'

Mia laughed. 'It's Andy's dick.'

'Why are you showing the bloody thing to me?'

'Thought you might be interested.'

'Why the hell would I be interested in your bloke's dick?'

'I dunno. He just sent it me.' Mia shrugged. 'Look, he sends me loads.'

'Stop it,' Vic said, 'make it stop.'

'You can always look away.'

'I can't. I can't look but I can't look away. Why? Why does he send you those?'

Mia shrugged. 'He just does.'

'Did you ask for them?'

'No, of course I didn't. Why would I?'

'So, he just sends you pics of his cock, unsolicited? Do you like them?'

'Um, yes, it means he's thinking about me.'

'It means he's having a wank without you.'

Mia bit her lower lip. 'S'pose.'

'As a matter of interest, how do you reply?'

'I don't.' Mia put her phone face down on the table while the barista cleared old cups away.

'Isn't he scared you'll show it to people?'

'I'd never do that.'

Vic raised his eyebrows. 'Hello.'

'Okay. But I've only ever shown them to you, the girls, and my mum.'

Vic's mouth hung open. 'You showed your mum?'

'No, I was joking about that.'

Vic recognised the little smile on Mia's lips, she was lying.

'God, I'd never dream of sending a picture of my dick to anyone.'

'I suppose you've never heard of this then.' Mia typed on the screen and turned her phone around again.

Vic grabbed the phone. 'Argh, Mia! What's this?'

'It's Rate My Cock. It's like Tinder but for cocks. Careful, you're liking those by swiping across like that.

Vic dropped the phone on the table.

'These are all selfies, yeah?'

'Of course they're selfies,' Mia said. 'Do you think people have a man-servant to photograph their phalluses?'

Vic picked up the phone and continued to scroll through the pictures of male genitalia. Mia looked at her friend's face. Vic was staring at the images with his mouth ajar.

'You are naïve at times, Vic.'

'I'm not naïve, it's just weird.'

'You're enjoying that more than I thought you would.'

'Why's he holding it next to a coke can and this one a Mars Bar?'

'Why do you think?'

Vic looked at her quizzically.

'To show how big it is, obviously.'

'Oh, right. So, size does matter.'

'It does but not in the way you're thinking. It's a Goldilocks thing. Too big and your eyes water, too small and you hardly notice it's there. So what you're looking for is something that's just right.'

'Do you prefer a coke can or a candle?'

'A candle but that's me. Some of my friends prefer a coke can. But it's not the size, it's what you do with it.'

'See, I've never understood that. What is there to do with it other than put it in and move it about?'

'True but it's what you do with the other parts of your body that's important, too. But you know this, right?'

'So, you should say, it's not *only* the size, it's what you do overall that's important?' Vic looked down at the phone again. 'Do you use this site?'

'Now and again, if I can't sleep.'

'Doesn't it give you nightmares? It's going to give me nightmares.'

'Fortunately, I like cock.' Mia smiled.

Vic's phone buzzed.

'Is someone sending you cock pics?'

Vic read the message, his brow furrowed. 'Odd.'

'What's up?'

'Kylie says she and Nat want a meeting with me.'

'What about?'

'I dunno, I guess I'll find out tomorrow.'

*

Vic had spent the day trying to write a routine suitable for ten-year-olds and had got nowhere. He took his coat off and shook the rain off. He forced a smile. In front of him were the woman he used to love more than anything in the world and the woman he currently despised more than anything in the world. He felt outnumbered; he should have brought Mia along with him. Someone coughed. Vic looked up at the waitress.

'A latte, please.'

'Soy milk or almond?'

'No cow?' Vic asked, the waitress shook her head. 'An Americano then, please.' Typical of Kylie to take them to a vegan place. 'What are you having?' He looked at the two women.

'We've already ordered,' they said together.

'Look, Vic,' Kyle began, 'we'll come straight to the point. Nat and I have been thinking and...'

That was never a good start to any conversation.

'... we know it's early days and we haven't spoken to Ellis about this yet. We wanted to talk to you first...'

Vic did not like where this was going. Were they moving away? Did they want sole custody?

'... and, of course, we will respect your right to say no.'

Bullshit. Vic knew if he said no to whatever they had planned he'd be engaging a solicitor within a week.

'And we haven't totally decided yet.'

For fuck sake, what happened to coming straight to the point?

'The thing is, we really enjoyed having Elis full time and, since Nat's playing a key role in El's upbringing, we thought it might be nice if we made it official.'

'Official? What do you mean official?

'Well if, you know, we...'

'I want to adopt Elis,' Natalie blurted.

Vic closed his eyes. He felt himself sliding beneath water, unable to stop the current dragging him down. He couldn't breathe. He grabbed hold of the table as Kylie's words drifted over his head.

'It wouldn't change anything, you'd still be his dad, it's just Nat would be his mum, too.'

'No,' he croaked. 'Absolutely not.'

'Vic, think about…'

He pushed himself up, knocking his chair to the ground. All eyes in the café turned towards him. 'No,' he cried. 'No… No… No…' He looked around for someone to throw him a lifebuoy. 'Just no…' Vic was aware the whole café was looking at him. 'No…' he said again.

'Vic, please, at least think about it.'

'Forget it.' He glared at two women sitting at the next table. 'These women are trying to steal my child.'

'Vic, calm down,' Natalie said.

'Don't tell me to calm down. You can fuck off! You can fuck right off. Fuck the fuck right off the both of you. You'll never take Elis.'

A man with a hipster beard strode across towards Vic. 'Mate, I think you'd better leave.'

'Who the fuck are you? It's none of your god damn business.'

'You're making it my business, now get out or I'll be forced to make you leave.'

Vic stared at the man. He thought for a moment he could take him. He clenched his fists and stuck his chest out. Socking someone in the jaw would be mighty satisfying. The woman who took his order came over but stood helpless as the two men squared up. Vic could feel the man's breath on his face and see crumbs in his otherwise perfectly sculpted beard.

'Vic, stop being a prick,' Kylie said.

'Typical man, thinks violence will solve everything.' Nat added.

Vic turned to Nat. 'I'm not the fucking bully here,' he spat. 'Go and crawl back under your rock.'

'I'll call the police,' the waitress said.

'C'mon, mate, time to go.' The hipster took Vic by the arm and ushered him to the door.

'The answer's no,' Vic yelled and let himself be led away.

*

'Don't worry, mate.' Ash looked up from his iPad, as Vic put two pints of Guinness down on the table and sat and took a long slurp of his pint. 'It says here they can only adopt if they have the blessing of the birth parent. You don't give the okay, there's no adoption. End of.' Ash scrolled further down the page and read on. 'Oh no, wait, hmm, it looks like they can apply for parental responsibility. They don't need you to agree to that, they just need a court order. Which you can oppose of course. Then the judge decides.'

'Great, like I can afford a lawyer.' Vic rolled his shoulders trying to release the tension. Took another mouthful of beer.

'Remember my mate, Chris, from Uni?'

'The chubby lad? Didn't like me much.'

'Aye, that's him. He's a bigwig lawyer now. If this goes any further, I'll get him to look at it for you.'

'I don't what's happened to Kylie. She's not the woman I married. She's become smug; like she's the better parent. God, I can imagine them,' muttered Vic, hunched over the dregs of his pint, 'chipping away, planting ideas into El's mind: Wouldn't it be nice to have two mummies? Wouldn't you like to live here permanently, so you don't have to go to that horrible flat with that terrible toilet paper and no games console? Wouldn't it be good to call Natalie Mum?'

'You don't know that.'

'I can fucking guess, Ash.'

'That's all it is, a guess.'

'Elis will want it so much he'll be asking me, begging me, to agree. If I say no, I'll be the bad guy and that'll make him want it even more. I can't win, I just can't fucking win.'

'He'll understand, mate. Just talk to him, tell him it would mean you wouldn't be his dad anymore. He wouldn't want that, would he?'

'Nice try, Ash, but they've already thought that through. They explained, ever so nicely and ever so calmly, that I would still be his dad, he'd be a lucky boy, he's have a dad and two mums.'

'Come on Vic, that's not…'

'I knew this would happen. It had to happen. They've made me surplus to requirements.'

'So, make yourself essential. Re-engage with Elis.' Ash took a swig of beer. 'You were the one who sent him to his mother's place for two weeks while you moped around in your pants. It's you who thinks you can't compete. It's you who's giving up.'

Vic toyed with his pint. 'You're right. I should give up. I'll let them have him, may as well let them adopt him. It's the only way to save my relationship with him.'

'That's not what I said,' Ash said but he was talking to a deaf mule.

Vic slumped in his seat and closed his eyes. His head thumped.

'You look like how I feel,' Mia said, putting two coffees down on the table.

'How do you do it all day? I only had one hour with them and I'm wiped out.'

'How did it go?'

'Tough crowd. But they laughed in all the right places and Elis looked proud as punch.'

'That's all that counts.'

'And I got paid for it.'

'Excellent.'

Vic's phone buzzed. 'Good old Ash,' he said.

'What's he done?

'He's talked to his lawyer friend. He says he's happy to help if it's needed.'

'He's a star at times.'

'And that's after I made a bit of a prick of myself in front of him the other day.' Vic told Mia all about their conversation.

'You were upset, Vic. You had every right to be a twat.'

They chatted about this and that for a while.

'Oh,' Vic said, putting his finger in the air, 'I know what I was going to ask you.'

'Sounds worrying,' Mia smiled.

'Oh no, not really. Well, slightly worrying, I suppose.' Vic felt his face redden.

'I'm intrigued.'

'Okay. This is it,' said Vic, staring into his coffee. 'All the women I've being seeing recently insist on having a shower before sex: is that normal?'

'Of course, it is.'

Vic looked up. 'Really? So, you do it, too?'

'Yes, most of the time.'

'When did that start? Was there a decree in *Cosmo*? An announcement on *Loose Women*? It never used to be like that. We used to get back home, drunk, and fumble into bed.'

'Oh, the good old, romantic days.'

'So, when did you start showering?'

'After I had Sid, I think. It's not official women's policy. I'm sure there are women out there who don't.'

'I've yet to meet them,' said Vic. 'Why have a shower before it though? It doesn't make sense.'

'It's nice to feel clean, isn't it?'

'Ah, well there I have to disagree. For me there's nothing better than a sweaty woman. It must be the pheromones but you lot want to wash them all away.'

'My lot?'

'You know what I mean.'

Mia shrugged. 'Look when I'm clean, I feel good, I can relax, not worry. And, because I'm relaxed, the sex is better.'

'But doesn't it take away the spontaneity?' Vic asked.

'Spontaneity's a man thing,' Mia said.

'Really?'

'You know the old adage, men want to get on with it, women want to take their time.'

'Oh yeah, that old chestnut.'

Mia smiled.

'So, sex is like shopping, or getting ready to go out?' Vic said.

Mia stuck her tongue out. 'You know what I mean. When did a woman ever have an orgasm during a quickie?'

Vic shrugged. 'Never I guess.'

'See.'

'So, you're telling me that being clean leads to orgasms.'

'No, not necessarily, but it increases the chances.'

Vic looked confused.

'Because we're not worrying about how we smell, our mind can stay focussed on the job in hand.'

'So why didn't you worry about it before Sid was born?'

'Because I wasn't expecting good sex back then. I suppose I was grateful to be considered attractive, in those days. How sad is that?' Mia peered into her coffee. 'But these days I know what I want and I'm bloody well going to get it. And having a shower is part of the experience.'

'And you expect us men to have one, too?'

'Naturally. We don't know where you've been. If you expect us to put your dick in our mouths, the least you can do is have the decency to make sure it's bloody clean.'

Vic smiled.

'So, stop your complaining, a little bit of water never hurt anyone.'

August 2016

'What do you reckon to the science museum for your birthday, Elis? We've been talking about going there for ages.'

Elis looked up from the TV. 'We're going trampolining, aren't we?'

'Are we? Oh, yes, of course we are. No problem, we'll do the museum another time.'

'Cool,' Elis said, turning his attention back to the cartoon.

Vic fingered his phone, wrote a message, deleted it and wrote it again. His finger hovered over Send but he put the phone down, went into the kitchen and put the kettle on. He rattled the spoon in the mug as he stirred; the tea overflowed the sides.

'Bugger it.'

Trampo-bloody-lining. Another body blow, another little victory for Kylie and Nat. Little things, one at a time. He took the tea back into the living room and watched Elis watching the television. He was lying on the floor with his chin in his hands biting his nails, exactly as Kylie used to do back when they were first dating.

'Stop biting your nails, Elis,' Vic said. Elis jumped and looked at his dad.

'Sorry,' Elis said.

It's not his fault. Vic summoned a smile. 'You don't want ugly, chewed up nails like your mother, do you?' he said, ruffling Elis's hair.

Vic deleted the message he'd composed and tried again.

» I hear we're going trampolining.

That sounded neutral enough. He pressed Send. His phone rang three minutes later.

'Hi Kylie,' he said, trying not to sound pissed off.

'I'm so sorry, I meant to call but I've been so busy and Nat saw this offer.'

Vic walked into the kitchen. Bloody Nat, it had to be Nat.

'Kylie, you're meant to ask me, not tell me.'

'I know but we had to book it, you know, to get the special rate.'

'Okay, it's done now. So, when is it?' Vic looked at his wall calendar.

'The Saturday before his birthday.'

'Saturday? I'm working in Oxford.'

'Well, can't you cancel? It's your son's birthday'.

'We agreed to try to do things on a Sunday.'

'It's one Saturday, Vic.'

'I only work Thursday, Friday and Saturday, Kylie, you know that.'

'But the deal was for a Saturday.'

Vic knew she was lying. Saturdays must be one of their busiest days, they wouldn't do deals on Saturdays.

'So, I have to give up a gig so you can save fifty quid?' Vic's voice was an octave higher.

'He's your son.'

'Fine. I'll see what I can do.'

Kylie three, Vic nil.

After Vic had dropped Elis in school on Friday morning he headed towards Coventry. The plan was to meet Tina at two, check into the hotel and have an afternoon of passion. Vic could then go off to his gig and Tina could head home. It had been Tina's idea, obviously. Vic would have preferred to get there at five, freshen up and do the show but he had to pick his battles.

Vic never knew if Tina orgasmed during sex and he didn't like to ask. With most of his women, he either knew or they were good actors but, with Tina, it seemed to be one long mini-orgasm without that one big moment. He kissed her head. Her face glowed as it always did after sex.

'You're the best,' Tina said and stroked Vic's head.

Vic lay in on his back, enjoying the noises of the afternoon drifting in through the open window.

'Penny for them?' Tina said.

'What?'

'What are you thinking about?' Tina rested her head on her arm and looked at Vic, her eyes sparkled.

'Trampolining.'

'What?'

'The trampolining. El's party next week, I told you. I'm wondering if I can go there and still get to my gig.'

'The party's a week tomorrow, you say?' Tina said.

'Yep,' Vic said.

'That solves it then, I can be there.'

'What?'

'I'm free. I'll come to the party, and then I can drive you to Oxford. That way you'll be nice and fresh for the show.'

'I don't really think that's a good idea,' Vic said.

'Why not?'

Vic rubbed his forehead and sighed.

'I don't want to introduce Elis to a new partner. Not until I'm sure it's right. It's been a hard journey for him already.'

Tina threw back the covers.

'Tina?'

Tina shrugged off Vic's hand and stood up. She glared down at him with her hands on hips. 'I'm nothing to you, am I? I'm just a shag. What do you think? That I want to be Elis's new mum? I don't. You're always complaining about Nat and Kylie, I thought you might like some moral support.'

'I get that, it's just, you know, I'm thinking of Elis and the message it would send.'

'Message? What message?'

'You know what message. We haven't been together long and…'

'I'd like to be part of your life, Vic. Not some kind of part-time lover.' She made sure she slammed the bathroom door.

'And that's exactly why I don't want to introduce you to my son,' Vic muttered.

*

The trampoline park was red. Red posters, red trampolines, red walls. The kids screamed and shouted as they bounced and Ed Sheeran screamed and shouted from the speakers. This was hell on earth.

What was he doing there? Kylie had barely acknowledged Vic's arrival, Elis waved but was too absorbed in the wonder of it all. Vic sipped a cup of tea and watched the kids bounce around, smiling and laughing. He had to admit it, trampolining was better than the science museum. The mums huddled in a group around Kylie and Nat. Vic looked around and caught sight of Dave. *Shit*, he thought, *don't come over, don't come over.*

'Ah, Hi, Dave,' he said.

'Hi, Vic,' Dave replied.

'No Louise?'

'No, Lou and I are going through a bit of a rocky patch.'

Vic kept his eyes on the kids.

'I think she's got a lover in tow.'

Vic swallowed. 'A lover?'

'If I catch the joker, I'll kill him.'

Vic nodded as he took another sip of tea

'Hey, it's not you, is it?' Dave said.

Vic spluttered and coughed. Tea sprayed from his nose. He snatched a paper napkin from a dispenser and dragged it across his mouth. 'Hah, good one.'

'I know. Couldn't be you, could it? Because then she'd be a lesbo, wouldn't she?' Dave threw his head back with laughter.

The kids were climbing off trampolines and Kylie was gathering them around. Kylie and Nat cut the birthday cake like they were bride and bride at a wedding. Vic checked his watch and slipped away. He'd got to the Severn Bridge when his phone rang. He pressed the little green button.

'Where the fuck did you disappear to?' Kylie voice filled the car.

'I told you I was leaving early, I've got to get to Oxford.'

'A simple goodbye would have been nice.'

'You were busy and, anyway, you fucking ignored me the whole fucking time.'

'Listen to yourself, Vic. You sound like a spoilt child. Elis was distraught.'

'He didn't even notice.'

'Are you calling me a liar?'

'Sorry,' Vic said. 'I didn't want to make a fuss.'

'Typical,' Kylie said. 'I won't invite you next year.' She hung up.

'Fuck you,' Vic said. 'Fuck, fuck, fuck you.' He slammed the steering wheel with his hand.

The phone rang again.

'What now?' he said. He glanced that the screen. It was Tina. He killed the call. Three minutes later, she called back. He took a breath and then hit the green button.

'Hi.'

'Hello gorgeous,' Tina said. 'How was the party?'

'Excellent. Just on my way to Oxford.'

'Great and you're coming to me after the gig, aren't you?'

Vic didn't answer.

'What's wrong?'

'Oh nothing, I'm just tired.'

'So, you're not coming? I made lasagne.'

'I'll be there,' Vic said, 'see you later.'

'Can't wait. Drive carefully.'

He massaged his forehead. Indicated and pulled into the services. Before he got out of the car, he hit the recall button.

'Hi,' Tina said.

'Look, Tina, I'm not going to come tonight. I'm not in the mood. I need some time alone.'

Vic waited for a response.

'Tina?' He could hear her breathing. 'Tina? Look I'm sorry but I've had a shit day and I'll be horrible company.'

'I thought you said the party was okay.'

'I lied.'

The line went dead.

'Fuck,' Vic said and slapped the steering wheel again.

*

'I'm forty-three. I know, I don't look it.'

Vic paused and the laugh came.

'I've noticed signs of ageing. For example, when I drop a coin, I look to see its value before I decide if it's worth bending down to pick it up; anything under fifty pence, not a chance.' A short pause; nothing.

He pressed on. 'And people are starting to look young, police officers, teachers, MILFs on porn sites. And, yes, the carpet matches the curtains, my cuffs match my collar…' Vic looked at a woman in the front row. 'I've got grey pubes, madam.'

A few people laughed.

'And then there's not understanding what youngsters mean. YOLO: you only live once. For youngsters, it means you take risks; for me it's shit. I only get one crack at this. No more risks. Sick means good. Fine, I get it. A sick video, a sick computer game, but I draw the line at a sick curry.' A small ripple of laughter. 'There are some advantages of getting older, though,' he continued, looking down at his chest. 'I've always been a breast man and now, look, I've got my own. I can spend hours playing with these bad boys. In fact, I'm off to play with them now. You've been wonderful, my name's Vic Bead, goodnight.'

Vic left the stage and wiped the sweat from his brow. The MC looked him in the eye as they shook hands. Vic smiled and headed backstage. He longed for a pint but it was going to be a long drive home.

'You know your problem,' Wally said to Vic.

'I didn't know I had a problem.'

'You share too much.'

'Do I?' Vic checked his phone. Nothing.

'It's too personal. No one wants to hear about the colour of your pubes.'

Vic continued to play with his phone, hoping Wally would leave him alone. 'They laughed, didn't they?'

'They did but you need to think about what your audience wants. You're trying to make them laugh, not seek therapy.'

Vic didn't look up.

'You're good but you could be much better. You need to hone your material. Why do people come to comedy clubs? They come to get pissed and have a laugh. Do people really want to learn about the sex life of a forty-year-old man? Does your routine really appeal to pissed up lads?'

'I don't want to appeal to pissed up lads, I'm not you.'

'But Vic, they're the audiences we get. There's no point aiming your humour at middle-class wankers when all we get in here is stag dos and hen parties. How much comedy do you watch?'

'Some.'

'Get yourself on YouTube, watch everyone, watch Monkhouse, watch Kay, watch McIntyre, watch them all, whether you like them or not.'

'Sorry, who died and made you my guru?' Vic asked.

'I'm only trying to help, offer some friendly advice,' Wally replied.

'Well don't.'

'Listen, pal, pull your neck in. You're just a jobbing comedian, doing an average job. I've seen folk like you come and go and it's the ones who listen that get somewhere. Arrogant twats, like you, end up playing the same shitty little clubs, like this one, until they retire.'

'Like you, you mean?'

'Aye, like me. But at least I'm top of the bill and not on second. The graveyard slot: not good enough to headline, not popular enough to have two gigs. There are younger acts than you with their own gigs; it's passing you by, Vic, you've stalled.'

Vic put his jacket on.

'You'd do well to listen to me. Jesus, I wish someone had taken the time to offer me advice when I was your age.'

'Screw you, Wally,' Vic said, he grabbed his coat and made his way to his car; a shitty end to a shitty day.

*

Despite not getting home until late, Vic was glad he'd not stayed at Tina's. Elis was staying with his mum overnight, so Vic had Sunday to himself. It felt like bliss.

He'd gone to the café for breakfast, before working his way through the Sunday paper. He got up to make a cup of tea and thought he should call Tina.

'Hi, there'

'Don't you hi there me, like there's nothing wrong.'

Vic sighed.

'Look, I said I'm sorry. I was feeling low and needed my own space, that's all.'

'I could have cheered you up. I could have kissed you better…' There was a huge intake of breath before Tina continued. 'But you didn't want to see me.'

'I didn't say that, Tina. Sometimes kisses don't make me better.'

'How do you think that makes me feel?'

'Oh, Tina.'

'I don't count, do I? Did you think about me? No, of course you didn't. You only ever think about yourself. You're selfish, Vic. You never call me, it's always me calling you.'

'I'm calling you now, aren't I?'

'Only after I called you three times. You were with her, weren't you?

'Who is her?'

'Your girlfriend, Mia.'

'No, I was—'

'Sometimes, I wonder what you're doing with me when you've got her.'

'How many times do I have to tell you, she's not my girlfriend?' Vic sighed. 'This is getting us nowhere, Mia.'

There was silence.

'Did you just call me Mia?'

'I, look, I'm—'

'I never want to see you again, you fucking bastard.'

Vic stared at the blank screen. 'Good bloody riddance.'

September 2016

Vic kicked the rugby ball high into the air and watched Elis chase after it and kick it back.

'Go long,' he shouted to Elis, before firing a sweet pass five metres over his son's head. 'I need to get fit,' Vic said to himself. He peeled off his sweatshirt and used it to wipe his brow. The ball trickled back to him. He kicked it high again, caught it himself, and passed the ball back to Elis.

'Let the ball come to you,' Vic said, miming the action and watching the ball spill from Elis's grasp.

Three girls walked across the field, two of them smoking, one licking on an ice-lolly. Vic caught himself sucking in his belly and puffing out his chest. *God, they're sixteen*, he thought, but he kept the belly sucked in. He looked at Elis trying to control the ball. Vic wasn't sure if he'd even noticed the girls. Elis stood up straight and drop-kicked the ball perfectly into Vic's arms. Elis punched the air like he'd just won the cup final and smiled. Vic spun a pass back to him and Elis caught it for the first time that day. Vic felt a surge of absurd pride. The girls walked on chatting amongst themselves, oblivious to the old man and the young boy trying to impress them. There might be a routine in that, Vic thought, as he slung another pass to Elis.

'Can we play football now, Dad?'

'Yeah, why not.' Vic put the rugby ball down and threw the football towards Elis. Elis trapped it with his left and fired it back with his right. 'Skills.' Vic nodded.

'See if you can tackle me,' Elis said as he ran at his dad with the ball glued to his feet. Vic stumbled, lunged and fell. Elis skipped over him. Struggling back up, Vic saw his son running at him again. He thought of all those football show-offs in school. Back then, he'd hack them to the ground. He stuck out a leg but remembered it was his son, and not Ryan Evans, just in time.

'Let's play penalties,' Vic said. 'We can use my sweater and the rugby ball to make the goal.

After their penalty shootout, they sat under a tree drinking a can of pop, Vic's phone buzzed. Two messages from Tina.

» *I can make it Tuesday evening.*

» *Sorry, that wasn't for you.*

He sent a message back.

» *OK, hope all's good.*

Back home, Vic walked into the living room and smiled at Elis. A sofa, an armchair, a beanbag but, like his mum, Elis was sprawled on the floor. He was laughing. No, not laughing, sobbing. He must have been like that for a while, because the iPad had gone to sleep in front of him.

'You okay, El?' Vic said but Elis didn't look up. 'Elis?'

A cartoon started on the TV screen.

Elis lowered his head onto his arm.

'Hey, what's wrong, kiddo?' Vic scooped him off the carpet and into the air, the iPad nearly whacking him in the face. 'Jesus, you're heavier than I remember.' He plonked Elis on the sofa, sat next to him and put his arm around him. He let him sob for a moment, while horrible thoughts about what might be upsetting Elis swam through his mind.

'Ethan Matthews calls me a freak,' Elis said, before wiping his nose on his sleeve.

'Who's Ethan Matthews?' Vic said.

'He's a boy in the other Year Six. Carys's brother. Every day he calls me freak cos Mum has a girlfriend. He says it's disgusting.'

Vic saw his chance. How easy would it be to build on a ten-year-old bully's prejudice and turn Elis against his mother and Natalie?

'Does it feel disgusting to you?'

On screen, a cartoon mouse dropped an iron on a cartoon cat's head. Elis sniffed

'Does it?'

'No,' Elis said.

'Do you think they love each other?'

Elis nodded.

'And do they love you?'

Elis nodded again. 'They give me ice cream.'

'Well, there you are, then,' Vic said, 'if they give you ice cream, they must love you.'

'And they give me cuddles and they help me with my homework,' Elis added.

Vic squeezed him. 'So, you're a lucky boy, aren't you?'

The cat stood on a shovel that sprang into his face. Elis giggled.

'Listen, next time he calls you a name, why don't you invite him for tea. Let him meet your mum and Nat and then he'll see it's perfectly normal.'

Elis looked up. 'No way, he's horrible.'

'Perhaps he needs someone to be nice to him,' Vic said.

'He should be nice to me, then.' Elis said.

Vic wanted to agree with him but he was playing the wise father. 'Sometimes it's not as easy as that,' Vic said.

They watched the TV screen.

'Dad, why *does* mum have a girlfriend?'

'That's a good question. Um...'

Elis's eyes widened as he stared at his father.

'Okay, let's see: some women love men, some women love women, some love both. Some men love men, some love women, some love both. Your mother loved me and now, well now, she loves Nat.'

'So, do you love men?'

Vic laughed. 'No, I'm in the loving women camp. What about you?'

'Boys are more fun, they play football, but Isabella Macintosh gives me butterflies.'

'Ah and who is Isabella Macintosh?'

'She's Dylan's older sister.'

'Does she know you like her?'

'No.' Elis hid himself in Vic's side.

'You should tell her.'

'Dad—'

On the television in front of them, the cartoon cat held the cartoon mouse by its tail.

'So, Mum loved you first?'

'Yes, very much. Especially around the time you were born.'

'But now she loves Natalie?'

'Yes. As I said, some people like both. There are no hard and fast rules. One day you might meet a boy who makes you feel how Isabella makes you feel. I could meet a man who makes me feel like your mother did. You never know.'

Elis looked down again. His forehead furrowed.

'If you and Mum loved each other so much, why don't you anymore?'

Vic scratched his chin. 'Love can be like a candle, Elis. When you first light it, you hope it will last forever but, eventually, it gets smaller and smaller, until there's no candle, no flame. Then you need to get a new candle. That's what happened with me and your mum. We ran out of wax.'

'That's sad.'

'Yep.'

'Will Mum and Nat run out of wax, too?'

'They might do, they might do, but they might be one of those oil candles where you can replace the oil, so the flame keeps burning. Then, they'll last forever.'

'I hope they're an oil candle,' Elis said.

'So, do I, Elis, so do I.' Vic gave him another squeeze. 'Now, what do you want for your tea?'

'Ice cream,' Elis said.

'Nice try but you can't have ice cream for your tea.' Vic said. 'You could, if you help me with dinner, have a small scoop for your pudding. How about a bolognaise?'

Elis nodded as they settled back to watch the end of the cartoon.

It had been one hell of a week. As well as Elis's bully, Vic had a broken washing machine to contend with, his agent had given him a bollocking, and he'd argued with Kylie about Christmas. For once, getting out and doing a show was a blessed relief. It hadn't gone badly either. Vic walked home, hands in pockets, mulling over his performance. The smell of chips overwhelmed his willpower. What the hell, he deserved a treat. He pushed open the door of the chippy and immediately recognised the red-haired figure waiting at the counter. He was about to leave but she turned her head at the sound of the door.

'Oh, hello,' she said. 'Are you stalking me?'

'Hi, Cariad. Technically, I'd say it was you stalking me. This is my patch.'

'Just been to the cinema.' Cariad smiled and pointed to the building across the street. Her smile was as lovely as the first day he'd seen it. 'What have you been up to?'

'Just had a gig.'

'How'd it go?'

'Not bad.'

'Three small chips,' said the man behind the counter.

'Thanks, Andros,' she said.

'Three?' Vic said.

'I've got the kids in the car.' She stroked Vic's arm. 'Call me. We should go out again.'

'Do you mean that?'

Cariad winked as she passed him. At the door, she turned and smiled again.

Do you mean that? What the fuck kind of question was that? If there was an Olympic gold for sounding desperate and pathetic, Vic was in with a shout. What did Cariad want? What was the wink? Fuck, this was daft. Why didn't people just say what they meant? He should call her. But, then again, maybe he shouldn't. Wasn't the definition of insanity doing the same thing over and over and expecting different results?

*

Vic and Ash had been to a game and had just entered the Ox and Cart for a quick pint.

'I don't mind losing,' Vic said, 'it's the performance.'

'Me and you could have done better.'

'We'd at least shown more commitment.' Vic smiled at Rosie, who smiled back at him.

'I'll get these.' Ash said. 'Two pints of Guinness, please, Rosie.'

'Anything for my two favourite customers.'

'We're old enough to be your dad,' Ash said.

'Well, I like a bit of grey.' Rosie winked at Vic and took the twenty pound note from Ash.

'How come you're not working tonight?' Ash said as they took their seats.

'No bookings this weekend. I did a last-minute cover slot last night but, otherwise, nothing.'

'No gigs on a Saturday? You need a new agent.'

'Funny that, she told me she needs a new client.'

'That bad?'

'No, she was just in a bad mood. Taking it out on me.'

'I'm going for a smoke,' Ash said.

Vic watched Rosie flirting with two customers as she served them. *That's how she is with everyone*, Vic thought, *it doesn't mean she fancies you. She's just doing her job.*

Ash settled back into his seat. Vic could feel the cold air on him.

'So, Kylie wants to take Elis to Nat's mum's place for Christmas,' Vic said, taking a swig of his pint.

'And?'

'She had him last year, this year it's my turn.'

'So, I hope you told her no,' said Ash, tapping the beer mat.

'I told her I'd think about it. But I don't know, it'll sound petty if I say no.'

'No, it won't. You should stand up to her more. She needs to hear no more often.'

'You think?'

'You know what she's doing, always pushing the boundaries.

I'm warning you, Vic, after this year, she'll be saying it's tradition that Elis is with her at Christmas and suddenly it'll be every year. Stand up for yourself. You both agreed rules, make her stick to them.'

'She'll say I'm being unreasonable.'

'Jesus, Vic. Will you listen to yourself? Man up. She's the one being unreasonable.'

'Maybe I should.'

'Not maybe, definitely,' said Ash, turning his cigarette packet over. He frowned. 'By the way, how are you doing with this parental responsibility thing?'

Vic shrugged. 'I think I'll just sign the forms.'

'Don't you dare. Make them go through the courts. And when they do, you can stand up and fight your corner. Think about it: if the three of you have parental responsibility, it will always be two against one. Whatever the decision, you'll always be out-voted.

'You're right but...'

'No buts, Vic. You've let that woman walk over you for too long. Time to toughen up.'

'Same again?' Vic nodded at the two empty glasses.

Vic watched Rosie pour the beers. His eyes drifted up and down her body. She smiled at him. Vic quickly looked away. Caught in the act. He avoided eye-contact as he paid and scurried back to his friend.

'Hey, did I tell you I saw Cariad yesterday?' Vic put the beers down and licked his fingers.

'You had a date? You dog.'

'Ha, I should be so lucky. No, I saw her in the chippy. She said I should call her.'

'And have you?'

Vic shrugged and took a mouthful of his beer. 'I'm not sure she meant it.'

'What have you got to lose? Ring her, what's the worst that can happen?'

'She'll say no and, well, I'm not sure I can handle the rejection.'

'Jesus, just do it. Send her a text now. I'll do it for you.' Ash leaned over and grabbed Vic's phone. Vic snatched it back.

'Okay, what shall I say?'

Between them they composed a message. Vic closed his eyes and pressed Send.

Sunday morning and Vic's head wasn't as bad as he'd feared. After leaving the pub, he had picked up a take-away and a bottle of red. He promised himself he'd only have one glass. He looked at the empty bottle, placed it in the recycling bin and then washed up last night's things. His phone lit up on the kitchen table. Vic looked at the screen.

'The Wicked Witch of the East.' He dried his hands and pressed the green button.

'Hi, Kylie,' he said, trying to put a smile in his voice.

'Hi, Vic, how are things?'

They chatted about Elis's parent's evening, and Gemma's party, before Kylie dropped the bombshell into the conversation. 'Oh, Vic, by the way,' she said, 'have you thought any more about Christmas?'

'Yeah, I spoke to Mum and she was devastated. She was really looking forward to having us all together at Christmas. So, sorry, I'm going to have to say no.' Vic gasped for breath. There was silence on the other end of the line.

'Okay, I suppose it is your turn,' Kylie said. 'It's just, well, I...'

'I think it's important we stick to the agreement, Kylie, don't you? That way you, me and Elis know where we are.' Vic could almost see Kylie biting her lip, trying to calm down. Should he back down?

'Oh, that's Nat,' Kylie said. 'I better go, we'll talk about this again. Okay?'

The phone went dead.

Vic smiled to himself and clenched his fist. He'd stood up to her and won. Now all he had to do was break the news to his mother that he and Elis would be joining her for Christmas, or to come up with a story for Kylie about why the plans had changed.

It had been four days since Vic had spoken to Kylie and he'd not heard a peep out of her since. That was good in a way, because it meant he'd not had a chance to back down, but it also worried him. What was she hatching?

He told Mia and she agreed with Ash that he'd done the right thing but it didn't make it any easier.

'I need a wee.' Vic said.

'I'm not stopping you. Off you go.' Mia checked her messages while Vic was away.

'What's up with you?' she said, as Vic sat back down.

'Nothing, why?'

'You look like you're in agony.'

'Is it that obvious?' Vic took a mouthful of coffee. 'Can I tell you something? It's a bit personal.'

'And when has that ever stopped you?'

'This is different. I've got a problem, down there, kind of aches most of the day and when I pee, fuck, it stings.'

'Have you been to the doctors?'

'Not yet.'

'Do you piss a lot?'

'All the bloody time and it stinks.'

'Too much info. Sounds like a urinary tract infection. Nothing to worry about.'

'Oh, thank fuck for that. I thought it was an STD.'

'Well, I'm no doctor. It might be gonorrhoea…'

'Very amusing.'

'I'm serious, you never know. You ought to get it checked out.'

'If it's this urinary tract thingy, how do I cure it?'

'Drink loads of water, stop wanking, and take some of these.' Mia rummaged around in her bag and placed a box of tablets on the table.

'Cranberry supplements?'

'They work wonders but still go to the doctor.'

'Yes, Mum.'

Vic's phone buzzed on the table. He turned it over, sighed and read it to Mia.

» *OK re xmas, but taking El to Germany for half-term.*

'Can they do that?' she asked.

Vic nodded. 'I think I need to sign a release form. Can't see any harm in it but it would have been nice if they'd asked, rather than presenting it to me as fact.'

Facebook. Vic scrolled down the page. Why was he addicted to this shit? He had one hundred things to do on a Saturday morning but here he was, checking in on people he barely knew and didn't care about. It was like nicotine. How many cigarettes had he actually enjoyed when he smoked? One in the morning, one after work, that sneaky one at 3 a.m, but he'd still smoked the other seventeen. How many posts did he truly like on Facebook? One a week? Yet he was still a twenty-visits-a-day man. More cats, more amazing acts of kindness, more political slogans bouncing around the echo chamber. Why did people share this stuff? Ah, there was Paul and Lucy, once again expressing how much they loved each other. Divorced in three months, Vic predicted. Then a photo of Elis. Vic smiled, he looked cute. He was about to scroll past when he noticed the tagline.

> *Great start to the day, in A&E waiting for an x-ray on the little fella's wrist.*

'Fucking hell.' He called Kylie's number. It rang and rang until finally he heard Kylie's recorded voice.

'Ring me, asap!' Vic said.

Twenty minutes later he tried again. Same response. He looked at the pics and tried to work out what hospital they were in. It was impossible. He tried Kylie's number a third time; it went to voicemail.

'Jesus, she's got time to post a picture but she can't answer her bloody phone.'

He looked at the photo again. An update message popped up.

All well, just soft tissue damage, off to get ice cream.

He called Kylie's number. Elis answered.

'You okay, scamp?'

'Yes, Dad. I fell off my scooter,' he said, his voice full of pride.

'No broken bones?'

'No but the X-ray machine was *amazing.*'

'Is your mum there?'

'Yes, wait a minute.'

'Hi, Vic,' said Kylie, her voice bright and breezy.

'Hi, Kylie.'

He waited.

'Vic?'

'When were you going to tell me?'

'Sorry, it was just such a palaver. You know?'

'No, I don't know, Kylie, that's the bloody point. You had time to post on Facebook but not to call me, his father.'

'Look, I've said I'm sorry. I didn't want to worry you.'

'If we were still married, would you have called me?'

'But we're not married, are we?'

'No but he's still my son and you'd expect me to tell you. For Christ's sake, Kylie, you told the world before telling me.

'It's just some tissue damage.'

'But you didn't know that, Kylie, did you? That's why you took him to the bloody hospital. Jesus, he could have been seriously hurt.'

'Stop being such a fusspot, no harm's done. I've got to go, we've just being served.'

'Fucking hell,' Vic said but Kylie had hung up.

Vic looked at his watch. Time for his own visit to the medical profession but he sure as hell wouldn't be posting updates on Facebook.

*

Obviously, the new Saturday morning opening hours hadn't caught on. The waiting room was empty apart from an old man in the corner, who looked like he might have died. He smelt like he might be dead, too. Vic tried not to breathe. The dead man was woken up by his own grunts. He smacked his lips, shot Vic a dirty look and closed his eyes. Vic picked up a copy of *Woman's Weekly* but put it down again, wiped his hands on his trousers. He looked at his watch and at the surgery door. 'Come on,' he said.

'Mr. Bead?'

Vic got up and glanced at the man in the corner. 'Don't mind him,' the doctor said, 'he just comes in here to get out of the cold.'

The doctor guided Vic to a seat and perched on the desk in front of him. 'So, what seems to be the matter?'

The matter seems to be that you're behaving like an overfamiliar, trendy newsreader and not like someone I want to get my pecker out in front of, Vic thought while he explained his symptoms.

'Any scabs, spots, discharge?'

'Nope,' Vic said.

'How many sexual partners have you had in the last year?'

Vic shrugged. 'A couple.'

'A couple means two or a couple means three?'

'Yes.'

'Which?'

'More like three.'

'I see. Condom?'

'No thanks, I've just eaten.'

The doctor sighed. 'Not heard that one before,' he said, the sarcasm heavy in his voice. 'Shall we try again? Do you use condoms?'

Vic cleared his throat. 'Most of the time.'

The doctor shook his head and typed something in Vic's notes.

'It's probably nothing to worry about, just a urinary tract infection.' He turned to the screen and started typing up a prescription. 'I'd like to run some tests and see how you are generally. You'll get an appointment from the surgery in the next few days. Come back and see me in a week if there's no change in your condition and, in the meantime, drink lots of water and rub this cream on the affected area twice a day.'

'You don't want a urine sample or to see it?' Vic asked.

'No thanks, I've just eaten.'

'Oh, *touché*.' Vic stood up.

'Oh and Mr. Bead, may I suggest you give some thought to your sexual behaviour? You're old enough to remember the start of the AIDS epidemic. It hasn't gone away, you know. And the instances of STDs are higher in the over-forties than in the under twenty-fives.'

'I didn't know that.'

'Also the majority of STDs are passed orally. So make sure you use those condoms, for sex and oral sex,' the doctor said. 'I know you think you're a comedian, Mr. Bead, but syphilis is no laughing matter.'

'Thank you, doctor.' Vic closed the door and made a wanker gesture. Who the hell did that quack think he was? Patronising bastard. It had reminded him of when he was bollocked by his head teacher for having a rather large love bite on his neck. *Promiscuity gets in the way of good grades,* Mr. Rawlings had said. Vic didn't tell him he'd done it to himself with a vacuum cleaner.

Vic tried to spend the rest of the afternoon writing. The evening gigs were in Newport, so he had time on his hands and the doctor had given him some ideas—

There are only three people it's okay to lie to: your children, a traffic warden and, of course, your doctor. We all do it. We round down alcohol, cigarettes and sexual partners; we round up fruit and veg. My doc asked me about fruit and veg portions, I had to think. A packet of crisps, a tin of beans and a Snickers bar. Three, I said. A day? he said. No, a week. If we all do this, it means the whole medical profession is based on lies. Who here eats five a day? It's impossible. But we tell the docs we do, he sees how unhealthy we are and puts it up to seven. I tell my doc I only drink fifteen beers a week—I really drink twenty-five—he sees that my liver is perfectly healthy, so thinks that's fine. But doctors want us to drink less, so they round down the limit. So, the doctors say the limit is ten. It's all lies and we've only ourselves to blame...

Vic read through what he had written and then ctl-alted his way to Facebook, Twitter, thought about going to YouPorn but remembered the advice Mia had given him, so went back to the Word document he'd been working on. He read it again and then put his finger on the delete key and kept it there until the screen was white again. It had potential but it needed more thought and fewer words. He went to make a cup of tea and have a glass of water. How could he make the doctor visit funny? How could he make a urinary tract infection funny? Did drunk lads really want to hear about painful pisses? Maybe Wally was right, maybe he had to go back to basics. He downed the glass of water in one and sat back at the computer. He slurped his tea and stared at the blank screen. He went to YouTube and typed in Monkhouse, then Allen, then Herring, Lee, Dee, Cooper...

'Fuck!' Vic looked at his watch, three hours he'd been watching YouTube videos. And what did he have to show for it? A brain that was scrambled with other people's ideas and no new material.

'Thanks for nothing, Wally,' Vic said, and started getting ready for the night.

October 2016

Vic sat in the kitchen, listening to the hum of cartoons through the walls. The flat was so much nicer when Elis was playing computer games, listening to music and watching telly all at the same time. Vic switched his computer on, typed in his security code and watched as the page loaded.

'What the fuck?' Vic started at the screen. 'What the actual fuck?'

He fished his phone out of his pocket. There had to be some kind of mistake. The recorded voice asked him for his details. A generic piece of classical music played as he waited for someone to take his call. 'C'mon, C'mon.'

'Armitage Bank, Marcus speaking, how can we help you today?'

'Hi, Marcus, it looks like someone's been taking money out of my account, three hundred quid, one pound at a time,' Vic said.

'Let me have a look.'

Marcus took Vic's details and Vic could hear the distant tap of computer keys

'Mr. Bead, do you own a tablet computer or smart phone?' Marcus asked.

'Yes but I haven't bought anything with it.'

'It looks like someone has been buying tokens on an app called, *Clash of the Farms*.'

'Clash of the what?'

'Farms.'

'Elis,' Vic said.

'Sorry?'

'Never mind. Why didn't someone tell me this was going on?'

'I'm afraid it's a app store account which you've verified, so this wasn't picked up by the fraud detectors.'

'Can I transfer some money from my saving account, please?'

'Certainly, I'll do that for you straight away. How much would you like to transfer?'

Vic plucked a number from the air.

'That's gone through. Is there anything else I can help you with?'

'No, that's it,' said Vic. He hung up. 'Elis, get in here now.'

Elis wandered into the kitchen with the iPad in his hand.

'Give me that,' Vic said.

'What?'

'Give me that bloody iPad.' He snatched it from Elis's hand.

'What's wrong, Dad?'

'You know very well what's wrong. Three hundred quid you've spent on that bloody farming game. Three hundred quid, Elis. That's our holiday up in smoke. What the hell were you doing?'

'I, I didn't know, Dad.'

'You didn't know, you didn't know? Of course you knew. What the hell were you...?'

Tears ran down Elis's face, as he ran from the kitchen.

Vic thumped the kitchen table. 'Shit.'

Ten minutes later Vic's phone buzzed. He looked at the screen.

'What?' Vic snapped, as he pressed the green button.

'Elis wants me to pick him up,' Kylie said.

'How the hell did he contact you?'

'He's got my old Nokia for emergencies.'

'And you didn't think to tell me?'

'Vic, he sounded really upset.'

'What did you say to him?'

'I said I'd call him back. What's happened?'

'He can't go crying to you every time I discipline him.'

'What's going on?'

'The little blighter spent three hundred quid on a bloody farming game.'

'Oh, I see, that's not good,' said Kylie. 'Hang on, how was he able to access your credit card details?'

'I put them in once, so he could buy some corn.'

'Well, that wasn't very clever, was it?'

'For Christ's sake, Kylie, I thought we agreed not to take sides. He knew what he was doing.'

'He's ten, Vic, I think he's been naïve rather than naughty. There was no need to shout at him.'

'Three hundred quid, Kylie. Maybe you can afford that with your middle-class girlfriend, but—'

'Oh, for god's sake, Vic, grow up. If you're short of money, why don't you get a proper job? I'm coming to get him.'

'No, you're bloody not. This is between me and him.'

'He's upset Vic.'

'And so he bloody well should be. Look, I'll talk to him, okay? Leaving him to stew for a moment won't do him any harm.'

There was a moment of silence.

'Do you need me to send you some money?'

'No, thank you. I'll survive.' Vic ended the call and let the phone fall out of his hand on to the table.

Elis stood in the kitchen doorway, staring at the floor. 'I'm sorry, Dad.'

'Come here.' Vic opened his arms and Elis crept forward.

'You're a scamp,' Vic said, as he hugged his son

'I didn't know, Dad. Honest.'

'Well, I guess we need to have a talk about money and the value of things.'

Vic could feel Elis's heartbeat.

'Go on, go watch TV.'

'Can I have the iPad back?'

'Don't push it.'

The next morning, after taking Elis to school, Vic went to the bank to see if there was any way of getting the money back. They promised him they'd look into it but they weren't hopeful. By the time he got home, the postman had been. Vic scooped up the envelopes from the mat. Bill, junk, junk, and a cream envelope, embossed with what looked like the name of a solicitors' firm

'Here we go,' Vic said. He'd been expecting this since the conversation in the café. He took a deep breath and sliced open the letter.

'No,' he said, as he read the contents. 'Over my dead body.'

An hour later Vic, was sitting in The Ox with Ash and his friend Chris.

'At least they've dropped the adoption idea,' said Ash.

'But they're still going for the parental responsibility,' said Vic, 'and, as you pointed out, that leaves me in the minority when it comes to all decisions.'

Chris had his glasses on his head and was reading through the letter.

'Standard stuff,' said Chris, as he pushed his glasses down. 'I'll get one of my staff to send a reply this afternoon saying you don't agree and, if they want to pursue this, they'll have to go through the courts.'

'Thanks,' Vic said.

'I'm not a family lawyer but, in my experience, the judge often sides with the father in these instances. Their lawyer will probably advise them to drop it.'

'See,' said Ash.

'Thanks. What do I owe you?'

A barman turned up with three plates of food.

Chris tucked in. 'Buy the lunch and we'll call it quits,' he said, his mouth full of burger. Swallowing, he added, 'If it goes to court, I can get fix you up with a reasonable family guy.'

'That's brilliant. I really appreciate it,' said Vic, as he tucked into his rib-eye steak. 'It's a relief to know there's someone on my side.'

Vic was trying to write new material when his phone rang, he looked at the screen and smiled as he pressed the green button.

'Hello, Kylie.'

'Vic, what the fuck?'

'What's the matter?'

'You know damn well what the matter is. I've just got a letter from your solicitor. I can't believe you're turning this down, Vic.'

That was quick, Vic thought, *I only had the meeting two days ago.*

'I told you in the café it wasn't going to happen. A fancy letter from a lawyer isn't going to scare me.'

'Fucking hell, Vic. We've agreed not to push to adopt. We just want Nat to have a legal role in Elis's life. She puts in the hours and the love, not to mention the money. She deserves this.'

'Sorry, Kylie, but I'm not going to agree to it.'

'Why are you doing this?'

'I'm protecting the relationship I have with my son.'

'Nothing will change.'

'Rubbish, it would always be two against one, so things would change.'

'Stop being so childish, Vic.'

'I'm not being childish, I'm being realistic.'

'Huh.'

'Kylie, I think it would be better if it was just me and you making the important decisions regarding Elis.'

'Nat's going to be so upset when she sees this. How am I going to tell her?'

'Not my problem.'

'You're a bastard. You're not gonna get away with this. I'll see you in court.'

Vic placed his phone on the table and went into the kitchen. He took a deep breath and ran himself a glass of water. He caught sight of his reflection in the window. He sucked in his stomach and puffed out his chest.

'Stay strong,' he said. 'Stay strong.'

That afternoon, Vic outlined the situation to Mia. 'I just said no.'

'I'm proud of you,' Mia said.

The barista called their drinks. 'I'll get them.' Mia said.

'I just wish we didn't need lawyers and the courts and

everything,' Vic said as Mia sat down.

'She'll come around. Did you agree to the holiday?'

Vic nodded.

'Good. You need to make a list of all the times you've compromised, to show you are not being petty.

'Good idea. So, how's the babysitting going?' Vic asked.

'The what?'

'Harry.'

'Oh, yes, that ended.'

'Oh no, why?'

Mia leaned in. 'He was hopeless in bed. Terrible. So much energy, so little skill.'

'Teenagers are often all fingers and thumbs,' Vic said.

'He's twenty-four. Anyway, it wasn't so much that, he...' Mia stared down at her coffee. 'He had all the moves but it was clinical, like he was reading from a script. And the positions he tried to get me in,' she exclaimed. 'I thought I was going to pull a muscle.'

'Porn,' Vic said.

'What?'

'Porn, he's learnt everything from porn. Back when we were first having sex we had to pick things up from instinct or school yard gossip. Now kids have hours and hours of tutorials out there.'

'But porn isn't real.'

'I know that, you know that, but the kids use it like *Minecraft* tutorials. I bet he never really got close to you either,' Vic said.

'How did you know?'

'He was leaving room for the camera.'

Mia laughed.

'But, if you think about it, you really ought to help him. It's only fair.'

'What the hell are you on about?'

'Well, if you throw him back into the water, as he is, how's he going to learn? The next woman that catches him is going to be equally disappointed. If you don't want him, the least you can do is show him the error of his ways.'

'Jesus Vic, I'm a teacher by day, I don't want to give lessons in bed. I'll tell you what, if you're so worried, I'll give him your number.'

'That reminds me. I've got a date with Cariad, tonight.'

'No way, she's found the keys?'

'Let's hope so.'

'Wow, look at you. You're really quite keen on her, aren't you?'

Mia left Vic and went straight to Andy's. As usual, they ended up in bed within minutes of her arrival.

Mia lay with her head on Andy's chest, watching his mobile phone. Despite it being face down on the bedside table, Mia could see it glow. She watched it fade and light up again. Andy, stretched next to her, moaned and ran his hand down her spine.

'You're delicious,' he said.

Mia watched the phone light up and fade again. Andy kissed her head and tried to sit up.

'Where are you going?' Mia said.

'I need to take this off,' he said, pointing to the condom. 'Then, I'll make some dinner.' He picked up his phone and pattered into the bathroom.

'Bastard,' Mia muttered to herself. She switched the bedside light on and started searching around for her clothes. She had no proof, it might have been his mother, or the bank, or his mate or… or… She put her knickers on. 'Bastard,' she said again, pulling her tights on. She wondered if it was just one or if there were many out there. No wonder he didn't care about her having Stan. It absolved him of responsibility. Gave him license to do what he wanted. He'd told her she was the only one but he was probably sitting on the edge of his bath right now, sending dick pics. She heard the toilet flush and the bathroom door open.

'Do you want a glass of water, or more wine?' Andy called, voice fading in the direction of the kitchen.

She pulled her dress on over her head and put her bangles on.

'No, thank you.' Mia picked up her phone. There was a message from Harry. She ignored it, opened the taxi app and booked a taxi.

'Oh, I thought you were staying for food,' Andy said as he entered the room with a glass of red in his hand. He set the glass down and tried to unzip Mia's dress.

Mia backed away and delivered her kamikaze line. 'I think my period's starting and I don't have tampons with me.'

'Oh, right. Want me to call you a taxi?'

Mia waved her phone and told him one was on the way

'Okay. Are you sure you won't stay?'

'I think I should go. I'll wait outside,' she said.

'See you soon, be good,' said Andy with a smile, as he put his arms around her and kissed the top of her head.

'Bye.'

Mia closed the front door and ran down the stairs out into the fresh air. She gulped and wiped away a tear just as the taxi rounded the corner.

If there was a better looking girl in the country, Vic had yet to meet her. Cariad's red hair glowed, her green eyes glistened and her smile captivated. She had her sunglasses perched on the top of her head and, to top it all off, she had fishnet tights and Adidas trainers. Vic was watching her every move for clues. Was the fact that she was playing with her hair a sign she was flirting? He had no idea.

'Do you get many hecklers?'

'One or two but people are usually put to sleep by my act, so there's no energy to heckle.'

'It must be terrible.'

'The show?'

'No, when they heckle.'

'Actually, I quite enjoy it. Gets you out of your comfort zone, gets the adrenaline pumping.'

'I don't know how you do it.'

'I don't know why I do it.'

'There you go with your 'Vic' humour. Always putting yourself down. You're better than you think you are.'

'How would you know?'

'I've seen your act?'

'Have you? When?'

'A while ago, after our last night out.'

Vic noted she hadn't called it a date. 'Why didn't you tell me?'

'I was with a group of frineds, I didn't want to embarrass you.'

'Is that why you didn't want to see me again?'

'There you go, putting yourself down again. Keep doing that and people will believe you. I told you, you were good. I'm not going to say it again and inflate your ego.'

'Thanks,' Vic said. 'Do you want another wine?'

Cariad nodded. 'But last one, I've got work in the morning.'

The rest of the evening passed all too quickly. Vic was still trying to spot signs that she might be interested but she was very guarded with her clues, or they were so subtle he was missing them.

They walked towards the taxi rank.

'Shall we do this again?' Vic said.

'Yes, I'd like that,' Cariad said, 'but I'm super busy at the moment. I'll call you.' She touched his face lightly and got in a waiting taxi.

'See you soon,' she said and waved as the taxi pulled away into the traffic. Vic had the feeling he was back on the roof of the multi-storey.

Mia and Vic stood at the counter, waiting for their coffees.

'I'll get these,' Mia said but Vic handed over a twenty pound note before she could get her purse out.

'Too late.'

'So, a week in Germany?' Mia said, as they walked over to an empty table.

'They left this morning.'

'Was he excited?'

'He was ecstatic. Although not sure a week in Berlin is going to be that exciting for a ten-year-old.'

'True but different food, different language, he'll love it. And you've got the week to yourself,' Mia said.

'True. I'd like to get some writing done but I'm suffering at the moment.'

'Really, why?'

'Dunno, just can't seem to write anything. I've got a few ideas but nothing seems to work when I sit in front of my computer.'

'Maybe you need to leave it for a few days.'

'I've tried that. Left it for days. Now it's been weeks.'

'Ah, not good.'

'No.'

'Why don't you go away yourself?'

'Money.'

Mia nodded.

'And no women to see?'

'I'm down to none.'

'No way.'

'Debbie's away and Tina threw her toys out of the pram. I haven't heard from her since.'

'What did you do?'

'I called her Mia. She went mental.'

'Fuck! That's bad. So, it's over?'

'She said so, although she did send a text the other day but then sent another one saying it wasn't meant for me.'

'Ah, the oldest trick in the digital age,' Mia said.

'What?'

'She's testing the waters. Be careful Vic.'

'Ha, ha, Ash told me to be careful, too.'

'Perhaps it's time to listen to us,' said Mia. 'And Cariad, how did it go last week?'

Vic sighed. 'I just don't get it,' Vic said, taking a swig of coffee. 'She said she'd call me but six days and nothing. Why did she agree on a date with me in the first place?'

'Maybe you bored her into submission,' Mia said.

'Very funny. No, come on, I'm being serious. Why get my hopes up?'

'She could have been trying to make up her mind. Maybe you didn't impress.'

'Kick a man when he's down, why don't you?'

'Or she could be in a bad place, you said her divorce had only just come through. She's got two kids. Maybe she's protecting you. At least she's not future faking you.'

'She's not what?'

'Promising you something and then not delivering. She's being honest, Vic. Unlike Andy. He's sleeping with other women and denying it.'

'And you know that for a fact, do you?'

'Let's call it women's intuition.'

'Right but is there any actual evidence?'

'Not yet, but I'm going around there this afternoon.'

Mia was sat up in bed. She'd had enough. As usual, Andy had disappeared to the toilet with his phone in his hand. She'd seen it glowing at least three times since he'd last checked it. Something was going on.

'So, who is she?' she asked as he got back into bed

'Who is who?'

'The woman you text every time you go to the toilet,' Mia said, her voice high and whiney.

'What *are* you talking about, woman?'

'Don't you 'woman' me.'

'Sorry but I've no idea what you are on about.'

'Why don't you simply admit it?' she said.

'Admit what?'

'Five minutes before you went to the toilet your phone lit up.'

'And that means I'm having an affair, does it?'

'No,' said Mia, 'but I'm curious. Why do you need to take it to the loo?'

'They're score alerts, I'm checking the football,' Andy said. 'I don't want to look at them when I'm with you.'

'Oh, give me a break. So, why the need to put the phone face down when you come back?' Mia asked. 'I'll tell you why,' she continued, 'it's so I can't see who's texting you.'

'I told you, it's score alerts. I put it face down because I don't want it to disturb us.'

They sat in silence for a while.

'You get plenty of messages too but I don't accuse you of having an affair,' Andy said.

'You know I have another lover. You tell me you don't.'

'Because I don't.' Andy shook his head. 'I can't win, the more I say I don't, the less you believe me.' Andy said.

'Leave your phone here next time you pee.'

'That means I'll be checking the football scores when I'm with you and you'll get pissed off with me for checking the internet instead of talking to you.

'So, show me.'

'Show you what?'

'These so-called football scores.'

Andy got his phone out and swiped it open. 'It's Saturday afternoon,' he said and showed her the screen.

'Okay,' Mia said. 'I'm sorry.'

'Come here.' Andy pulled Mia towards him and gave her a big kiss.

'I've got to go,' Mia said, trying to escape from his clutches.

'Hey, how about I cook you a meal on Thursday?'

'Yeah, that'd be great.'

'And how about a quickie before you go.' Andy kissed her again and Mia decided to let him have his fun.

Vic worried that Mia was getting herself into trouble. It was like picking at a scab. The more you picked the more it hurt. Sometimes it was best to just leave it alone and enjoy it for what it was.

He checked his phone again. Still nothing.

How long before he could send Kylie a message without looking over-anxious? There were no reports of car crashes on the M4, or planes disappearing between the UK and Berlin. So, he could assume they'd got there safely but one text to say all was okay wouldn't hurt. This was typical of Kylie. If Vic didn't send her a text to say Elis was home from school, she went up the wall but, when Elis was with her, she never let Vic know all was well. He checked the phone again, despite there being no beep or vibration. He checked arrivals at Berlin airport online. The plane had landed two hours ago, two bloody hours. She really was taking the piss.

Rain began to fall and, although it was only 3 p.m, it was already dark. What if they'd been picked up by a rogue taxi and the driver had kidnapped and murdered them in a field on the outskirts of Berlin, leaving their bodies to the crows? What if the taxi had crashed on the way in to Berlin and they were critically ill in a German hospital?

'Stop it,' Vic said.

He tried to distract himself by reading through his material for later. These wild fantasies were hiding his real fear, that they hadn't gone to Berlin at all. The fear that they'd gone somewhere else and were never planning on coming back. He wished he'd never signed the permission form. He paced around the living room.

He couldn't breathe. He opened the window. Hail stones clattered into the room. He closed the window. Sweat was beginning to form on his brow and his stomach felt tight. Where the fuck was she? He stared out onto the street, hoping to see his ex-wife and child walking through the storm. His phone beeped. He snatched it from the table and saw the message was from Tina. He threw it onto the sofa and watched it bounce onto the floor. He swore and scrabbled to retrieve it. He composed a message.

» *Hi, did you arrive safely?*

Did that sound casual enough? He shrugged and pressed Send.

Grey ticks appeared to confirm it had been received, but they didn't turn blue; delivered but not read. He willed them to turn blue. They stayed stubbornly grey.

'Check your fucking phone,' he said.

Maybe he could go onto Facebook and ask if anyone had heard from Kylie, or he could phone her mum? He was overreacting. He knew what Kylie was like. He returned to the window and watched the people hurrying through the downpour. He looked at the phone, ticks still grey. Fuck it, he was phoning her.

It rang three times before she answered.

'Hi, Vic, what's wrong?'

'Nothing, just checking you'd landed safely.'

'Jesus, Vic, you had me scared. I thought there was something wrong.'

Vic took a deep breath. 'Well, I'm so sorry to worry you but it's the first time my son has been on a plane without me, so I thought you might have thought to let me know you'd got there safely.'

'Oh yes, everything's fine.'

'Can I speak to him?'

'Um, he's...'

'Can I speak to my son, Kylie?'

He heard Kylie call Elis.

'Hi, Dad,'

'Hi Elis, how's Berlin?'

'It's massive, Dad, the buildings are *huge*, and the plane was amazing.'

'Great, what time is it there?'

'Er, Mum, what time is it?'

Vic heard Kylie's curt reply.

'It's twenty-five minutes past four, Dad.'

'Wow, it's only half past three here, so, you're in the future. Have a good time and remember I want a photo a day, okay?'

'Yes, Dad.'

Vic rubbed his forehead and sighed as he unscrewed the top from a bottle of red and took a huge gulp.

November 2016

'Do you want a glass of wine?' Andy called from the kitchen.

'Yes, please. White, if you have it.' Mia looked up from her phone to see Andy come in with a glass in his hand.

'There you are, Madam.' Andy put the wine down and gave Mia a kiss. 'It'll be about ten minutes, okay?'

'Smells great,' she said.

'I always do,' Andy said.

'I meant the food.'

Andy blew her a kiss and went back into the kitchen. Mia noticed Andy's phone was lying on the coffee table. She looked at it. Her fingers itched. It was in touching distance begging to reveal its secrets. She shouldn't, she knew she shouldn't. No, she should leave it well alone. But, then again, wouldn't it be good to know for sure? If he was telling the truth, she could stop being so suspicious but, if he was lying, she'd know what she was dealing with. She put her phone down and took a mouthful of wine. What to do?

Her fingers reached for his mobile.

'You okay in there?'

She snatched her hand away. 'Yeah, fine,' she said and listened closely to see if he was coming in the room. Andy started singing. Mia gabbed his mobile and hit the Home button.

Please enter your six-digit access code…

'Bastard.' She'd watched him a million times swipe left and the phone opened. When had he put in a code? What was he hiding? She placed the device back on the table and took another sip of wine. She'd find out that damn code and catch him with his pants down.

Vic's phone buzzed just as Ash was putting two beers down on the table. 'That's my freedom over,' he said.

'Back are they?'

'Yeah, just touched down.'

'And she let you know this time?'

'I think I got my point across,' Vic said. He took a swig of beer.

Ash looked around. 'Dead in here, isn't it?'

'Always is. They'll sell it for flats one of these days.'

'It's bound to happen. And, talking of the inevitable, have you and Mia got it on yet?'

'Give it a rest, will you?'

'I've been thinking,' Ash said, 'I think you're Mia's intellectual fluffer.'

'Her what?'

'Don't tell me you don't know what a fluffer is.'

'Enlighten me.'

'In the porn industry, they hire people to,' Ash coughed, 'prepare the stars for action. That's a fluffler.'

'Right, so how does that relate to me and Mia?'

'After her coffee with you, she always goes off to meet Stan or Andy, doesn't she?'

'Yeah, so what?'

'Well, she obviously needs intellectual titillation from you, before going to get the physical stimulation from her men.'

'You don't half talk some rubbish at times, Ash.'

'Why's it rubbish?'

'I am sure Stan and Andy are more than capable of doing whatever it is you are claiming I do.'

'Nonsense. Christ knows what Mia sees in Stan. We both know he's emotionally autistic. And Mia's the first to admit Andy's not the sharpest tool in the box. I mean, he's a fucking woodwork teacher. So, she needs you for the mental side of things.'

Vic shook his head and took another swig of beer. He smiled at Rosie, who was collecting the empties from their table. He watched her walk away like a catwalk model.

'I mean, it's a compliment,' Ash continued.

'Oh yeah, thanks. You're saying I can mentally turn woman on but I'm not up to the physical job.'

'Without you, the other two wouldn't be getting any. You're facilitating their sex lives. A modern-day Cyrano.'

'And I don't even get as much as a 'Thanks',' Vic said.

'Well, I think many fluffers go on to be big stars, so you never know.'

'Does Lily know you are such an expert on porn?'

'I think she's probably guessed,' said Ash, as he stood up . 'I'll be back it a tick. I need a smoke.'

Vic nodded and watched Rosie going about her business. He felt a sudden rush of sadness knowing he'd never be that age again and, more importantly, knowing he'd never get his hands on a body that age again.

'Would you ever date a twenty-one year old?' Vic asked when Ash returned from outside.

'Chance would be a fine thing,' Ash said. 'Sadly, I haven't got a magic wand to make Lily twenty-one again. Why? Who have you got your eye on?'

'Oh, no one. I was just thinking about how wide my span is. I'm early forties so—What? Twenty years either way?'

'You'd shag a sixty-year-old?'

'I'm not saying I would but I wouldn't rule it out. I think that would be less weird than a twenty year old.'

'But you said twenty-one, you were very specific. Who do you have your eye on?'

Vic's face reddened.

'No one, I'm just thinking aloud.'

'It wouldn't be the lovely Rosie, would it?'

'Keep your voice down, you idiot.' Vic hissed. Rosie was serving one of the old fellas. She looked over and smiled at the pair of them.

'She's closer to Elis's age than mine,' Vic said.

'Hmm, true. That doesn't paint it in a good light.' Ash looked at his friend. 'Look at your puppy dog eyes. You've got it bad. Want me to set you two up?'

'No, you caused me enough troubles with Cariad.'

They drank in silence for a minute or two.

'I think twenty-one is okay,' Ash said, 'as long as you don't initiate it.'

'What do you mean?'

'If you come on to her, it's creepy but, if she comes on to you, then it's okay.'

'Sounds reasonable. So, I've just got to find a way to get her to make a move.'

'Good luck with that. I'm still trying to get my head around the thought of a sixty-year-old.'

'There's some very sexy sixty-year-old women.'

'But it sounds so ancient.'

'It's only seventeen years older than us, mate. When we were seventeen, we'd have loved a thirty-four-year-old.'

'True, I suppose. But sixty?'

'Goldie Hawn, Helen Mirren, both over sixty. Tracey Ulman is late fifties.'

'True but they've had work done, haven't they? Stick to your twenty-year-olds.'

'If I can get them to come on to me.' Vic smiled.

December 2016

Vic opened the café door and saw Mia at the counter. She smiled when she saw him.

'I've got your usual,' she said. Vic nodded and then pointed at an empty table.

'How's life?' Mia asked as she put the two coffees on the table.
'Not bad.'

'How are you?'

'Same old. I see you've been busy.'

'What?'

'You've set up a new website. I like it,' Mia said. 'It shows you've finally started listening to me.'

'No, I haven't.' Vic poured some sugar into his coffee. 'What makes you say that?'

'Well, someone has.' Mia tapped on her phone and turned it around so Vic could see his own face staring back at him.

'Vicbead dot org,' he read. 'That's a bit odd.'

Vic scrolled through the photos, touched on a tab called Interviews and read all about how getting over his wife was hard. 'I never gave this interview,' he said. 'It's weird, it's kind of made up but with things I would say.' He continued reading. 'Are you behind this? Is it a wind up?'

'Do you think I've got the time or the inclination to do that?'
'No but if not you, then who?'

'Your agent?'

Vic shook his head. 'She'd have told me.'

'Your super fan, Tina?'

'She hates me at the moment.'

'But she knows enough about you to fake an interview.'

'True but there're pictures here from gigs she wasn't even at.'

'As far as you know.'

'Look, there's one from last week. It's three weeks since we last spoke. She's not going to come to my gigs and not let me know, is she?' Vic tapped the Reviews tab and started reading. 'The reviews are good,' he said.

'Must be Tina, then. She's the only one who actually likes your stuff.'

'Oi, other people like my comedy, you know.'

'Sorry.'

Vic continued scrolling. 'This is creepy.'

'It is a little but it's good creepy. I've been nagging you for ages for you to get more than a Facebook page and your agent's page. Now you've got it. Free publicity.'

'Except I can't control it.'

'True but it's positive.'

Vic continued to stare at the screen, occasionally following links.

'Jesus, it's even got my upcoming gigs. I hardly know them myself. Is she watching me?' Vic looked over his shoulder and around the cafe.

'Relax, Tina—'

'If it *is* Tina.'

'—whatever. Whoever it is, they probably just searched the clubs' websites, or contacted your agent. You've got a super fan, not a stalker.'

Vic put the phone down.

'Talking of stalking,' Mia said, 'if you were Andy, what would your code be on your screen lock?'

'Why?'

'I need to get in to the secret palace. I want to prove he's got other women.'

'You sure you want to know?'

Mia nodded.

'Have you tried his birthday?'

'Yep. And the first six digits of his phone number.'

'Your birthday?'

Mia nodded.

'Who does he support?'

'What?'

'He's a football fan, isn't he? What's his team?'

'Cardiff City.'

'Okay.' Vic scratched his chin. 'Try 192710 or 192701.'

'Why?'

'It's the year city won the FA Cup and the score.'

'Jesus, that's random.'

'I know three City fans with that as their pin.'

'Men.' Mia shook her head. 'I'm seeing him later. I'll try it.'

'Why are you so convinced he has another woman?'

'There are four reasons.'

'Go on.'

Mia counted on her fingers: 'One, the phone lights up all the time. He says it's football updates, but I don't believe him.'

'He might have notifications on. I have them for the cricket.'

Mia pulled a face. 'Two, some nights he goes to bed at ten. Sends me a text telling me he's knackered and needs an early night.'

'He might be knackered.'

'Or he might be with another woman and she's gone to the toilet. He's letting me know not to disturb him.'

'Or he might be tired. Okay, so let's say that's two.'

'Three, he never tells me who he's out with—'Just a friend, just friends'—no names, nothing specific.'

'He might think you don't know them, so it's not relevant.'

'Yeah right.'

'And four?'

'He suddenly got a screen lock on his phone. Just out of the blue.'

'Maybe he updated his operating system, security codes are compulsory now.'

'Or maybe he's hiding secrets. And five.'

'I thought you said four.'

'Well, there's five. I'm a woman, I can change my mind, so five: I have a sixth sense.'

'You see dead people?'

'No, I just know these things.'

'That's probably the most damning evidence. Are you sure you want to know for sure?'

'It's not that I want to know, Vic, it's that I have to know.

What was that number again?'

'192710.'

Mia lay in Andy's bed, panting. Despite his faults, he was good at that. She stroked his chest and looked at the wispy hair. Oh, she wished she could trust him. It would make life so much easier.

'Thanks,' she said.

Andy laughed. 'You're welcome.' He kissed her hand. 'Back in a minute. I'm going to take this off.'

He left his phone. Bloody hell, this was her chance. Mia snatched up the phone and typed the number Vic had given her.

192701. Nothing.

192710. Again, the phone shook its refusal.

'Some help you were, Vic,' Mia mumbled.

She heard the toilet flush. *Don't forget to wash your hands*, she thought.

011927.

Nothing

101927.

The phone opened. Mia felt her stomach flip. At the same time, she heard the clunk of the bathroom door.

'Andy, be a love and get me some wine.'

'Of course, lovely.'

Message: Lorna. She opened the message stream. It was more a photo stream.

Tits.

Dick.

Tits.

Dick.

Stimulating conversation it was not.

'Bastard,' she said, as she realised that his intimate photos were the same ones he sent her.

She looked for more evidence. Her messages were beneath Lorna's, and then his mum and some bloke called Stu. She hid the window and checked to see what app was last opened. Tinder!

He had six conversations with six women ongoing.

 » Looks like you need a little spanking.

This guy was a serial sexter. She thumped the bed and looked up at the sound of the door being kicked open. Andy stood, motionless, two glasses in his hands.

'What the fuck are you doing with my phone?'

'What the fuck are you up to?'

'I said, what are you doing with my phone?'

'Are you sleeping with this Lorna or just sending pics of your glorious manhood?'

'What right do you have to go into my phone? And how the fuck do you know my code?'

'Answer my question. Who is Lorna? Are you shagging her? I've got a right to know.'

'Give me that.'

Mia threw the phone at Andy. It bounced off his chest.

'Now look what you've done, you—' Andy put down the glasses and snatched an old t-shirt that was on a chair and got down to clean the carpet.

'How many are there? How many are you fucking? You told me it was football scores. So, come on, what's the fucking score?'

Andy scrubbed the wine.

'You care more about the carpet than me!'

'It's going to stain.'

'Who cares?' They stared at each other. 'Don't you care about disease? If you fucking give me an STD, I'll fucking kill you. You fucking, selfish bastard.'

'You went in my phone.'

'Do they know about me? Or am I football scores, too?'

'Oh, listen to prim and proper over there. It's not like you're all sweetness and light. Does Stan know about me?'

'That's not the fucking point. You know about him. I haven't lied to you.' She hesitated, thinking this wasn't strictly true. But, no, she hadn't lied. Okay, she may have omitted to mention Harry but that wasn't lying, not really. 'Anyway,' she continued, dragging on her clothes, 'you're the one sneaking around like a dirty pervert, shagging anything that moves.'

'Mia, it's not like that.'

'Just fuck off, Andy, just fuck the fuck right off.' Mia grabbed her bag and headed for the door. Andy reached for her arm.

'It's just harmless fun. I'm just sending texts.'

'Harmless, call that harmless? You'll be dickless if you're not careful. Then what will you send photos of?'

'It's just banter.'

'Banter? Banter is being casually racist, not sending pics of your dick via text.' She shoved Andy away and slammed the door.

Standing outside, she pulled her coat around herself and shivered. It was only 8 p.m, but the street was deserted. She didn't want to be alone. Stan was playing darts and Vic was performing. She scrolled through her contacts.

'Hi, are you busy?'

'No, not really.'

'Fancy a glass of wine?'

'What? Now?' Harry asked.

'Yes but if you're not free.'

'I'm free.'

'Good, my place in an hour. Oh and bring the wine.'

As Mia walked home through the rain, she deleted Andy's number and all his messages.

Vic turned the collar down on his shirt, checked his flies and then grabbed his keys. A quick walk to the shops might get the ideas moving in his mind. There was a new routine brewing in there, somewhere, but he needed to think of something else for a while and let it work itself out. He felt the rain on his face as soon as he closed the front door. He hesitated for a moment. Should he go back and get a coat? No, he was only going to buy milk. A bit of rain never hurt anyone.

He locked the door and turned around. Was that Tina loitering across the road? It was. She was wearing a red coat with a hood, protecting her blonde hair from the elements.

'Tina,' he called, as he jogged towards her, 'what are you doing here?'

'Oh, hi, Vic. How are you?' She kissed him on the cheek.

'Yeah, I'm fine but… Surprised to see you.'

'Oh, I was just in the area. Thought I'd walk down the street for old times' sake.'

'Right, well, um, I was just going to get a coffee, do you want one?'

'Love one.'

Before Vic could lead Tina towards the High Street, she'd marched across the road and stood on Vic's doorstep.

'C'mon, I'm getting soaked here,' she said.

'So how have you been?' Tina asked as she nosed her way around the flat.

'Not bad, a few new comedy ideas, a few new bookings. Yeah, it's going okay.'

'Got together with Mia yet?'

Vic sighed. 'So, what have you been up to?'

'Nothing much. I've been missing you,' she said, as she nestled up against him.

'Tina?'

'What?' She laid her head on his shoulder.

Vic took a deep breath. It would be easy to have sex with her now. So, so easy. Her body warmth produced familiar stirrings. But no, he mustn't. He didn't want to go through the aftermath again. Best to keep it on a friendly footing.

'We shouldn't,' he said.

'But I want to.' Tina's eyes were wide open and one hand went to the top button of her blouse. 'Come on, it would be fun.'

'Yes, it would be.' Vic moved away and poured some water into the cafeteria. The grounds sizzled. 'But…'

'No buts.' Tina nuzzled into him again.

'Let's drink our coffee.' Vic pressed down the plunger immediately and poured the resulting weak coffee into two cups. 'I haven't got any milk.'

'That's okay,' Tina said and took one cup into the living room. She sat on the sofa and looked at Vic's computer.

'Hey,' Vic said, trying to close the lid. 'That's private.'

'Let me see.' She smiled, as she began to read a section aloud. 'This is good,' she said, 'but look, you can edit this bit.' She highlighted a section on the screen. 'Remember, choose every word carefully and read aloud what you've written.'

'Thank you, Michael Macyntyre.' Vic snapped the lid of the computer shut and sat down across from Tina.

'Come here.' Tina patted the sofa next to him.

'Look Tina, I don't think this is sensible. I hurt you last time. You're looking for something different from me.'

'How do you know what I'm looking for?' She crossed her legs, flashing the tops of her stockings. 'I just want you one more time.' She adjusted one of her heels and stood up and walked over towards Vic. She took his coffee off him and put it on the table, sat on his lap and kissed him. Their tongues fought.

'Tina, this isn't a good idea.'

Tina kissed him again. 'Yes, it is, it's a very good idea.'

Vic's hand wandered up her thigh and found the flesh at the top of her stockings. Tina moaned.

When Vic eventually came back with his pint of milk he could still smell Tina's perfume in the air. He sat on the sofa and closed his eyes. Why had he let himself get dragged into that? Did he have no self-control? She'd said she just wanted it to be a one-off. Vic hoped that, this time, she meant it. He had an hour to do some work before he had to collect Elis. He opened up his laptop and read what he'd written earlier in the day. He hated to admit it but Tina had been right. He deleted the offending line and checked his phone. He swallowed: three messages from Tina already.

Two days later Mia and Vic sat opposite each other in the café, looking at their phones. Like synchronised swimmers, they both shook their heads and turned their mobiles face down on the table. They both took swigs of coffee and looked around the café.

'I'm not sure I like this place anymore,' Vic said.

'It's getting a bit hipsterish, isn't it?' Mia agreed.

'And why do business people insist on having meetings in coffee shops? Their companies pay thousands for offices and yet they nip over the road to the café.'

Mia's phone buzzed.

'You're popular.'

Mia shook her head.

'I think I might have done something stupid,' Mia said.

'That makes two of us,' Vic said. 'Let's hear yours first.'

'I tried those numbers you gave me on Andy's phone.'

'Oh yes and?'

'One of them worked. And guess what? The bastard's sending dick pics to some tart called Lorna. *And* he's sexting countless girls on Tinder. I didn't have time to check Whatsapp or anything else, so god knows how many he's got.'

'What a twat.'

'And, get this, he's sending her the same dick photos he sent to me. You'd think he'd take a new photo for each girl but no, I get his sloppy seconds. Second-hand dick pics.

'Oh fuck, I'm sorry.' Vic put his hand on Mia's arm. 'What did you do?'

'I went ballistic, threw his phone at him, stormed out.'

'Good for you.'

'And I've deleted his number from my phone. I never want to see the bastard again. I should have cut his prick off and sent a photo of that to the sluts.'

Vic frowned. 'Well, assuming you didn't actually cut his prick off, none of that sounds too stupid.'

'It's what happened next that's stupid.' Mia paused to take a mouthful of coffee. 'When I left him, I texted Harry.'

'The teenager?'

Mia shot Vic a 'not now' look. 'I just didn't want to be alone, any port and all that. He came over and one thing led to an orgasm. For him at least.'

'Well, at least you had some fun.'

'Yes, only now I hate myself, and that—' she pointed at her phone which had just buzzed again— 'is the twentieth message he's sent since.'

'Ah.'

'I told him it was a one-off. I thought that would be the end of it but…' Right on cue her phone buzzed. 'I'm trying to ignore him but he's like a kid with a drum kit. He's assuming we're now an item, for God's sake.'

'Sounds like we have the same issue,' Vic said, as his phone buzzed again.

'Oh God, please tell me it's not Tina.'

Vic nodded.

'But, Vic, why? You know she's bad news.'

'She was outside my house. Just standing there in the rain. She invited herself in for coffee and the next thing I know she was all over me.'

'She lives in Reading; what the fuck was she doing just passing your place? Didn't any alarm bells start ringing in that thick head of yours?'

'Obviously not.' Vic sipped some coffee. 'I told her I didn't want to do anything but she wouldn't take no for an answer. I told her this couldn't go anywhere, she said she didn't want it to, but, of course, she wants to see me again.'

They sat in silence for a minute, sipping their coffees.

'What are you going to do?' Mia asked.

Vic shrugged. 'I don't know. You?'

'I'm just ignoring him. That's what you should do. She's no good.'

'I'm enchanted by her. She's sexy.'

'I've said this before and I'll say it again, be careful, Vic.'

'And Andy, what are you going to do about him?'

'That's over, done, history. I've severed the limb. I'm not going back there. I knew he was up to something. He could have just told me.'

'Oh right and you would have coped with that, would you?'

'Probably not but at least he wouldn't have been doing it behind my back.'

'True.'

'That's what hurts, it's humiliating. He said it was football scores.'

'Bastard.' Vic shook his head.

Vic looked up at the sound of the café door tinkling. A man stood in the doorway, clutching a bunch of flowers bigger than his head.

'Look,' Vic said.

Mia looked around. 'What the fuck is he doing here?'

'I'll leave you to it.' Vic slid out of his seat and grabbed his coat. 'I'll call you later.'

Andy smiled at Vic as they passed each other.

'These are for you.'

Mia didn't take the bouquet. She was too busy putting her coat on.

'Mia.'

'Fuck off Andy. A bunch of supermarket flowers is not going to get you out of this.'

'They're not supermarket...'

'Sorry, Andy. Maybe Lorna would be impressed with cheap flowers but I'm not.'

'Mia, you've got it all wrong.'

Mia marched out the door, leaving Andy with everyone's eyes on him.

'These cost me fifty quid,' he said to himself.

Vic was wondering if he should have left Mia with Andy, or if he should have stayed around for moral support. It was odds-on they'd end up in bed. Mia had even less willpower than him. He got into his car and checked his phone; another message from Tina.

'For fuck sake,' he mumbled.

» Why don't you ever text me?

Vic rolled his eyes, put the phone back onto the passenger seat and started the engine. Bloody woman. He couldn't win; if he texted her, he was leading her on, if he didn't, he was ignoring her. As he drove, the phone buzzed again and again and a third time. The lights turned red. He put the handbrake on and picked up the phone.

» You took advantage of me. Sex might be a game to you but it is something special to me. I'm not one of your whores

» I never want to see you again.

» Pig.

The lights turned green. Vic shook his head. What did she want from him? Three more bleeps. He pulled up outside his flat and picked up the phone.

» Pig.

» Bastard.

» You've broken my heart. I hope you're happy now.

'Don't answer,' Vic said to himself. 'She's a nutter.'

He got out of the car and let himself into the flat, put the milk into the fridge and read the messages again.

He wasn't a pig. She was fucking reinventing the past. He'd told her it wasn't going to lead anywhere but fuck knows what she'd heard.

» I didn't mean to hurt you. I told you I wasn't looking for anything serious. Sorry.

He looked at the message, pressed Send and realised he was running late. Debbie would be here any minute. Diversion therapy.

His phone buzzed.

» You played with my emotions, Vic. Goodbye.

Vic moved some of Elis's toys into his room and checked the place looked presentable. He didn't have time for a proper tidy but Debbie rarely looked further than the bedroom. He'd just finished washing up when the doorbell rang.

'Hi, Vic.'

'Hi, Debs, come in. Whiskey or wine?' Vic looked up. 'Take

you coat off, make yourself at home.'

'I'm not stopping.' She played with a button.

'What's up?'

'Vic, there's no easy way of saying this. I've met someone and I think it might go somewhere so, well, I think I should start the relationship with a clean slate.'

'You've met someone? Who? When? How?'

'That doesn't matter. I'm sorry, you know I like you,' said Debs as her eyes filled with tears. 'But this is going nowhere and well, I need more.'

Vic handed Debbie a tissue.

'Thanks,' she said. She wiped her eyes, smudging her make-up.

'Yeah… No, it's cool, no problem,' Vic said. He put his arms around her. 'I completely understand.' He kissed her on the head and tried to move her into the bedroom.

'No Vic, don't. It wouldn't be fair. I should go.' She didn't move. They stood and hugged for a few minutes before Debbie prised herself away.

At the door, Debbie looked back. 'Thank you, Vic.' And then *clunk*, she was gone.

Vic poured himself a glass of wine and paced the room. He looked out of the window and saw Debbie marching away. 'Well, whoever this new guy is, he's a lucky man,' he said and slumped down onto the sofa. He put his head back and closed his eyes. No strings, they'd both agreed, but strings always develop. He thought about phoning someone, anyone, to chat about anything. Kylie's was the last number he called. She used to be his best friend. He couldn't call her now. Mia? She'd understand.

His phone buzzed in his hand.

'Hi, Mia, I was just thinking about you.'

'I know, I felt it.'

'Wow, really?'

'Actually, I just got a text from Debbie.'

'Ah.'

'Are you okay?'

'I'm fine.'

'Are you sure? I don't want you wallowing in self-pity, listening to the Cure or something.'

'Mia, don't fuss, I'm fine. It was a causal relationship. No drama.'

'If you need me, you know where I am.'

'Mia, it's cool.'

He ended the call, put his head back again and closed his eyes.

'Fuck.'

First Tina and now Debbie. He'd managed to lose two women in a day. That was some going.

January 2017

Somehow, not having women to worry about gave Vic a clearer mind. He'd had a couple of cracking ideas during the day and was busy trying to get them down on paper, before the cloud descended again—

I feel sorry for young boys, nowadays. The Internet has ruined porn. Ruined it. Half the thrill of porn, when I was a kid, was the ritual around acquiring it. It was a military operation. Starting with the reconnaissance mission. Seeking out a newsagent that looked quiet and where the top shelves were no more than a tiptoe out of reach. Then you had to prepare your equipment. Fake ID, in case you got asked for it. A bag to bring the catch home in, exact change in the back pocket, and, of course, tissues ready on the bed for when you got to the safety of base. A big coat could be useful, in case there needed to be an emergency withdrawal from the shop.

The day of action. Timing was important, two or three in the afternoon was the quietest. Walk past the newsagents once or twice, to check it was empty. Check the street for potential customers and then, when the coast was clear, dart in, grab your copy of Fiesta, *slap the change on the counter, shove the magazine into the bag and exit, stage left.*

There were things that might make you abort the mission. Someone coming in the shop meant another magazine was picked up and purchased. My dad became quite worried about me at one time, I had so many copies of Train Spotter World. *Also, I didn't like it if it was a woman behind the counter.*

Finally, it was the 80s and I was like Thatcher—my biggest fear was inflation. Imagine having to scrabble around for another fifty pence because the cover price had gone up.

Once the mission had been accomplished, the sense of anticipation on the walk home was unbearable. What was beyond the cover? What would they be wearing? Any fishnets? Heels? What would the stories be about? I'd already have an erection by the time I got to the front door.

But the threat wasn't over. I swear my mum knew where I'd been. Maybe the sight of me leaving home with a spurious bag and a big coat in the middle of summer gave it away, or my flustered look when I opened the front door.

Anyway, she always had a task for me when I got in.

But finally, finally, the bliss of the magazine.

These days kids have it so easy. Check the bedroom door is locked, log onto the private browser and that's it, sorted.

Back then it was more innocent, too, just pictures of naked ladies and you had to imagine the rest. These days there's no imagination needed. It's all there. Where's the fun?

Vic read through what he had written. It was good but there was something missing. He remembered what Tina had said about every word counting. He needed to edit it. He leaned back and rubbed his neck. Perhaps a bit of cyberslacking first, though. He clicked on Facebook.

A little red dot showed Vic that someone called Kim had left a comment on his Facebook fan page. He quickly clicked on the link.

A terrible smutty comedian, with the grand total of zero jokes. His misogynistic 'comedy' is spiteful and degrading. Ladies, if you go to see this comedian, the joke is on you. Literally and metaphorically.

Right, so, not a fan.

He clicked on Kim's profile. Her picture was a bunch of flowers. She belonged to one or two comedy appreciation groups but the rest of the profile was hidden. Another red dot appeared, and another one. Both comments from Kim.

Worst gig ever—feel sorry for his ex-wife.

You're the reason the word shite was invented.

Vic scratched his chin. He took screen shots of the messages and then deleted them.

He thought back to the last gig he'd done. Had he gone off-script and upset people? He couldn't remember it if he had. Another red dot appeared.

Coward—Deleting my comments. Can't handle criticism?

Vic deleted it again and looked to see if he could block her. He shivered. He went to the windows, making sure they were firmly closed. This Kim was out there somewhere and she didn't like him.

He drew the curtains and went to check on Elis. He was fine, sleeping soundly.

Back in the living room, he tried to think. What could have upset her? Okay, his routines had become more laddish recently but he was usually the butt of the jokes; he always came out of it worse. Who was this Kim? Was she real? It could be a dummy account. That meant it could be anyone. Wally, Tina or Debbie. Maybe it was Kylie, or Nat playing games because he refused to agree to their demands. Surely Kylie wouldn't do that to him but Nat? He wouldn't put it past her. It made sense, the stuff about feeling sorry for the ex-wife. He thumped the settee. It had to be bloody Nat.

Mia sat in the café wondering if she'd done the right thing. She stirred her coffee while watching the door. After eighty texts and a similar number of missed calls, she'd finally agreed to meet Andy. He seemed genuinely sorry and, what's more, he'd managed to catch her with her guard down. She remembered the first time she'd sat here waiting for him. She'd been so determined that it would just be coffee but things had escalated quickly. He was a smooth-talking bastard. She'd be more resolute this time.

Mia watched him come through the door, his muscles bulging in his T-shirt. *No, Mia*, she thought. He was going to have to do more than look ripped to get her back. No flowers this time, she noted, his standards were slipping.

'Thanks for coming. Can I get you anything?'

Mia shook her head, her arms folded across her chest.

He went to the counter to order.

''Thanks for coming'…?' Mia mumbled. *What is this*, she thought, *a bloody job interview?* Was he going to ask her where she saw herself in five years' time?

Placing his coffee on the table, Andy smiled. 'So, how are you?' He leant forward and put his hand on her knee. She pushed it away. 'Sorry, force of habit,' he said. He looked around the café. 'Look, Mia, I was an idiot. I shouldn't have been chatting to other people. But believe me, it was only chatting. I never met them or anything. Look—' he got out his phone— 'I've deleted all the apps, deleted all the chats. No more fooling around. From now on only you, I promise.'

Mia folded her arms and stared at him. 'Why should I believe you? You're a liar. Fucking football results. Did you think I was that gullible?'

Andy looked at the floor.

Mia continued to stare at him. *Trying the contrite lover routine now, are you?* she thought. *Don't try the puppy dog eyes with me.*

'I'm sorry, I got carried away, I can't say much more but I've learnt my lesson and I miss you and …'

'And you lied.' *Don't smile*, Mia told herself.

'I've removed my security code, you can get into my phone any time. Okay?'

'Why would I want to get into your phone?'

'So that you know I'm not chatting to anyone else.'

'I don't care. You can do what you want. None of my business.'

'Mia, I'm asking if we can get back together.'

'I know what you're asking.'

'So?'

'I'll think about it.' Her arms were still crossed. After a minute, she picked up his phone. He was telling the truth, there was no code, no Tinder, no messages from Lorna. She put the phone back on the table. 'Impressive. It must've hurt.'

'It was worth it for you.'

'Creep.'

'Mia, I'm serious, I miss you. I'm sorry.'

Mia directed her gaze towards the barista performing his magic, before turning back to face Andy.

'So, you've deleted all the apps? And told Lorna it's over?'

Andy nodded.

Mia looked away again.

'Why don't we go back to mine?' Andy said. 'I've got some prosecco in the fridge.' He put his hand on Mia's knee under the table. This time, she didn't brush him away.

*

Vic and Mia were sitting in the window of the café, stirring their coffee and staring out of the rainy window.

'Why don't they all roll?' Vic asked, tracing a raindrop with his finger.

'I was just thinking the same thing. Some are in control, some are just holding on, while others come crashing down, taking others in their wake.' They watched them. 'Which one's next to fall?'

'That one.' As Vic pointed to it, it ran down the window wiping out countless other raindrops.'

'You win.' Mia said. 'Are you okay about Debbie?'

'Yeah, I've hardly given it a second thought. Who's this new guy she's with?'

'I don't know. She's being very secretive. But she seems happy.'

'Good, I'm glad,' he said, taking a sip of coffee. 'Hey, do you happen to know anyone called Kim?'

'Kim? I don't think so. Why?'

'I got this a couple of days ago.' Vic showed Mia the screenshots of her Facebook posts. 'Swipe right for more,' he said.

'Wow, they're a bit harsh, even for you.' Mia said. 'Who sent these?'

'Kim. But who the hell is Kim?'

'Whoever she is, she doesn't like you.'

'Give it here.'

Vic fiddled with his phone and passed it back to Mia.

'Have a look at her profile.'

'There's not much on it,' Mia said.

'But it looks legit, doesn't it?' Vic said.

Mia nodded. 'I wouldn't worry. She's just some random woman who thinks she has the right to slag off a comedian that she doesn't like.'

'It freaks me out, knowing she's out there somewhere.'

'Stop being a baby, it's a couple of messages. Could it be a fake account?'

'I don't know,' Vic said. 'If you set up a fake account, why would you like different pages.'

'Don't you have to when you sign up?'

Vic shrugged. 'I thought it might be Kylie, or Nat, at first, but it seems unlikely, even for Nat.'

'Could it be your friend, Tina?'

'I wondered about that. But if she's behind the website, she's not going to praise me on one site and slag me on another, is she?'

'That woman is capable of anything,' Mia said. 'Have you checked the website recently?'

The both picked up their phones.

'No and, look, here's a review of the Swindon gig, the one Kim slagged off. It's a belter.'

'Weird,' Mia said. 'Can you report this Kim to Facebook?'

'I didn't think about that, but I deleted the comments and I've blocked her. She can't access my page anymore.'

'Good.'

Mia's phone buzzed.

'Hi, I can't talk right now. I'm with Vic. Yes, okay, see you later. Bye, bye.'

'Stan?'

'Nope'

'Harry?'

Mia shook her head again. 'Andy,' she said. 'I met him yesterday.'

'What? You're as bad as me! I thought that was over. What happened to severing the limb?'

'He apologised and deleted everything. He was really sorry.'

'I don't believe that,' Vic said. 'He's had his ego damaged. He had to prove to himself he could get you back.'

'No, he really was contrite. And you know I can't resist him, he's my Tina.'

'Be careful.'

'That's my line. Look, I'll be fine, I'm a big girl now.'

'Big girls make mistakes, too,' Vic said.

A gust of wind crashed into the window causing two more raindrops to lose traction and start falling.

'I've got to go. I've got that meeting with Kylie about Elis's school.'

'Oh, good luck.'

'Thanks. Thankfully, she's not bringing Nat.'

Mia smiled. 'Only one wicked witch.'

'Then I'm meeting Ash later. Do you want to come?'

'Where's Elis?'

'He's with Kylie; I was meant to have a show tonight but it got cancelled last minute. Gives me a chance to see Ash.'

'I've got a pile of marking, I'll leave you boys to it. Next time, maybe.'

'Okay, you know where we are if you change your mind. Lunch, Thursday?'

'Yep.'

Vic had suggested meeting Kylie in the same café that he'd met Mia but she'd insisted on going to a veggie place she was mad about. Vic shook off the rain and sat down.

'So, secondary school already, eh? Our little boy is growing up,' Vic said. 'I quite like the look of the school at the end of my street. Mia works there and...'

Kylie laughed. 'Too late, I've put his name down for Taff Vale High School.'

'You've what?'

Kylie stared at Vic across the table. Her lips were so thin they were barely there, her brow had deep frown lines. 'This isn't garden furniture, Vic. We're talking about our son's future.'

'I know but that doesn't give you the right to make decisions without me.'

'I wouldn't need to if you were a bit more proactive.'

'How much more proactive can I be? You texted me two days ago. I did the research and arranged this meeting only to find the decision's already been made.'

'Ha, your research simply involved finding out which secondary school was closest to your flat.' Kylie crossed her arms.

'Right, pot calling the kettle silver. I suppose it's only coincidence that the school you are having kittens about is near you.'

'It is a coincidence, Vic, and you should know it. Everyone knows that's the best school around. Top of the league tables, with an excellent OFSTED report, it's a brilliant school.'

Vic puffed out his cheeks. 'Listen to yourself. Now it's you treating Elis like some kind of commodity. Life isn't all about league tables. What if Elis turns out to be creative, or sporty, and he's stuck in some academic hellhole?'

'The only hellhole around here is that dump near you. Have you seen their scores? Are you really saying you don't want Elis to have the best possible start in life?'

'Hey, Mia works there, it's not that bad and she says its improving. Anyway, I'm saying it's not as black and white as you are making it out to be. There are other things to consider. Will having Mia there help him settle? Which school are his friends going to? What are the teachers like? League tables only give a snapshot of—'

'Well, it's too late now. As I said, I've put that as our first choice. Your hellhole didn't even make the top three.'

'Bloody hell, Kylie, can't you see this is wrong? You've made the decision, you've ignored me. I just—'

'Nat and I are taking him to an open day on Friday.'

'Right, what time?'

'Why?'

'I want to come.'

'There's no need.'

'Of course there's a need. He's my son, Kylie.'

'It's at eleven.'

'I'll see you there. Now, if you don't mind, I've got a date.' Vic pushed his chair back, left some money on the table and walked out of the café.

Vic hurried down the street. His date was with Ash but there was no harm in letting Kylie think differently. He'd known Kylie was in a hurry, so making her stop and pay for the drinks put a smile on his face. He hated himself for being petty but on the other hand small moral victories were cathartic.

Vic looked down the taps and back again. Since when had The Ox and Cart turned into a hipster place? There were more craft beers than normal beers.

'What will it be?' Rosie smiled at him.

'Guinness, I guess.'

'Don't want to try the Hog's Bottom IPA?'

'I'd rather eat my own arm.'

'Not a fan?'

'I just think they all taste the same. But there's always some poor sap who's fallen for it and will give a spiel about getting a hint of pomegranate in this one, or a touch of anti-freeze in that one. As a matter of interest, how long have these barrels been open? They must be going stale. The punters probably think it's a great new brewing process, bringing out a delicate mushroomy palate, whereas, in reality, it's just mould.'

Rosie laughed as she started to pour his beers. 'The geezers that do my head in are the ones who insist on trying four different ones before ordering. But the boss says it's good for business.'

Vic looked around the bar. 'I can see it's working. I can barely move for hipster beards.'

'Been quiet all week. I think it's the weather. That'll be £3.75, please.'

Vic handed over a fiver and, as he waited for change, his gaze was drawn to Rosie's flat stomach beneath her crop top.

Handing Vic his change, she gave him another dazzling smile. 'Are you on your own?'

'No, I'm meeting Ash.' Vic got his phone out to check for messages. 'He should be here by now.'

'That's a shame. I'm getting off in an hour, I was hoping you'd buy me a drink.'

'Excuse me?'

'Well, you come in here every week, all smiles and flirts, and then nothing happens.'

'I didn't think you'd be interested in an oldie like me.'

'You're not that old,' she said, as she glanced over his shoulder, 'Guinness for you, too?'

'Lovely. You get this Vic. I'll be back in a mo',' said Ash, pointing towards the toilet.

'My day off is Thursday,' Rosie said.

'Oh?' Vic said.

'Wanna do something then?'

'Um yeah, why not? What do you fancy?'

'How about I come to yours about two, some Netflix and chill.'

Vic handed over the money for the drink. 'I'll download Netflix.'

'Give me your address.'

Vic wrote it down, along with his telephone number, and sauntered over towards an empty table.

'What are you grinning at?' Ash said as he picked up his pint.

'Nothing, why?'

'You look like a cat that's been let loose in a dairy.'

'Rosie just asked me out.'

'Fuck off!' Ash looked across at Rosie who was serving the only other customer in the bar. 'That Rosie, you mean? The twenty-one year old Rosie? I fucking hate you at times, Vic.'

'Jealous?'

'Of you having a date with the gorgeous Rosie, whatever gave you that impression?'

'You've got Lily, you don't need to be messing about.'

'I know and you know I wouldn't give her and the kids up for anything. But when I see you and your women,' Ash again looked at Rosie, 'Jesus, what I'd give to get my hands on someone like that.'

'Those are the good days, then there are the days when you wake up at three a.m. and there's no one there next to you or, worse, you're in a woman's bed on the other side of town and all you want to do is break wind. The days when you think you're never going to find that one person. The days when you still feel that piece of jigsaw is missing. Or the cold sweats of having to perform for a new lover.'

'Jesus, listen to you, you, miserable sod. You've just been asked out by a hot twenty-one year old and you're already whinging.'

'Sorry, you're right. It's not a bad life.'

'Not a bad life; it's a bloody *brilliant* life. Just make sure you give me a blow by blow account.'

'Will do,' Vic said.

'Changing the subject, how are things with Kylie?'

'Don't ask.'

'That good, eh?'

Vic blew out his cheeks. 'Worse. It's toxic. I had a meeting with her today. She's a nightmare,' he said, outlining the conversation he'd had his ex. 'How has it come to this? She used to be my favourite person in the world. Now she acts like I don't exist.'

'She's got a point though.'

'Oh, you're not taking her side, are you?'

'Mate, it's not about sides. Most people would kill to get their kid into that school. You know as well as I do that it's the best one in town. Okay, so it's closer to hers but it's not that far from yours.'

'True but shouldn't we be considering where his friends are going?'

'It's one factor, yes.'

'And shouldn't she have spoken to me before putting his name down?'

'I agree, she should have discussed it. It's just not the end of the world.'

'She's making decisions without me.

'But she wasn't spiting on you. She's acting in Elis's best interests, Vic. She's got his name down for one of the most sought after schools in town. You have to learn to pick your battles. This one is not worth the effort. It's a win-win. Agree to this, you look good, and you save your energy for bigger battles along the way.'

'Hiya, sorry I'm a bit late, I was cleaning.'

Mia was sitting in the corner of a greasy spoon café with a mug of builder's tea in front of her. She looked at her watch.

'You're bang on time. Hang on, did you say you've been cleaning?'

'Yes.'

'Right, so what's the special occasion?'

'I've got Rosie coming around.'

'Rosie?'

'The barmaid from the Ox.'

'Vic? She's what, twenty?' Mia shook her head. 'And you took the piss about me and Harry.'

'She's twenty-one, actually, and she came on to me,' Vic said. 'You dog.'

'Invited herself around for a movie. I even signed up for Netflix.'

'Wow, she must be special if you're spending money on that.'

'Free trial. So, how are you?'

'Yes, all good. Shall we order?' Mia signalled the waitress. 'Do you know what you're having?'

Vic nodded.

'I know what I was going to ask you,' Mia said, when the waitress had gone. 'How do I get on Tinder?'

'Why do you want to get on Tinder? Not got enough men?' Vic unwrapped his cutlery.

'Andy said he'd deleted it,' Mia said.

'And you don't believe him?

'I do, but—' Mia hesitated. 'It's just, well, it's better to be safe than sorry, isn't it?'

'And, if he's still there?'

'I don't know, I'll deal with that as and when. So, do you know how to get on Tinder or not?'

162

'I think it's via Facebook,' Vic said.

'Listen to you pretending you don't know.'

Vic smiled.

'But that's bad,' Mia said, 'that means I can't set up a fake account.'

'Maybe it's changed. Download the app and we'll have a look.'

'Oh, great—it's via Facebook or phone number, this could work,' said Mia as she tapped away. 'I'm in,' she said. She looked at the screen 'Now what? Shit, it says upload a photo.'

'Just take a picture of that coffee cup.' Vic said.

Mia looked at him. 'A coffee cup?'

'Yes, loads of women have random objects as their profile pic.'

'Okay, so, what about a fake name?'

'How about Kia,' Vic said.

'Isn't that too close.'

'That's the beauty of it.'

'Kia it is, then. Right, that's me set for the night.'

When Vic got home, he looked at his flat. It had taken him three hours to clean it this morning and it still looked a mess. What would she think? Why did he care? He readjusted the throw on the sofa and straightened a book on the bookshelf. The doorbell rang. He took a deep breath. The butterflies in his stomach were doing a merry dance. This was it.

'Rosie,' he said, as he opened the front door.

'Hi.'

Vic stood and stared. Her long brown hair was scrapped back, her big brown eyes smiled and, to his great delight, she was still wearing her crop top with jeans; jeans that she must have poured herself into. He wondered how long it had taken her to get them on and, more importantly, how long would it take to get them off.

Eventually, he managed to splutter, 'Wow!'

'Are you going to let me in, then?'

'Sorry, yes come in.' He caught a waft of perfume as she went by. 'Tea, coffee, or would you prefer wine?'

'Later.' Rosie grabbed his arm and kissed him.

It was all tongues and teeth. Vic tried to make his mouth fit hers but they didn't match.

He genuinely hadn't been expecting this. He'd thought Netflix and chill actually meant they'd be watching a movie. He stifled a laugh. This situation was perfect for his speaking a different language routine.

'Where's the bedroom?' Rosie said.

Vic led the way.

They lay on the bed kissing. The jeans had been surprisingly easy to remove.

He wanted to show Rosie that this old dog had all the tricks. He may not have the guns or the energy of youth but it was experience that counted. But, despite the kisses on the neck, the shoulder massages and his gentle nibbling of her nipples, Rosie didn't respond as passionately as Tina or Debbie or Amanda would have done. She barely touched him in return.

Was she enjoying it? Fuck, she wasn't a virgin, was she? Maybe she was scared. *How do you broach a subject like that? Stop thinking,* he told himself, *just enjoy. Make the most of it.*

He kissed her again and ran his hands over her body. He looked at her lithe shape and at his own beer belly; his hands looked enormous. This suddenly felt all kinds of wrong. He eased her away and took a breath, but she pulled him back and kissed him again. She hadn't wanted a shower. Why hadn't she wanted a shower? Perhaps he should suggest one. It might relax him, it might give him time to think, it might allow him to back out. What was he doing? Should he stop?

'I've got condoms.' she said.

'Me too,' Vic replied.

'Put one on, then.'

Rosie was gone within twenty minutes of him finishing. The sex had been one-sided. He'd put all the effort in, he'd climaxed, she hadn't. But she'd seemed happy enough when she left.

Vic could get used to this: the perfect-looking woman, with low expectations in bed and who didn't hang around after the event. Bingo.

The television was babbling away but Mia paid it no attention. She was busy swiping left and right on her mobile phone. Being able to check out pecs and biceps from the safety of her own sweat pants was quite therapeutic. She mostly swiped left, consigning would-be creeps to the rubbish bin but, occasionally, a stunning smile, or a well-defined pec, had her swiping right. Not that she'd ever meet any of them but what harm could it do?

A red dot appeared in the top right of the screen.

One new match.

Brian, thirty-five. Accountant. Red hair, shirt and tie. She couldn't even remember swiping right.

    » Hi babe, what's up?

'C'mon Brian, you can do better than that,' Mia said and went back to swiping.

A new message from Brian came in.

    » Fancy some fun?

Interesting. She presumed the fun he was referring to didn't involve going to see a Michael Buble concert. Mia didn't even have a proper profile pic, so this guy was willing to shag a cup of coffee. She returned to the profiles. Left, left, left, right, left, left. New match.

Craig, thirty. Bricklayer. Topless photo, duckface. Crap speller.

    » Hey, sweatheart, stop swipping, youve found me.

Mia unmatched.

A new message from Brian arrived along with three more likes.

    » Hey, send us your Whatsapp number and I'll send you some pictures of my pride and joy.

'Oh, give me a break,' Mia said as she unmatched Brian.

Three more swipes and then a face she recognised.

There he was. Dressed to impress, flashing that smile. She stared at his face. Should she swipe right or left? Her thumb hovered over the screen, right or left? She took a mouthful of wine.

If she swiped right and he matched, she'd have proof he was still using the site. If she rejected him, she'd never know. She held her breath. What if she swiped right and he didn't match? That would mean one of two things. It could be that he wasn't using the site, or it might mean she'd been rejected by her own lover. She closed her eyes and moved her thumb to the right.

But there was no little red dot to say they'd matched. Nothing.

She put her phone down. What now? She'd discovered the bastard was still there but she had no plan. She was seeing him tomorrow. Should she confront him about it? But she'd have to admit she had been on the site, spying on him. She had every right to spy, after the way he'd behaved, but he wouldn't see it like that.

What if she told him a friend had seen him on there? Yes, that might just work.

She went back to swiping. A red dot appeared. Was it him? No? Mike, forty-five. Customer Service Manager.

» *Hey sugar tits, fancy a bit of me?*

Mia unmatched Mike, and deleted the app. She'd had enough.

'I love this place,' Vic said. 'School didn't use to look like this. This looks more like an interactive museum. Do you like it, El?'

Elis nodded, looking nervously at the big boys and girls, in smart uniforms, serving tea and coffee.

'You've changed your tune,' Kylie said. 'I thought this was an academic hellhole.'

'Well, a man's allowed to change his mind, isn't he? Or does feminism only work one way?'

Nat tutted.

'Did you see those whiteboards? They didn't have them in my day.'

'They didn't have electricity in your day, Dad.' Elis said.

'Nope, just slate and chalk, and it did me no harm.'

Natalie tutted again.

'Ah, Mr and Mrs Bead.'

A thirty-something woman approached them. She looked like the cute one from Bananarama.

'Actually it's—' Kylie began.

'Yes,' Vic said.

'And this must be Elis. I'm Miss Evans, the deputy head. I understand you've already put Elis's name down on the register.'

'Yes,' Vic said, 'we have but, actually, it's Mr Bead and Miss Carter—' Vic had clocked that the deputy head was a 'miss'— 'we're divorced.'

'Oh, I see. Mr Bead and Miss Carter and—sorry, you are?'

'I'm Natalie Miles, Kylie's partner.'

'Okay, so Mr Bead, Miss Cooper and Miss Miles.'

'It's Ms Miles,' Nat said.

The teacher gave Vic a weak smile.

Vic raised his eyebrows.

'Right, well, I'm sure Elis will be very happy here, if he gets a place.' She turned her attention to Elis. 'So, young man, what's your favourite subject?'

'Maths and computers,' Elis said.

'Excellent. I hope you've enjoyed your look around and, if you have any questions, you know where we are.' She smiled at Vic again, as she left to greet other parents.

'That's exactly what's wrong in this world,' Nat said.

'What? The fact that deputy head teachers are younger than us?' asked Vic.

'She's not younger than me,' Nat replied. 'I meant her assumption that you two were married. And did you notice the way she only spoke to the man? Like we don't have a brain. I'm not sure I want Elis to come to a school where they reinforce gender stereotypes so freely.'

'But the OFSTED report is so good,' said Vic. 'And, anyway, it's not your decision. Hey, Elis, shall we go and ask Miss Evans about the computer resources?'

'Yeah, okay.'

'What are you smiling at?' Nat asked when Vic and Elis returned.

'Nothing, just great to see Elis on the computers. I think he really impressed Miss Evans.'

'Bet he wasn't the only one trying to impress her,' Nat said.

'Jealous?'

Vic had to admit that his chat with Miss Evans had been rather good fun, but he wasn't going to tell Nat.'

'Oh, Kylie, before I forget, could you have Elis on Monday, after school, for an hour? I have a doctor's appointment. If not, I can arrange for Mia…'

'No problem, I'll collect him,' Nat said. 'We'll give him his tea—that'll be nice, won't it, Elis?

'Great, thanks,' Vic said. 'I'll pick him up about seven.'

'Hi, come in,' Andy said, wielding a chopping knife. 'Dinner's almost ready.' He pecked Mia's cheek and walked back towards the kitchen. 'You look lovely. Help yourself to some wine.'

Mia took a bottle of white from the fridge, poured herself a large glass and topped up his.

'So…' Mia looked at Andy, willing herself to stay calm.

Andy looked up from the pan but continued to stir the sauce. 'What's up?'

Mia took a breath. 'Martha said she saw your profile on Tinder yesterday.'

He looked back down at the food as it bubbled.

'Really?' he said. 'Did she swipe right?' He smiled at Mia.

'That's not the point, you told me you'd left the site.'

'I deleted the app. I thought that deleted the account. You can check my phone if you like.'

'I don't need to check,' Mia said, although her fingers itched.

'Look, I know I was wrong and I understand why you don't trust me, but I've changed. Not having you in my life made me realise how stupid I'd been. I've given all that up, I promise.'

Andy turned the heat off under the sauce and put his arms around Mia. 'I promise.' He kissed her forehead and her nose before trying to kiss her on the lips.

Mia turned her head away but allowed him to hug her. She didn't believe him. She wanted to, she wanted to give him the benefit of the doubt and she knew, if she could convince herself of his innocence, she could trust him.

Fuck, she was being an idiot.

He kissed her neck and ran his hands over her back.

'The sauce will burn,' Mia said.

'It's okay, I've turned it off.' Andy put his hands on her face and looked in to her eyes. Mia knew dinner was going to be a little later than planned.

She closed her eyes and rested her head on Andy's chest. She could hear his heart beat slowing down. *Oscar for Mia*, she thought. She only felt a little guilty; he'd put in all that effort, he deserved to think he'd satisfied her. She squeezed him a little closer and felt his hand in her hair. He kissed her head and she started to drift off.

'What that?' Mia said, through drowsy eyes.

'The neighbours' phone,' Andy said. 'They have it turned up loud.'

The ringing eventually stopped. Mia tried to settle on Andy's chest again but, this time, she couldn't get comfy. The ringing started again.

'What the fuck?' Mia sat up and looked at her phone. 'You should tell them.'

'I have. Deaf as posts they are.'

'Are you sure it's coming from next door?'

The ringing stopped.

'I need a wee and then I'll restart dinner,' said Andy, as he headed towards the bathroom.

Mia moved to the end of the bed and watched him. He stopped in the living room, opened his bag and took out a phone, fiddled with the side buttons and dropped it back into the bag before continuing into the bathroom.

'Bastard,' Mia said. She got out of bed and snuck into the

living room. She reached for his second phone.

3 Missed Calls—Lorna

'Fucking bitch.'

She could hear the water splashing into the bowl. 'Fucking liar.'

She went back into the bedroom and took his other phone from the bedside table. She opened the photos and scrolled through them and there they were. Andy and some cow enjoying a cocktail together; Andy and the same girl in different clothes and a different bar. The next photo confirmed that she wasn't his sister. She started to get dressed.

Clutching a bottle of red, Andy breezed in and asked, 'Want some more wine before I resume cook—?'

'What did Lorna want?'

'Who?'

'Fuck off, Andy. What do you take me for? The neighbours' phone? Really?' She held up one phone and did her best impression of him. 'Look, I've deleted her number. What I didn't tell you, however, was that I bought a new phone.' She held up the other one, then reached for her clothes. 'This time it's over. I hope you're happy with her.'

'Mia, wait, I…'

But Mia was gone.

Vic was beginning to think the doctor didn't like him; the feeling was mutual. Was medical school three years of how to build a superiority complex, three of how to patronise and one of beginners' medicine?

'I'm pleased to say the test results are mostly fine, Mr Bead. But how much do you drink?'

'Depends on how thirsty I am.'

The doctor peered at Vic over his glasses.

'Tough crowd,' Vic said.

'Mr Bead, this is not a performance. It would help if you took this seriously. How many units of alcohol do you drink in a week?'

'Probably more than I should.'

'Mr Bead. Your liver's somewhat compromised. This could be because of the amount of alcohol you drink. It could be something else, of course. At the moment, it's nothing to worry about but I advise you to drink more water, drink less alcohol, and consider taking zinc supplements. Oh, and it might be useful to lose a pound or two, too. We'll do more tests in a year, okay?'

Every time Vic went to the doctors he was told to give up something; maybe he should give up going to the doctor.

That could go into his routine, thought Vic, as he made his way to the chemists.

Vic looked at the tablets and looked at the website. It told him zinc was a natural remedy; it improved liver function. It also boosted the immune system and was good for the heart and gut. There was one side effect that captured his attention; it improved your sperm count.

What Vic didn't want was his little soldiers to be more active. Christ, women didn't like condoms; the last thing he needed was one of his men going rogue and launching a lone wolf attack. He hoped they lollygagged around like moody teenagers. Nature's own contraceptive.

Should he take these pills or not? Liver problems versus fatherhood. What would be worse? What the hell did a 'compromised liver' mean anyway? Further tests in a year. Couldn't be too serious. Vic looked up the symptoms of liver disease. It didn't look great but, then again, parenthood lasted a lifetime. Talking of which, he needed to collect Elis.

February 2017

Meet me in Missoula, Rosie had said. Vic had agreed, not having a clue what, or where, Missoula was. He told himself this was all part of the fun of having a twenty-something lover. He was discovering a whole new world.

But, as he stood outside the place, he wished he'd been more attentive. The music was making his ears bleed even from here and, by the looks of the smokers huddled in the smoking zone, Vic was going to be the oldest here by about twenty years.

He hated it as soon as he pushed the door open. It was hot and dark with flashing disco lights, it smelt of aftershave and perfume and hair product. Vic was glad of the smoking ban because one match and the whole place would go up in flames. It was 5.30 p.m. on a Thursday, but the weekend was well underway. He worked his way through the crowd; Rosie was nowhere to be seen.

'Pint of cider please, mate,' Vic yelled.

'Two pounds fifty,' the barman shouted at him.

'How much?'

'Happy hour, five till ten, all drinks half price.'

Vic took a sip of his cider. He'd fought the urge to point out that five till ten was more than an hour, but the thought that the prices went up to a fiver after ten filled him with horror. No wonder the place was busy now.

He could feel people's eyes on him. *Who's let the old man in?* He searched the faces. Where the hell was she? He checked his phone. No messages.

'Vic.'

Vic looked around but couldn't see the source of his name.

'Vic.'

Someone tapped him on the shoulder. He turned and stared, mouth open. Rosie usually wore a touch of make-up in the pub but not this much. She looked like a cheap ventriloquist dummy, and she was four inches taller than usual, too.

'Hiya,' he said.

She kissed him and Vic was sure all eyes were watching him. 'Blimey, Rosie, how many have you had?' he asked.

'Just a couple.' She giggled. 'Come and meet my friends.' She tottered off, holding onto his hand, dragging him along in her wake.

'This is Vic,' Rosie said. 'This is Olivia and Olivia, they're on my course.'

'Which one is which,' Vic said, laughing.

The two Olivia's gave him a stony glare.

Rosie continued to hold onto Vic's hand as they stood chatting.

'So, like, it's like, you know just, like wrong,' Olivia One said.

'No, yeah, I know, right, it's just, right, when it's like that, right, you know?' Olivia Two added.

'Yeah, no, you're so right, it's like, not easy, right but, like, I don't know,' said Rosie, turning towards Vic. 'What do you think?'

'Um, I'm not sure, it's like…' Damn it, this non-language was catching.

'See, I told you he was a, like a cutie, didn't I?' Rosie said and kissed Vic, tongues and all.

Both Olivia's looked like they might throw up.

As the girls continued to talk in their strange code, Vic recognised a remix of a tune he'd known when he was their age. He sang along. Sweat was dripping down his back. He took a mouthful of cider and looked around. It seemed as if everyone was watching his every move.

'Hey, right, we're going to do these later, I brought, like, one for you.' Rosie opened her bag to reveal four laughing gas canisters and a small bottle of vodka.

Vic's head thumped. He didn't want to do laughing gas. Was it dangerous? He could see the headline, *Comedian Dies of Laughing Gas!* His shirt was stuck to his back and his pint was tepid. Vic dug his phone out of his pocket.

'Shit,' he said.

'What's wrong, sweetie?'

'A message from my ex, she needs me to have Elis tonight, after all. I've got to go. I'll call you tomorrow.'

'Buy us a round of cocktails before you go,' Rosie said, draping herself over him.

What the hell, it was happy hours. 'Come on then. Help me carry them.' He paid for the cocktails and got a sloppy kiss in return.

'Have fun,' Vic said.

'I will.' Rosie's eyes sparkled over the top of her cocktail umbrella.

Vic almost ran out of the bar into the street. He sent a text to Mia and headed home.

Mia looked at the text from Vic.

» Missoula a nightmare. Heading home.

She laughed. That boy was chasing a dream that had died twenty years ago. She hoped his mid-life crisis would not involve skinny jeans and a tattoo. She took a mouthful of wine.

Now she was free of Andy, Mia thought she might as well reinstall Tinder. Just to see what was out there. She discovered that, in her absence, she or, rather, her alter-ego, Kia, had collected several new fans. A twenty-one year old body builder, with more muscles than brains, was trying to convince her she needed some young cock in her life. Mia unmatched him straight away. Two businessmen both declared upfront that they were married, because they wanted to be honest. *Not that honest to the poor wives*, Mia thought. She rejected them both. There was also a message from her 'wonderful' Andy. She looked at the date he sent it. It was before they'd split up. Further proof, if any were needed, that he was the scummiest of scum bags. She read his message;

» Hi beautiful, so glad we matched. Looking for some fun?

A shiver ran down her spine. She felt sick. Should she reply? See what his patter was like? Lead him on a little bit? She'd think about it.

She deleted a few more unsuitable matches before pausing over Geraint. Thirty-eight, normal looking, fresh-faced. She read his message.

» Hi Kia. Nice photo. How's your week treating you?

She shouldn't reply. She knew it. She'd had enough of men. She didn't need another one. But he was the only one who'd used her, albeit fake, name *and* he had a nice face and he'd asked her a question. She shouldn't reply.

» *Not bad, how's yours?*

Why did women take men clothes shopping with them? It could only ever end in tears. They wanted a second opinion but no man worth his salt would be honest. Only a fool would say it makes your arse look like the Burj Khalifa.

Vic stood outside the changing rooms, listening to some generic music. They'd originally agreed to meet for coffee and yet here he was, in Top Shop. He checked his watch and closed his eyes. Thirty bloody minutes wasted in this dump.

'So, what do you think?' asked Rosie, emerging from the changing rooms.

'It's… um,' Vic said.

'You don't like it?'

'It's lovely, there's just not much of it,' Vic said.

'That's the whole point, Grandad.' Rosie twirled, looking at herself in the mirror. She disappeared back into the cubicle.

'Does your daughter have everything she needs?' asked a smiling shop assistant, standing millimetres from Vic's shoulder.

'Oh, she's not my—yes I think she does,' said Vic, as he felt his face become warm.

Rosie reappeared in her street clothes, that 'dress' on a hanger.

'So, are you going to buy that one, then?' Vic said.

'I don't know. I really like it but…' She looked at the price tag. 'It's pretty expensive and I don't get paid until next week.'

Vic looked at her, and at the 'dress'.

'It's so nice, though,' she said, holding it up to the light.

Fuck, Vic thought, *she wants me to buy it for her.*

'I bet they won't have it next week. Don't you think it looked lovely on me?' She kissed him.

She does, she wants me to buy it for her. 'Yeah, it did.' Vic caught a glimpse of the price tag.

'And wouldn't you like to peel it off me?' She said, draping herself over Vic.

It was forty quid. Could he afford forty quid? He had that Tuesday night gig lined up; that was some bonus money. Oh, what the hell, if it would make her happy— 'Why don't I buy it for you?' he said.

He avoided eye-contact with the shop assistant as swiped his credit card but you didn't have to be a genius to read her mind.

'Let's skip the coffee and go to your place,' Rosie said. 'I'll show you how grateful I am.'

'Okay,' Vic said, thinking to himself that he could murder a coffee.

All the way home, Vic could feel eyes on him. Watching him walking arm and arm with a girl half his age. What did they think? He could hear the whispers. *Pervy old man with a young girl.* Rosie clung to his arm like a limpet. She was proud of her catch. Vic should have been proud but he wanted the ground to open up and swallow him.

Rosie sat up in bed looking at her phone.

'This bag would go lovely with that dress.' She showed a picture to Vic.

'Bloody hell, two hundred quid for a handbag?'

'That's nothing,' Rosie said. 'Look at this one.'

'Five hundred pounds? That's a bloody joke.'

'It's fashion,' she said, lips pouting.

'Jesus, Rosie, you work in a pub.'

'Well, that's why I've got you.' She kissed him and pulled him down under the covers.

Vic lay looking at the ceiling, wondering what was wrong with him. He was meant to be in post-coital bliss but this wasn't bliss. He thought of Ash; what would he say if he knew Vic was in bed, next to a naked, twenty-one year old and bored shitless? What would he say if he knew Vic was in bed, next to a naked, twenty-one year old and thinking of Ash?

He closed his eyes and hoped she wouldn't want to do it again. But at least doing it was better than conversation. He was sick to death of hearing about this handbag range, or that lipstick, or the new album from Sam Smith. He looked down at Rosie's head, currently resting on his chest and stroked her hair.

Rosie's phone buzzed on the bedside table.

'Hi, babes,' she said, as she sat herself up. 'Not much, a bit of studying that's all. You?'

Vic heard a male voice but couldn't pick out the words.

'The weekend, of course, I can't wait to see you... About two fifteen, I think. Will you be there to meet me? Okay great... See you then... I love you, too.' Rosie blew kisses down the phone, kissed Vic and snuggled back down onto his chest.

'Who was that?' Vic asked.

'Steve,' Rosie said.

'Oh?'

'My boyfriend.'

'You've got a boyfriend?' Vic sat up in bed.

'Yeah, of course. Why, is that a problem?'

'No, I just thought... If he's your boyfriend, what am I?'

Rosie laughed and kissed Vic on the lips. 'You're silly, that's what you are.'

'No, seriously, Rosie.'

'Don't worry. He's up in Birmingham Uni. You're the daddy here.' Rosie kissed Vic again.

'And he knows about me?'

'No, he'd fucking kill me, and you,' she said, reaching for her phone again. 'Look.'

'He's a big boy,' Vic said.

'Very,' Rosie giggled. She tried to kiss him but Vic moved away.

'You okay?'

'Yeah, bit of a shock, I suppose.'

'Sorry, I thought I'd told you about him. And, anyway, this was only ever going to be friends with benefits. You're twenty years older than me.'

'Can't argue with that,' he said as he dragged himself off the bed and made his way to the bathroom

'Have you thought anymore about that bag?' Rosie said when Vic walked back into his bedroom.

'What bag?' Vic said.

'The one I showed you? That handbag.'

'Not really, why?'

'I thought you might like to buy it for me.'

'Is it your birthday?'

'No but I thought you might like to reward me for being such a good little girl.'

'Oh, right, well.'

'Look, it's lovely,' she said, handing Vic her phone.

He looked. He'd seen similar bags in the market but they didn't cost two hundred quid.

'I can't afford that,' Vic said.

'I thought you were a big shot comedian.'

'I'm *a* comedian,' said Vic. 'Let's agree that, if I ever get on *Mock the Week*, I'll buy it for you. Now, bring your delicious little body over here.'

'I've got to go,' she said. 'I've got work later.'

'I thought you started at seven.'

'Yes, no, I, um, well, I need to go home first.'

'See you after the weekend?'

'Maybe.'

Vic played scenes from the afternoon over in his mind as he waited for Mia. There was only one logical conclusion.

The door opened and he waved at Mia as she came in the café. She headed to the counter but Vic managed to catch her attention.

'Skinny latte.' He pointed at the mug.

'Oh lovely, thanks. How are you?'

'Ups and downs.'

'Same here.'

'Oh yeah, Andy. Are you okay?'

'Do you know that bastard was active on Tinder?'

'You're better off without him, Mia. This time no going back, promise me?'

Mia nodded. 'How's it going with Rosie?'

'I think you're going to enjoy this,' Vic said and took a mouthful of coffee.

'Do tell.'

'Guess where she's going this weekend.'

Mia shrugged.

'To spend time with her boyfriend in Birmingham.'

'She's got a boyfriend? What're you, then?'

'I'm coming to that. She suggested I buy this for her.'

Vic showed Mia the handbag on his phone.

'For 'being a good girl',' he added.

Mia wiped her mouth with a napkin. 'You're not going to buy it, are you?'

Vic shook his head. 'No way. Anyway, I can't afford it. I've already bought her a dress.'

'And I assume you pay for dinner and drinks and everything?'

Vic nodded.

Mia smiled.

'What?'

'I never had you down as a sugar daddy.'

'That's what she thinks I am, isn't it?'

'You've got to end it, Vic. Get out of there while your bank balance is still in equilibrium.'

'But she's twenty-one.'

'And I bet she's boring, and crap in bed, and you're embarrassed to be seen out with her.'

'How do you know?'

'It's textbook stuff, Vic. She's playing you for a fool.'

'And you? What are you going to do now you're left with only Stan?'

'I'm working on it.' Mia smiled. 'With the help of Tinder.'

'I thought you said that was all jocks sending pics of cocks.'

'Every thorn has its rose,' Mia said.

Vic spent the entire weekend wondering how to dump Rosie. It had been ages since he'd dumped anyone. Kylie, Toni, Debbie, even Tina, had all dumped him. He'd like to send her a text, get it over with. Was that frowned upon? He thought it probably was. In twenty years' time, people would look back and laugh at the idea that dumping someone by text was such a bad thing. *Poor Sophia, not only did Jackson finish with her, he did it face-to-face, the heartless brute...*

So why didn't he just text her? Type a simple message, press Send, and it would all be over. Who cared what Olivia One and Olivia Two thought? Future Rosie would thank him. But he was old-school. He gritted his teeth and, preparing himself to face the awkward silences, the poorly chosen words, and the tears, he typed his message.

» Fancy a coffee?

He stared at it for a moment before pressing Send.

A coffee was a perfect solution. In public, so no histrionics. He'd order an espresso, so he could gulp it down, say his piece, and walk away while Rosie still had plenty of latte left. He checked his phone. It told him the message had been read.

Doubt seeped into mind. Without Rosie, there'd be no one. He'd run out of people. Debbie seemed happy with her new bloke. Tina was god knows where. Louise had left Dave for the guy who installed her new boiler. She constantly reminded Vic that it could have been him, if only he'd had the balls. Amanda had got together with one of the younger comedians. Annie was getting married. And then there was Cariad—had he missed the boat? Those who had graduated from the school of divorce at the same time as him had all gone on to the university of second marriage. Maybe he could give that deputy-head a call, Miss Evans. She seemed to like him or maybe she was just doing her job. Christ, it was so difficult to tell. Where did being friendly stop and flirting start?

Did he really want to split up with Rosie? Maybe he could afford a handbag or a dress, so as not to be alone. *God listen to yourself*, Vic thought.

There was another option. He picked his phone up and typed

a message.

» *Hi, how are you?*

He pressed Send just as his phone bleeped.

» *Don't fancy a coffee. In fact, don't think we shud c each other anymore. u cant give me what I need xxx*

Fuck, Rosie had dumped him by text; the bloody bitch. And kisses on a dumping text, really?

Vic fancied a pint. Elis was staying at Kylie's an extra day, because of some birthday party. After a quick text exchange, Vic pulled on his coat. Ash could just about make time, as long as it was only one, so Vic knew they'd have at least two.

Just as he was leaving Vic's phone bleeped again. A message from Tina.

» *Hello.*

Vic walked into the pub and saw Rosie behind the bar. Of course, she'd be there, what was he thinking? *Play it cool*, he said to himself.

'Walk Like An Egyptian' was playing on the jukebox. That's who Rosie looked like; Susana Hoffs in her prime. It had been bugging him all this time. He smiled at her and spotted Ash at a table in the corner, two pints on the table already.

'I've been thinking,' Ash began.

'Steady on,' Vic smiled.

'Okay, I won't tell you.'

'Come on. Let's hear your wonderful wisdom.'

'I was thinking about you and Kylie, about what you said last time, about you and her being best friends.'

'Past tense.'

'Exactly, so, why don't you play on that?'

'What do you mean?'

'Well, how often do you two sit down and have a conversation? A proper conversation. Not two minutes over the phone, not over Elis's head, not with Nat chipping in.'

'We had that one about school but it was more like an

argument, rather than a conversation.'

'See!'

'Not really, no.'

'You need to find the time for the two of you to be alone. Remind her of the *you* she fell in love with. Not the tetchy, miserable sod that she's doing battles with.

'I thought you were meant to be on my side. I'm only defensive because of her.'

'I know and that's why you need to have a proper conversation.'

'Do you think it will work?'

'I don't know but it has to be worth a try, doesn't it? Go to a café; without Elis, without Nat, just the two of you. Have a heart-to-heart. What have you got to lose?'

'The price of a latte.'

'You tight bastard. Talking of which, it's your round.'

'Can you go?'

'Things not well in the garden of Rosie?'

Vic shook his head.

'Don't tell me you've blown that already. What happened?'

Vic handed Ash a ten-pound note. 'Get the beers in and I'll tell you.'

He watched his friend chat to his ex-lover at the bar and hoped he was behaving.

'Come on, then,' said Ash as he put the pints and change on the table. 'Spill the beans.'

Vic told him about Rosie, Rosie's handbag, and Rosie's boyfriend.

'Okay, I'll let you off. I'll give Lily a little while longer, then.'

'So you should. Everything alright there?'

'Yes, all good,' Ash said. 'Nothing changes.'

'Busy this weekend?' asked Vic.

'Busier at the weekends than at work. Kid's parties, ballet, football, shopping, it's hectic. You?'

'Gigs in Swansea on Friday and Saturday, then meeting Tina on Sunday.'

'Tina? I thought that was…'

'It was but we got chatting today. Decided to give it one more try.'

'Be careful with that one, Vic.'

March 2017

'Listen.'

Tina put a finger to her lips and stopped Vic mid-sentence.

Vic couldn't hear anything other than the general hubbub of the café.

'What am I listening to?'

'Ssh.' Tina closed her eyes and stared at the ceiling. 'It's our song.' She snuggled up to him.

Vic listened but all he could hear were the faint strains of some generic tune on the café speakers.

'We have a song?'

'Don't you remember?' Tina asked when the instrumental kicked in. 'It was playing in the foyer of the hotel on the first night we got together. I told you I loved this song and you said you did, too.'

'Did I?' Vic scratched his head. 'Right.' He wasn't sure he'd ever heard the song before. *The things I say to get a shag*, Vic thought to himself. 'Who's it by again?'

'Listen,' she said, as the vocals started again. 'It's so romantic.'

Vic tapped his phone to open Shazam but it was no use; the song faded just as the app loaded.

'He's brilliant, isn't he?'

'Not really my cup of tea, to be honest,' Vic said.

'Oh, come on Vic, even if you don't like the music, you have to appreciate the words.'

'If you say so,' Vic said and took a mouthful of coffee.

'You're always so negative. Stop trying to be so cool. You're not trying to impress little Miss Perfect now, you know.'

'Who?'

'Miss Sunshine Out of Her Behind, Mia.'

'Jesus, Tina, why are you obsessed with Mia. She's my best friend.'

'Me, obsessed? Me? That's rich. Every other word you mutter is Mia. I see you liked her post on Facebook again.'

Vic shrugged.

'And you don't even like dogs.'

'Sometimes, Tina, people use Facebook to say, 'Hey don't forget me.'' Vic banged his coffee cup down. 'For God's sake, a Facebook like is a digital hug for a friend in need, that's all.'

'You never *like* my posts.'

'I do,' Vic said but he knew he didn't.

'You don't, never.'

'Tina, I…'

'You just don't care, that's what. You're too busy ogling Miss Sunshine Ass.'

'This is nonsense. There isn't and never has been anything between me and Mia. I don't need to like your posts because I talk to you more often.' Vic glanced at their two empty cups. 'Come on, let's go,' he said.

'Where?'

'Well, I thought you were going to show me what you've got on under that dress.'

'You're only with me for the sex.'

True enough, Vic thought. 'Nonsense,' he said.

Vic lay in the darkness, listening to his stomach rumbling and Tina snoring. He would give anything to be alone right now. He watched the light in his room change as a car went past. His stomach groaned again. Vic could feel it slowly inflating like a stubborn bouncy castle. Alone, he'd happily let the air out but, with Tina next to him, he had to hold it in. He shut his eyes and hoped sleep would override his bodily functions but it was no use. The gurgles grew louder, the urge to break wind stronger.

'Where are you going?' Tina mumbled.

'Just the toilet,' Vic said.

'Don't leave,' she reached out towards him.

'I have to.'

Sitting on the toilet, Vic still couldn't relax. He knew the walls were paper thin and, despite the hum of the fan, Vic's trumpeting would be clearly heard in the bedroom. But it didn't matter, anyway, because now that he was sitting here in the cold, all urges had gone. He flushed the loo, washed his hands, and climbed back into the warmth of the bed. Tina mumbled something unintelligible. No sooner had he closed his eyes, his belly started chatting again and the need to fart returned. If there was a god, he was obviously a sadistic bastard.

Farting was like saying 'I love you'. There comes a time in a relationship when it was okay to do it but knowing when that time was was one of the mysteries of the universe. Both parties had to break wind/say I love you at exactly the same time, or else there was an awkward imbalance. Vic's stomach rumbled. *There might be a routine in this*, thought Vic as his eyes grew heavy. Convinced that Tina was now unconscious, he let out a little parp and fell asleep.

Vic woke up with a bloated stomach and a feeling that he'd had a good idea last night. But, try as he might, he could neither release the trapped wind or remember the idea. Tina was already in the bathroom doing whatever she did in there.

The bathroom door opened. 'Oh, you're awake, are you?' Tina said as she crawled onto the bed and tried to kiss him.

Vic pulled away. 'I'll just go and clean my teeth,' he said.

He washed his face and let out a little fart as the water was running. His stomach felt a little better. The water cooled his face. What was that idea?

Wandering back into the bedroom, Tina smiled and said, 'Come here.'

Oh, shit, thought Vic, *what now? With this gut?*

'You go on top,' he said as he closed his eyes and tried to remember his idea.

'I've got to go,' Tina said, almost as soon as Vic had finished.

'Already?' Vic hoped it sounded genuine. 'Hey, by the way, I'm working in Slough on Thursday. One night only.'

'Do you want to stay at mine, then?'

'Yeah, why not. That would be nice.'

Tina kissed him and then kissed him again.

'Thanks, Vic,' she said, as she headed for the front door.

'Um, you're welcome.'

The moment the door closed, he headed to the bathroom.

Finally, alone, he sat on the loo and relaxed. The moment the trapped wind escaped with gale force, he recalled the perfectly formed, I love you/breaking wind routine. Sitting on the loo, he quickly typed it into his phone before he forgot again.

Vic looked in the rear-view mirror. Elis was strapped into his car seat, playing a game on Vic's phone.

'Good day in school?' Vic asked.

'Yeah.'

'Do anything fun?'

'Not really.'

Vic indicated and turned left. Some right wing politician was pontificating on the radio about the negative impact of immigration. Vic pressed a button to change to a music station. He recognised the song immediately.

'Hey Elis, open Shazam on my phone, will you?' Vic looked in the mirror. 'El, I'm talking to you.'

'What?'

'Open Shazam and find out what this song is, will you?'

'Dad…'

'Come on, it will only take you two minutes. You can pause the game.'

'You really don't know what this is?' Elis said, not breaking concentration.

'No,' Vic said. 'Why, do you?'

'I thought you liked rubbish music. Everyone knows this is Ed Sheeran.'

'Oh, Ed Sheeran, I've heard of him. What's it called?'

Elis rolled his eyes. '"Thinking Out Loud".'

'I thought you only liked cool stuff, El. How do you know that?'

'It's only the most popular song in the world. All the girls sing it in school.' Elis looked back down at the phone and sang along in a high-pitched voice.

'I take it you don't like it.'

'No, it sucks. Nat says Ed Sheeran should be tried for crimes against humanity.'

For once, Vic could agree with the darling Natalie. Shit, it was bad enough having a 'song' but, to discover it was an Ed Sheeran song beggared belief. Half the bloody world must have an Ed Sheeran song as 'their song'.

'Yesss,' Elis said.

Vic looked in the mirror and saw his son doing a celebratory jig in the back seat.

'What's up?'

'I just got to level sixteen. Luke's only on level twelve.'

'Well done,' Vic said, despite having no clue what level sixteen was, apart from the simple fact that it was four levels higher than the mighty Luke had managed.

'I'll send mum a text.'

As Vic pulled up outside their flat, he heard himself say, 'You never send me a text telling me your news when you're with your mother.' *Shit*, he thought, *I'm beginning to sound like Tina.*

'Yes, I do.' Elis said.

But he didn't.

Vic wished he hadn't agreed to go to Tina's after the show. He yawned; it would have been a long drive home but at least his own bed would have been waiting for him. Oh well, too late now. He walked up the garden path and the front door swung open.

'Hello lovely,' said Tina as she threw her arms around him. 'How did the show go?'

'Yeah, not bad. The new stuff is taking time to bed in.'

'You were brilliant.'

'Were you there, then?'

Tina cleared hr throat. 'I mean, I'm sure you were, you always are. Are you hungry?'

'Not really,' he said.

'Good.' Tina lead him towards her bedroom.

As they stood, naked, Tina wriggled away and sighed. 'I need to lose some weight, look,' she groaned, grabbing some of her tummy between thumb and forefinger. 'Pinching more than an inch.'

'Don't be daft,' Vic said. 'You're perfect.'

'No, I'm not. Look,' she said, standing sideways so a small paunch stuck out. Vic pulled her towards him, knelt and kissed the offending belly.

'This is gorgeous,' he said, trying to bite it.

'Get off, I need a shower,' she said, backing away into the bathroom.

Vic shook his head. *Women*, he thought. Tina was probably right; a pound off here or there would do no harm but the same could be said about everyone. He looked down at his own belly. Not just a pound off needed there; a whole half-price sale was in order.

As soon as he heard the shower start, he checked his messages.

'Hey look,' Vic said, handing his phone to Tina when she came back from the bathroom.

She glanced down at the phone as the towel fell off her head. 'What is it?'

'It's a sofa to 5K challenge. Thought you might be interested.'

'Why would I be interested in that?'

'You said you wanted to lose weight; this is a good way to exercise and have fun.'

'Five minutes ago you said I was gorgeous as I was.'

'You are. But I'm just saying,' Vic sighed. '*You* said you wanted to lose weight and I thought, well, I thought you might like to try this challenge.'

'If you think I'm fat, why don't you just say it? Come on, stop being a coward, say it.'

Vic shook his head.

'Enough with the passive aggression, Vic. Say it!'

Vic sighed.

Tina turned her back to him and let the towel drop to the floor. 'See, I'm gross,' she said, staring at herself in the mirror.

'Tina, that's not what I meant and you know it. I was just saying that if you think you need to lose weight, this might be an idea.'

Tina kept inspecting her body grabbing bits between finger and thumb.

'Gross,' she said.

'You're being stupid.'

'Oh, so stupid and fat—it's all coming out now. Anything else? Wanna add in ugly? Boring?'

'Oh, for God's sake, Tina, I didn't…'

'So, at least I know, now,' she cried as she stomped back into the bathroom. 'The man I love thinks I'm an ugly, stupid, boring blob.'

Why was she vacuuming on a Friday night? With a heart-felt sigh, Mia slumped into an armchair and checked her phone. Tinder was doing her head in. Every man she'd liked had immediately wanted to send her pictures of his dick.

Except Geraint. He seemed normal.

> *Hi, how are you Kia?*

> *Not bad, you?*

> *I'm assuming you're not actually a coffee cup. So, what do you really look like?*

> *I can't send photos on here.*

> *So, let's chat on WhatsApp.*

She hesitated. She always resisted sending men her number but this was Geraint.

Within minutes she had a message. He looked even better in his WhatsApp picture. She looked through her snaps, found one where she thought she looked presentable and sent it.

> *Oh, and by the way my name's Mia.*

> *Wow, gorgeous. Pleased to meet you Mia. Got one showing a little more?*

» *I thought you were different.*

» *Sorry, but you've got to try your luck, haven't you?*

» *Well I've got one in my bikini, I might send it, if you're good.*

» *Oh, I'm good.*

» *LOL*

They chatted for a while longer and then Geraint tried his luck again.

'What the hell?' Mia said. She found the photo on her phone and sent it.

» *Wow, the things I would love to do to that body.*

» *Oi, talk to the eyes.*

» *Seriously, you're gorgeous.*

» *So, what would you do?*

» *I'd start by kissing…*

Mia got up, moved into the bedroom and shut the door. Sid wouldn't be back for at least another hour but she didn't want to take any chances.

Twenty minutes later, Mia lay on the bed trying to catch her breath. She'd thought Andy was a good lover but this guy was amazing, and he was in a different postcode. How did he do it?

» *Did you enjoy that?*

» *Amazing, are you as good in real life?*

» *Better. Send me a photo.*

Mia held the camera phone above her and clicked her naked torso. She hoped the look on her face would tell Geraint exactly how much she'd enjoyed it. She pressed Send and smiled.

April 2017

Vic and Elis were waiting for the pizza delivery to come. It had been a long day and Vic hadn't felt like cooking and Elis hadn't needed asking twice. As ever, Elis was in the middle of a mission to get to a level he'd never reached before.

'Dad—' he looked up from Vic's iPhone— 'which is better, iPhone or Samsung?'

'Good question. I think the first one you use is the best.'

'Huh?'

'Well, my first smart phone was an Apple. I tried to use an Android tablet and hated it. Couldn't get used to the operating system. So, the first one you use is the best. What are you giggling at?'

'Look!'

Elis showed Vic a video of him telling Elis all about his views on iPhones, but he had cat's ears and whiskers.

'How did you do that?'

'Magic.'

'Elis?'

'It's a new app, Dad. I just downloaded it.'

'Elis, what did I tell you about downloading apps without my permission?'

'It was free.' He giggled again.

'I don't care, you ask my permission.'

Elis giggled again.

'Elis!'

'Sorry, Dad, but look—'

And there was Vic telling his son off, with a bow in his hair.

'Elis, I'm being serious. Ask my permission before downloading anything, okay?'

'Yes, Dad. Sorry, Dad. I can't wait until I get my own smart phone.'

'Saving up, are you?'

'Mum said I can have one when the baby's born,' said Elis,

giggling again, as he showed his father a video of himself with a viper's tongue.

'When what baby is born?'

'Nat's baby.'

'You're telling me Nat's pregnant?'

'Not yet but they keep talking about it.'

There were so many questions but most of them were not appropriate to ask a ten-year-old.

'Apparently, her brother is going to be the father. Cool, eh?'

'Her brother?'

'Yep, Uncle Mark.'

'Well, technically, he's not your uncle, is he?'

'Whatever.'

'And you are okay with this, are you?'

'Yes. I'm going to have a brother or sister. Someone to play with.'

'Half-brother or sister.'

'Although, I hope it's a brother.'

'Yeah, there's already enough women in that house.'

'What?'

'Nothing, kiddo. Nothing.'

Elis shrugged, looked back down at his father's phone and giggled.

Vic stared at the TV but he wasn't watching it.

So, Kylie and Nat were going to start a family. What was wrong with the one they had? Vic knew that it was none of his business but he felt like he should have been told, or even consulted. After all, it was something that would massively change his son's life and had the potential to change his own. Didn't Vic have an interest in that? Was he being unreasonable? And what was all this stuff about her brother? Nonsense, surely. Elis must have got it wrong.

He looked down at his son, still engrossed in the mindless app, and wondered if Elis really was okay with it? He said he'd have someone to play with, but he can't have thought it through. By the time the baby reached playing age, Elis would a teenager and, more to the point, Elis would no longer be number one.

He'd become a glorified babysitter.

The more Vic thought about it, the less he liked it. It seemed strange, Elis having a brother with completely different DNA. What if the father was a murderer or an alcoholic?

'Hey, Elis, can I have my phone a mo'?'

'I'm playing.'

'C'mon, you can use the iPad.'

Elis thrust the phone into Vic's hand. 'It's not fair.'

Vic went into the kitchen and called Kylie.

'Hi, Vic, what's up? All okay with Elis?'

'Hi, Kylie, yeah, all's fine but he's just told me something odd and I thought I'd check in with you.'

'Go on.'

'Well, he said Nat's having a baby with her brother.'

'That boy's got a gob on him.'

'So, it's true.'

'Not exactly. We're looking into the options of IVF and we've been sounding Elis out about having a baby brother or sister.'

'And the stuff about Mark?'

'The idea is that we use one of my eggs and Mark's sperm. That way it has some of both our DNA. Nat's going to host because she's never been pregnant before.'

'I see,' Vic said. 'And when were you going to tell me?'

'Nothing's happened yet, Vic, and we don't need your permission.'

'Possibly not but...'

'It's really none of your business.'

'I beg to differ. It's going to radically change my son's life and, as his father, I think I have a right to—'

'No, Vic, you don't get any say in this,' said Kylie. 'Anyway, he's fine with it. So, nothing to worry about.'

'He says he's fine with it, Kylie, but he clearly hasn't thought it through.'

'What that's supposed to mean?'

'It's obvious. There'll be one child who'll yours and Nat's and one who's yours and mine. You're bound to treat them differently.'

'Fuck it, Vic, you're inventing problems. Why don't you stop thinking? Look, Nat and I wanted parental responsibility so both our children would be equal in law. But no, you didn't want that, did you? I've had it with you and your petty mind.'

Vic stared at the blank screen and sighed.

He opened the message app.

> » *Hi Mia, fancy coming round for glass of wine later?*
> » *I'll be there about 8.*
> » *Great, can you bring the wine?*

'Dad, can I have the phone back now?'

The doorbell rang. Pizza to the rescue.

Having just listened to Kylie's plans, Mia frowned. 'I do understand, Vic, really I do…'

'But?'

'Well, I…' *How to put this?* thought Mia. 'You're right but, also, you're wrong. I agree, it might be tough for Elis, but I'm afraid there's nothing you can do about it. There's no law saying they can't do it. Most kids have step-brothers and step-sisters. It's the new normal. Christ, some of the relationships I hear about in school are mind boggling. Welcome to the 21st Century.'

They listened to Elis playing computer games in his bedroom.

'Ten more minutes, Elis,' Vic yelled, as he refilled Mia's glass. 'It just feels weird, having no input on something that will change Elis's life drastically.'

'Don't worry. He'll survive. It's amazing how quickly kids adapt to change. Look how he got used to the new situation after the divorce.'

'Yeah, he coped with that but this might be one step too far.'

'He'll be fine, as long as you are. But, if you project your worries on him, he'll get stressed. Let him see it as a magical event. Then, *if* problems do arise, be there for him. And you never know, it might be an opportunity for you.'

'Opportunity?'

'Elis will be a young teenager and will have a screaming,

vomiting, smelly baby in the house. They'll tell him to turn his music down, turn off the video games. Suddenly, *your* place will be the cool place.'

'You could be right.'

'I am right. You wait and see,' said Mia. 'So, how's it going with Tina?'

Vic tutted.

'That good?'

'She does my head in. It's like she lives in a parallel universe. She accuses me of things that have never happened.'

'Like what?'

'The other day, *she* said she was fat, by the end of the conversation it was *me* who had called her fat. Then, apparently, I like your Facebook posts because me and you are a couple.'

'Time to get shot, Vic.'

'But then I'll miss her. The problem is, I'm in love with the thought of her. When we're apart, I want to see her but, as soon as we're together…' Vic shook his head.

'That's why Geraint's perfect.'

'Ah, your Internet lover.'

Mia dropped her voice. 'It's the best sex I've ever had.'

'It isn't sex, it's sext.'

'I don't care what you call it, it's amazing.'

'And are you going to meet this dude?'

'I don't know. That might ruin it.'

'He might be a schoolboy, or an old man, or he might even be a woman.'

'He's none of those. We've spoken in the phone. He has a very sexy voice.'

'You're crazy. For all you know, he could be trawling Tinder, gathering pictures and publishing them on a website.'

'Shit, I never thought of that.'

'No, please tell me you haven't sent naked photos.'

'Just one or two, or five.'

'Mia! You're a school teacher, you can't go around sending naked photos to complete strangers.'

'I'm sure it will be fine.' Mia looked at her watch. 'Hey, I better go. I've got work tomorrow.'

'Okay, let me pay for your cab.'

'No, it's fine. I'll walk. Be cool, Vic. Don't worry.'

Vic had spent the whole night, the whole day, and the whole of the drive to Bristol, thinking about Elis and the new baby. He knew Mia was right but he couldn't get over the fact that his son would have a brother when he was with his mother but, when he was with Vic, Elis would be an only child. It wasn't right.

Sitting backstage, Vic listened to himself being introduced and realised he hadn't thought about his act. This was going to be a disaster.

He walked out on stage, sweat dripping from his brow before he'd even begun.

Twenty-three minutes later his whole shirt was sopping wet. He replaced the mic into the stand and bowed.

'Thank you very much, I've been Vic Bead, enjoy the rest of your evening. Good night.'

Vic walked off stage to cheers and whoops.

'Ladies and Gentlemen, Vic Bead,' shouted the MC, encouraging more cheering.

Vic went into the little room backstage and did a fist pump. 'Yes,' he grunted. *Maybe that was the secret to success, think less before a show*, he thought.

'I see you took my advice on the material, then,' Wally said, sitting in his usual seat backstage.

Vic took a swig of his beer.

'Much better now you're not whinging about your ex-wife. Welcome back, the real Vic Bead.'

'Don't flatter yourself, Wal,' Vic said.

Wally smiled and turned away.

Vic knew Wally was right, in part, but he wasn't going to let that prick take credit for it.

'Hey, Vic.' The manager popped his head around the door. 'There's a woman asking for you. She's in the bar, says she's your girlfriend.'

'Girlfriend? Right, thanks.'

Vic wondered if it might be Toni, the comedian's groupie, but, when he arrived he saw it was Tina, arms folded across her chest, eyes icy.

Looks don't kill people, crazy lovers do, Vic thought.

'Hi, Tina,' he said, in a bright cheery voice. 'I didn't know you were in town tonight. Why didn't you tell me?'

'Shall we go outside?'

'Sure.'

They stepped out, into the smokers' section.

'What's wrong?' asked Vic.

'Like you don't know.'

'I haven't got a clue.'

'Your new material—humiliating, just humiliating.'

'What are you talking about?'

'You don't like our song, that's fine, but you could have just told me rather than tell the whole world.'

'It's not that I don't like it,' Vic said, 'it simply gave me an idea for material.'

'That's all I am to you, isn't it? A source for your bloody stupid material, someone to ridicule on stage.'

'I didn't ridicule you.'

'Our whole relationship is a joke to you, isn't it?'

'No, Tina. It's not you. It's, well, it's a grotesque version of you, mixed with other people I know and—'

'Now you're saying I'm grotesque?'

'No, that's not what I said. I write comedy. I warned you at the beginning I often use a version of my real life in my material.' Vic shrugged. 'What are you doing here, anyway?'

'I go to all your gigs, Vic. How else would I be able to write the reviews for the website?'

'So it *is* you. That's creepy.'

'Creepy? It's not creepy. I love you ,Vic, I love you. But obviously, I'm wrong to say that. Should I just fart it?'

'Tina—' Vic tried to put his hand on her shoulder but she pulled away. 'Are you Kim, too?'

'Kim, who the fuck is Kim? Another one of your fancy women?'

'I don't have fancy women, Tina.'

'How do you know about the website anyway? It was supposed to be a surprise,' said Tina, wiping her eyes and smudging her make-up.

'Mia showed it to me.'

'Oh, little Miss Perfect. I should have known.'

'For fuck sake Tina, this isn't about Mia.'

'I bet you don't write routines about her, though, do you?'

'Actually, there are bits of her in there but, as I've said countless times before, Mia never has, and never will be, my girlfriend.'

'Maybe not physically but you've been having an emotional affair with her for years.'

'You what?'

'That's why no one else can get close to you. No one else is good enough. You're in love with Mia, Vic. You just want sex from me, and your countless other women, because you can't get into her knickers.'

'For the last time, Mia and I are friends, we have been since Uni. Men and women can be friends, you know?'

'Ha.'

'Tina, you're confusing your over-active imagination with reality.'

'I can only say what I see. You'll never find happiness with her in your life.'

'You're crazy.'

'Grotesque, creepy and now crazy. It's over Vic. And this time for good. Don't come crying back to me when you're lonely, or when some twenty-one year old dumps you.'

'What?'

'You heard.'

Vic swallowed, how did Tina knew about Rosie?

'I hate you.'

Vic watched her stomp away. He headed back inside, promising himself this time there would be no going back.

He stood at the bar watching Jessie deliver her set. It was the first time he'd been on the same bill as her but he'd heard all about her. Everyone said she was about to take off and he could see why.

'Ladies and Gentlemen, Jessie Hulme.'

The crowd whooped and cheered.

The lights came up to signal the interval. Vic finished his lager and ordered another one before the bar became overrun with comedy fans.

'Hi, Vic.'

Vic turned. Standing next to him was a woman, about his age, with short dark wavy hair, slightly chubby cheeks and a charming, if rather goofy smile. She looked like Nena of 99 Red Balloons fame.

'Hi,' he said.

'You were great tonight. You don't remember me, do you?'

Vic shook his head.

'Jenny Clarke, I was in the year below you at school.'

'Oh, hi. Yes, I remember you,' said Vic. 'You're a long way from home.'

'Over for a hen do.'

'Yours?'

'God no, never again. Do you remember Heather Bryant?' Jenny pointed to a gaggle of women. 'It's her wedding. She's the one in the veil. Then there's Liz Michaels, with the devil's horns, and Michelle James, with the halo.'

'Ah, Michelle, didn't she use to go out with Tommy?'

'That's right, she did.'

'What ever happened to him?'

'Dead.'

'Really? Shit.' Vic bowed his head for a moment. 'Are you having a good night?'

'It's okay.'

A loud laugh filled the room. 'That's Dawn,' Jenny said. 'The cheerleader of the group. Somewhat overbearing.'

'I'm sure I've heard that laugh before,' said Vic with a slight frown. 'Are you staying at the Holiday Inn?'

'Yep.'

'I think I heard you arrive. No sleep for me, then.'

'We'll be as quiet as pissed mice by then.'

'That's what I'm worried about.' Vic smiled.

The lights dimmed and the MC came bounding onto the stage.

Jenny smiled at him and went back to her seat.

Vic put his empty pint glass down and slipped out. He could do without watching Wally tonight.

Vic was sitting on the hotel bed, draining the dregs from his last remaining can of lager. He flicked through the channels, looking for something to entertain him. Why did Tina always manage to dump him when there was other crap going on in his life?

There was a gentle tap on the door. *Bloody hell*, he thought, *has Tina changed her mind?* He pulled his trousers on and looked through the spy hole. Jenny.

'Thought you might like a nightcap, help you sleep,' she said, holding up four cans of gin and tonic.

'Where are the others?'

'They went to some nightclub. I couldn't be arsed. Are you going to invite me in?'

'Sorry, yes, come in.'

They drank and talked about people Vic could barely remember and teachers he'd rather forget.

'I always fancied you,' Jenny blurted as she leaned towards him.

Vic doubted that very much. He lent in and gave her a sloppy kiss. Within minutes they were naked.

A soft click woke him. He felt like he'd been through a washer-dryer. He desperately needed a glass of water but didn't want to move. The room was bathed in bright light. He held his head, thoughts in a jumble; babies, Tina, Jenny, lager, gin, sex. His eyes focused on a discarded condom wrapper. There was no note or phone number. He groaned. His head thumped and his stomach grumbled. He reached for his phone and typed in Jenny's name into Facebook. There she was: Jenny (Daniels) Clarke, married to Kevin Clarke, a man who, as far as Vic could remember, was in prison for GBH. Was that why she had snuck

201

away without waking him? What if she regretted it. What if… God, what had he done? Vic was sweating. He got out of bed and staggered into the bathroom where he dropped to his knees and threw up.

In the shower, all he could think about was Jenny going to the police to report him. What would he tell Elis? How could he prove his innocence? Her word against his and in today's climate… And even if he did prove it, Kevin Clarke would be waiting for him on release. As soon as he stepped out of the shower, he threw up again. What if Jenny had told her friends and, any minute now, a posse of women stormed his room to wreak revenge on the man who had taken advantage of their drunk friend? Vic lay on the bed, wishing he knew how to say no.

There were two reasons why Vic left breakfast until the last possible moment; one, he wasn't entirely sure he could deal with the smell of food, let along eating any and, two, he wanted to avoid a room full of clucking hens.

The smell of food was surprisingly good. The sight of many pale-faced women sat at various tables, on the other hand, wasn't. He tried to avoid eye-contact as he headed for the buffet.

'That's the comedian from last night,' he heard the woman who Jenny had identified as Dawn blurt out.

Vic looked around and smiled. At least they weren't lynching him.

'Come to do us a private show, have you?'

Vic searched the faces. His eyes found Jenny, she winked at him.

He smiled, loaded bacon onto his plate but before he could find a seat, a wave of nausea came over him. He slammed his plate down and made a hasty exit.

'Hi Vic,' Mia said. 'Sorry, I ordered already, I've only got about forty-five minutes.'

'I thought you were free this afternoon.'

'I am but I have to cover registration for a colleague.'

'Sounds fun,' said Vic and ordered a coffee.

'How was Bristol? Any sign of whatshername, that Transvision Vamp woman?'

'Toni, no, but Tina showed up and then stormed off.'

'What happened?'

'She decided my show was a humiliation and you and I are at it like rabbits.'

'Just the usual, then.'

Vic laughed. 'I think it might be final this time, though.'

'I've heard that before.'

'And then a little dalliance with an old school friend.'

'Male or female?'

'Very funny.'

'You're an old dog, Vic Bead.'

Vic smiled.

A waitress brought Mia's food.

'Are you sure you won't have anything to eat?'

'No, I'm fine,' Vic said.

'So, I've been thinking,' said Mia. 'Which would you rather: Tina to leave, or to die?'

Vic looked at her. 'Is this a joke?'

'No. Answer the question.'

'Well, leave me, of course. I wouldn't wish death on anyone.'

'Really? I think I'd prefer the death option. Is that strange?'

'A little.'

'Think about it. Andy's out there somewhere, shagging Lorna, or whoever his latest bint is. He's in school flirting with the women in the maths department and the dinner ladies. It's killing me. If he were dead, I'd be upset, obviously, but at least I wouldn't be filled with the sort of jealousy that makes me want to cut his balls off. I'd have only fond memories.'

'Are you trying a new routine on me?' Vic said.

'Ha, ha, no. I was just thinking. Do you remember when I gave up Facebook?'

'Oh yeah, how long did that last? About three days?'

'Four but that's not the point, is it? The point is, you can delete it from your phone, shut down your account, but it's still

203

there. The account lies dormant.' She took a mouthful of coffee. 'Your friends tell you what fun they're having on it. So, of course, you go back to it. The only way I could give up Facebook would be if it didn't exist anymore. Do you see?'

'Not really, no.'

'It's the same with Andy, and you with Tina. We know they're poisonous, we know it's wrong, but they are still there, lurking in the background. If they were dead, we'd have to move on.'

'This is the craziest thing I've ever heard. But do you know what? You're right. Can I use it in a routine?'

'Be my guest. So, how shall we kill Tina and Andy, then?'

'Oh, I've thought of over a hundred ways to kill Tina.' Vic said.

'You are joking… right?'

Vic grinned. 'How's Tinderboy.'

'Good.' Mia looked at her watch. 'Oh, look at that, I have to get back to school. I'll tell you next time.'

Free lesson and the staffroom to herself. Mia looked at the pile of marking sitting on her desk, sighed, took a sip of tea and opened her emails. One from Geraint. She smiled.

A little story for you.

Mia opened the attachment.

Irma looked fantastic in her long flowing black dress, black fishnet stockings and her new, drop-dead gorgeous, high-heels. It was the first time anyone else would see her wearing them, although she'd worn them a few times home alone when she'd wanted to feel sexy. Now she was waiting for him. He'd told her what to wear and where to stand.

She didn't know what he had in store for her, but she shivered now at the thought of his touch.

There it was, the rap on the door she'd been waiting for. She stood in the middle of the room and took a deep breath. He let himself in, and approached her. She longed for a smile, or a kiss, but he just circled her, inspecting her. He had a glint in his eye that scared and thrilled her in equal measure. He stood behind her, silence filled the room, he lent in towards her, she could feel his hot breath on her neck and her own heart thumping in her chest.

He whispered in her ear, his voice thicker, lower than usual.

'Do what I say, and you won't get hurt, disobey me and I can't guarantee your safety.'

Her knees buckled.

'Take off your dress.'

She meekly did as she was told, mesmerised by his voice.

'Now stand still. Let me look at you.' His voice was lower than ever, a hot breathy whisper.

He circled her again, inspecting her body. There was a smile of approval on the corner of his lips. His eyes devoured her.

Goosebumps appeared on her body. She realised that the only part of him to touch her so far was his breath and yet she was more turned on than she could ever remember. What were his plans for her? What did he mean 'can't guarantee your safety'? Part of her wanted to disobey him to see what the punishment might entail. But, most of all, she wanted him to touch her, feel skin on skin, the warmth of the embrace.

He stood behind her, close, so she could feel his presence, feel his breath, but not his touch.

He whispered again, telling her she was beautiful, telling her how he longed to kiss her but still he didn't touch.

The hairs on her neck stood up, her knees still weak. She sensed he was smiling, enjoying putting her through this torture. She was smiling too, enjoying being the object of his desire.

'You okay Mia?'

Mia looked up to see Mike Johns, the chemistry teacher, staring at her.

'Um… I'm fine, Mike, I'm fine,' she said. 'Just um… reading a really funny email.'

'Brilliant, I could do with a laugh. Can I see it?'

'No, it's nothing really, just a silly family thing.'

The chemistry teacher shrugged and Mia decided she'd better put her phone away before it got her into trouble.

*

After Mia had gone back to school, Vic stayed in the café for another coffee and to do some work. Looking around, as he was ordering another coffee, he saw a face he recognised waiting in the queue behind him.

'Hi, it's Miss Evans, isn't it?' Vic said to the woman behind him in the queue.

'Yes, you're, Mr... um, don't tell me—son who loves computers, wife who loves women.'

'Nicely put,' Vic Smiled. 'Vic, Vic Bead,' he said, as he put his hand out.

'Tiffany,' she said, shaking his hand. 'What's wrong?'

'Nothing, it's just, well, Tiffany seems like a young name.'

'What's that supposed to mean?' She crossed her arms.

'Sorry, I mean, I suppose it's not a name you'd expect for a deputy head.'

'Keep digging.'

'No school today?'

'I had a dental appointment, not going back in.'

Vic picked up his coffee. 'Wanna join me?'

'Only if you promise not to discuss my name, my age, the school or your son's chances of getting there. Okay?'

'Fair enough.'

They went back to Vic's table and sat down.

'So, your wife left you for a woman.'

'I should have put that off limits, too.'

'Must be hard. I probably shouldn't say this but your ex-wife's girlfriend looks rather fierce.'

'She hated you. Said you reinforce gender stereotypes.'

'Oh yeah, being the youngest female deputy head in the county is a terrible role model.'

Vic laughed. 'I thought I was left of centre but she makes Marx look like Maggie.'

'You should be a comedian.'

'I am.'

'Really?'

'Yep. You married?'

'Divorced. It's just me and Izzy now.'

'Nice name.'

'It's Isabella, really, but everyone calls her Izzy.'

'How old?'

'Seven.'

'Nice.'

'So, tell me about being a comedian. It must be tough.'

'So's being a deputy head teacher.'

'At least I don't have to make them laugh,' she said, taking a sip of coffee. 'What's it like when no one laughs?'

'Lonely. You cry alone in a hotel room.'

Tiffany touched Vic's arm. 'But it must be great when the whole room is laughing.'

'I wish I knew.'

Tiffany laughed just a little too loud.

Her phone buzzed on the table. 'I better go. That's Matt.'

'Matt?'

'My boyfriend.'

'Oh, I see, right, well, of course.'

'We should do this again,' Tiff said. 'Are you on WhatsApp?'

'Yeah.'

'What's your number?'

How come she kept the boyfriend secret for so long? She'd had plenty chance to mention him but she'd clearly said it was just her and Izzy . He'd thought she'd been flirting with him. Had she been flirting?

Ten minutes later, Vic's phone buzzed. A message from an unknown number.

    » Thanks for coffee, let's do it again. Tiff.

Vic had had one of those weeks where nothing of any significance had happened. He hoped Mia had some gossip because he had nothing.

'So, how are things with your secret Internet lover?' Vic asked.

'Hotting up,' Mia said. 'He's gone all *Fifty Shades* on me.'

'Really?'

Mia nodded.

'Is that good or bad?' Vic asked.

'I like it. He's sending me these kinky stories, look.' Mia picked up her phone and handed it to Vic.

> *Irma sat in her chair, wearing nothing but her new red high-heeled shoes. She'd bought them early that day and wanted to treat Carlos to something special.*

'Bloody hell,' Vic said. 'Who the hell are Carlos and Irma?'

'It's me and him, isn't it?'

'Or, its generic, so he can send it to anyone.'

'You always have to ruin things.'

'Or add a bit of reality,' he said, as he continued to read.

> *She knew he'd be home in soon. She was ready for him. She heard the key in the lock. This was it. He came into the room and saw her, naked, legs slightly apart, touching herself.*
>
> *'Wow' was all he could say as he took a step towards her.*
>
> *'Stay there,' Irma ordered, 'watch me.' Her voice was stern but sexy. She fixed him with her eyes as she rubbed herself deliberately.*
>
> *'Take off your shirt,' Irma said.*
>
> *Carlos responded, peeling off his shirt.*
>
> *'Now the trousers, but slowly.'*
>
> *As Carlos took off his trousers, Irma smiled, pleased to see the outline of the effect she was having on him through his trunks. He took a step closer.*
>
> *'Turn around,' she said, her breath heavier as she spoke. 'Take them off,' she ordered as she continued to play with herself. 'Don't touch yourself,' she said.*

Vic looked up. 'This is shite,' he said.

'No, it's not, it's fun.'

'So, he wants you to dominate him? It's *Fifty Shades* in reverse.'

'No, he switches, sometimes the man's in charge, sometimes the woman.'

'Right.' Vic handed the phone back. 'And you like this?'

'It's kinda kooky.'

'It's kinda kinky. And this is what he's into, is it? Domination stuff?'

'He doesn't explicitly say so but all his stories are about it. For example, today's story was about pegging.'

'Pegging?'

'The woman wears a strap on and …'

'Okay, I get the picture. Sounds painful.'

'Yes.'

'What pleasure would a woman get out of that?'

'The power I suppose. I dunno.'

They contemplated that for a moment.

'Would you do it?' asked Vic.

'I'd probably giggle but I'd give it a go.'

'You do know why *Fifty Shades of Grey* wouldn't work in real life, don't you?'

'Do tell.' Mia picked up her coffee cup and warmed her hands with it.

'Second-hand sex toys.'

'What?'

'Well, let me ask you this. If you started dating a man and he whipped out a vibrator, would you be happy to use it?'

Mia shrugged.

'You wouldn't, would you? Because you wouldn't know where it had been. Literally. If a man introduces a sex toy to a woman, it has to be box fresh. They're like teddy bears. You can't give a new flame your old flame's teddy bear.'

'Same rule for rabbits as for teddies' Mia said.

'Well put. So, Miss Whatsherface in *Fifty Shades* would go into the dungeon and see those toys and say, 'Are these new?' It's going to cost a fortune each time you get a new woman. We're not all Christian Grey-style millionaires'

'This is a new routine, isn't it?'

'Maybe.'

'Can't we ever just have coffee?'

'What do you think?'

'It needs work.'

'Thanks. Do you think you'll meet this guy?'

'I'm tempted.'

'Sounds like a pervert to me. You told me he sounded normal.'

'Define normal.'

'Good point.'

'Anything happening with you?'

'Nothing, zilch. I tried to get a date with the deputy head from Elis's new school but she's not having it.'

'Why not?'

'She says she got a boyfriend but I wonder if I can still...'

'Dangerous territory, Vic.'

Vic smiled.

'What are you doing this weekend?'

'I'm off to Huddersfield, Friday and Saturday, and then a Sunday lunch gig in Coventry on the way back. You?'

'I'm seeing Stan on Friday. Then no plans.'

'You could come to Huddersfield.'

'I think, I'll pass.'

Vic was sitting back stage at the comedy club. He wrote a few cues on his arm just in case he forgot any of the new stuff. His phone lit up on the table.

> *Hi Vic.*
> *Hi Tiff. What are you up to?*
> *Nothing, just watching TV*
> *Cool. I'm in Huddersfield. Just about to go on stage.*
> *Exciting. Good luck.*
> *Thanks. Really love the new photo on Instagram.*
> *You're sweet. I thought I looked fat.*
> *No way. You look amazing.*
> *Blushing now. Good luck with the show.*

Two hundred people had laughed exactly when Vic wanted them to. For that twenty-five minutes, he'd been the main man. He could still hear the laughter, the applause was still ringing in his brain but, sadly, the endorphins were fading.

He took a swig of wine.

At least with bad gigs there was someone or something to

blame; tiredness from the long drive, the prick in the front row with his arms crossed, the heckler, the venue, the MC, or, of course, his own material. A bad gig gave something concrete to reflect on and a sense that it could get better. A good gig, on the other hand, led to this—a shitty, empty hotel room in Huddersfield, with no one to share the elation with. All he had was an over-priced bottle of cheap wine from the twenty-four-hour garage, and Babe Station.

Vic checked his phone again. Still nothing. Not even a 'good night' from Elis or a 'how do I look?' from Tiff. He turned the light off and pulled the duvet over him. There had been a time when he loved these big hotel beds. He'd stretch out and make sure he used every single inch. Today it felt empty and cold.

Two drunks argued as they passed the hotel; an emergency vehicle screeched passed, filling his room with a flash of blue; a toilet flushed above or next to him. He checked his phone again, the room filling with digital light. But nothing had changed in two minutes, thirty seconds since he'd last checked.

Mia should have been sleeping, too, but Geraint was keeping her awake.

> *Have you ever been watched having sex?*
> *No.*
> *Would you like to be?*
> *Not really. Why?*
> *If I chose a man for you, could I watch you and him together?*
> *Really? We haven't even met.*
> *Don't you think it would be horny, performing for me?*
> *I'd be embarrassed.*
> *I'd like to watch you.*
> *We'll see. Have you done any of this stuff before?*
> *Only with my wife.*
> *You're married?*
> *Yes. Does it matter?*
> *I don't know. Does she know about this?*

» No, not exactly.

» Not exactly?

» She says I can have my fun as long as I don't tell her.

» She's not into it?

» No.

» How many other women do you have?

» None, only you.

» Really?

» Yes.

» I've a question. Be honest.

» Okay.

» Are you a sub or a dom?

» Both.

» Liar, you're a sub.

» You're right.

» So?

» So what?

» You want me to dominate you?

» Yes.

Mia let that sink in for a moment.

» Would you like to get a coffee?

» Yes

» So, name your time and place.

» Geraint?

» Geraint?

Vic bounced into the comedy club. He was ready for action. It'd been a great day, laying aroun, and chatting to Tiff via WhatsApp. Now, he just had to repeat the success of last night. His phone buzzed. Vic smiled.

» Had my haircut, today. What do you think?

Vic look at the photo.

» Very stylish.

» Thanks, you're so sweet. Izzy had one too.

Ping, another photograph.

» *As beautiful as her mother.*
» *You're lovely. What are you up to?*
» *Just about to go on stage.*
» *Good luck.*

Vic smiled and heard his name being called. He bounded on to the stage. 'Hello Huddersfield.'

Vic walked back to the hotel at a snail's pace. How could the same venue, the same routine, the same bill, produce totally different results? Last night, he'd left the stage with laughter chasing him; tonight there was nothing but polite applause. To top it off, there were no messages from Tiff, or Elis. He slumped on the bed. The room seemed to have become smaller since last night. The air was staler and the hotel needed to sack their cleaner.

Vic tried to replay both nights through his mind. Had he hit punchlines differently? Paused in the wrong places? Had his body language been different? There hadn't been any hecklers, no obvious trouble makers, and yet tonight's crowd hadn't laughed as much. Maybe they hadn't been drunk enough, or they'd been too drunk.

He got undressed and went into the bathroom. The man in the mirror had black bags under red eyes. His skin looked grey. He sighed and started cleaning his teeth. Did the money in his wallet justify putting himself through this? Was it time to give it up? But then what? Back to the nine-to-five?

He closed his eyes and leaned onto the edge of the sink as he recalled his past life.

He'd been oh-so-happy then, hadn't he? Working with casual racists and full-time homophobes in an office that suffocated him. Surely this was better than that, wasn't it? With another sigh, he washed his face and went back into the bedroom.

A notification told him he had a comment on his Fan Page.

Loved the show tonight.

Elisa Barnet. He knew that name. One of Kylie's friends? Someone he went to university with? No, he remembered; she was a comedy reviewer and booker and she'd taken the time to comment on his show. Bloody hell, he thought, as his phone buzzed.

» *Hope the show was went well tonight. Tiff xx*
» *It was fine. You're looking lovely.*
» *How do you know?*
» *You always do.*
» *Thanks, smiling now. Sweet dreams. xx*
» *You too.*

The phone vibrated just as Vic was about to enter the café. It was another message from Tiff. He smiled, slipped the phone away and held the door open for a woman with a four-by-four buggy. Mia was at the counter.

'Americano?'

Vic nodded.

'How was Huddersfield?' Mia asked, handing over a twenty pound note to the barista.

'A long way away. How was your weekend?'

Mia looked around for a table. 'Not bad. Stan made one of his killer curries on Friday night, so spent most of Saturday close to the loo.'

'Too much info,' said Vic with a grimace. 'Hey, do you remember I told you about Tiffany?'

'The one that parked you?'

'No, that was Cariad.'

'I can't keep up. So, who was Tiffany?'

'Deputy head at the school Elis is going to go to. Looks like the cute one from Bananarama. Lovely coffee together, lots of flirtation, then dropped the boyfriend bombshell.'

'Ah, yes, I remember.'

'Well, since then we've been chatting on WhatsApp.'

Mia rolled her eyes.

'Tell me—if she has a boyfriend, why does she want to talk to me?'

'Maybe she likes you, thinks of you as a friend.'

'But do friends send each other the kiss emoticon or the one with love hearts for eyes? I've never been great at reading signs but surely those are pretty obvious.'

Mia stirred her coffee. 'I bet she invites compliments, doesn't she? Says she feels fat or her hair looks awful.'

'Have you been reading my messages?'

'I don't have to. I know what she's up to. You're her surrogate,' Mia said, clinking the spoon on the side of her cup.

'Surrogate?'

'Surrogate or substitute, whatever you want to call it. You know what it's like, you've been in a relationship for a long time, partner takes you for granted, along comes a keen pup who makes you feel special. But you don't want to drop the original, so...'

'Oh, great, a back-up plan.'

'Not quite, just someone to do the odd-jobs the main man forgets to do. But, hey, it's not all bad. It's a level or two down from being parked and at least she's talking to you. I reckon she'll keep you on a lead for a bit, feed you enough titbits to keep you happy, and then either you'll get bored, or she'll find someone else.'

'A surrogate for the surrogate?'

'Exactly.'

'Does the surrogate ever take the place of the original?'

Mia shook her head. 'It's unusual.'

'Do you have one?'

'Oh, I've had plenty. Harry, for example.'

'But you slept with him, didn't you? So, there's hope for me.'

'Sorry, mate—' Mia shook her head— 'I'm an exception.'

'I think I'd prefer to be parked.'

'Ignore her texts, then.'

'Have you seen her?' Vic opened a photo on Instagram. 'She's lovely.'

Mia shook her head and smiled. 'You're a lost cause, Vic.'

'Talking of leashes, any news from your 'lover'?'

'Geraint? Man, he gets weirder and weirder.'

'Why, what's he up to now?'

'He asked if I'd let him choose a man for me and then watch us, you know, perform.'

'Jesus, you haven't even slept with him yet and he's pairing you off with another guy?'

'I know, it's odd, isn't it?'

'Why do you entertain his perversions?'

'He's interesting. All the other guys online just want to tell you how they'll fuck you senseless.'

'And he tells you how someone else will fuck you senseless.'

'No, he has an air of mystery.'

'He's got an air of having watched far too much PornHub.'

'At least it shows some effort. Why do men think we will be turned on by how big and stiff their dick is? We don't care. But this is different, he's seducing me with words and he can spell.'

'He's setting himself up though, isn't he? I mean, he's good between the sheets of paper but is he going to any good between actual sheets?'

'Well, I hope I'm going to find out soon.'

'So, you've agreed to meet him?'

'We had this amazing, intense conversation the other day. It ended with me challenging him to meet me. I'm waiting for his answer.'

'Take a panic alarm.'

'I'll be fine, he's a pussycat.'

» Geraint?

» Geraint?

Mia looked at her silent phone and shook her head. She had to admit it, he was gone.

May 2017

Despite living in this city for much of his life, there were still large swathes that were a mystery to Vic. His phone told him he'd arrived at the pub but there was no sign of it. He checked the email from his agent again.

Duke of Carlise Pub, ask for Eric.

He should have taken a taxi. He looked around and eventually managed to pick out the place through the drizzle.

There was a bored-looking man behind the bar and an old fella with a copy of *The Echo* spread across one table. Otherwise it was empty.

'Is Eric around?' Vic said.

The barman looked up and went out the back. Vic heard him shout out for Eric.

A lithe man, with glasses, appeared behind the bar. 'Hi,' he said, 'you're Vic, right?'

Vic nodded and held out his hand.

'I presume you're the comedian and not the stripper.' Eric threw his head back. His laugh sounded like a dying dog.

'Stripper?' Vic said. 'I was told it was a curry night.'

'That's right—Hot and Saucey, the best curry and strip night around.'

'Right…'

'It works like this; we feed them, then you get twenty minutes, then the stripper, then a break. Then you again, for ten, and then the stripper will do something naughty with one of the men in the audience.'

'Right…'

'That's not a problem, is it?'

'A problem?'

'I hope you're not one of those bloody feminists.'

'Me, no,' said Vic, as he imagined Eric copping a feel of the stripper and saying it was just banter.

'Great. Well, the event is in here.'

Eric led the way into the large back room.

'Don't worry about the music or lights, I've got a kid who does that. Just go on and do your bit. You can prepare in here—' He showed him a smaller store room off the side. 'You'll get a helping of curry, of course.'

'Thanks,' Vic said.

'Hope you like it hot. Can I get you anything?'

'A cup of tea would be great.'

Eric disappeared.

'Fuck, wank, shit,' Vic muttered as he glanced at the notes on his arm. Could he still do it? Maybe he could get the new porn stuff in. And the dick pics routine; it wasn't ready but it was better than the break-up material. Maybe he could try the *Fifty Shades* stuff. No, that wasn't ready either. 'Think of the money,' he said to himself.

'Hiya.'

Vic turned to see one of the Olivias standing in the doorway.

'Hello. It's Olivia, isn't it?'

The girl stared at him blankly.

'We met in that club, I was with Rosie.'

'Oh, right,' she said, not looking any the wiser.

'What are you doing here?'

'I'm the stripper.'

'Oh, right. Sorry, I didn't…'

Olivia crossed her arms. 'It pays for my university, better than working in Tesco.'

'No, yes, right, of course. No, it's cool. Anyway, I'll be introducing you, so what would you like me to say?'

'My working name is Lisa. So just call me Lisa. Oh and, please, don't tell Rosie.'

'Do you want the good news or the bad news? The bad news is the stripper couldn't make it tonight. The good news is we've found a replacement. Me.'

Vic started to undo the buttons on his shirt.

There were mock boos and wolf whistles.

He'd won them over. Now for the routine. *Think of the money,* he told himself as he launched into the 'buying porn' material. It wasn't going down too badly. In fact, there were laughs in all the right places. But Vic could tell they were getting impatient.

'And now, Gentlemen, the time has come. You've seen the tit, now it's time for tits.' Vic silently promised to pay his fee to a women's charity. 'Please, welcome to the stage the wonderful, the lovely, the gorgeous, the delectable—'

'Get on with it.'

'Put your hands together, and keep them above the table, for… Lisa!'

Vic watched Olivia/Lisa gyrate on-stage for the braying crowd. He thought of Rosie opening her legs for him, expecting to get dresses instead of kisses in return. What had the world come to? Students selling their bodies to get themselves through university. Had it always been thus? Perhaps his classmates had been strippers, or had sugar daddies. They wouldn't advertise it, would they? He looked at the men in the audience. Treating women as objects, to be screamed at and touched by the mob. Vic hated it. He shouldn't be watching but… he was a man and Oliva/Lisa was mesmerising. All curves and slinky moves. She smiled and teased and wiggled in a way Vic had never seen before. She poured baby oil onto her tanned skin and rubbed it in. She was amazing. She swayed in front of the men and then gave a flick of her hips, taking her body just out of reach. Vic stared at her, obsessed with her beauty but angry at himself.

The song was coming to an end. She did a little bow to the audience before dancing off to a round of whoops and whistles.

'Gentlemen, another big hand for…Ol… O… oh, so lovely, Lisa. We're going to take a short break, for you guys to sort yourselves out. We'll be back in fifteen minutes.'

At the end of the show, Eric ushered the men into the main bar to spend more money, leaving Vic and Olivia to finish their drinks back stage.

'Can we share a cab? There's always one or two outside who think, cos I'm a stripper, I'm fair game.'

'It'd be my pleasure.'

'See?' said Olivia, nodding towards a man standing by the pub door.

He made a move towards her but aborted when he saw Vic.

'You're never tempted? Sorry, I shouldn't have asked that.'

'Not with the audience, you'd get a reputation. But it does get me horny.'

'Does it now?'

'Rosie said you were good. Shall we go to yours?' said Olivia, licking her lips.

Vic looked at her, knowing that if she'd asked him mid-strip he'd have said yes. He closed his eyes and imagined the body he'd seen earlier in his bed.

'I don't think I should; Rosie's friend and all that.'

'Okay, I'll just have to hope my boyfriend's still up, then. You can drop me here, driver.' She got out of the car.

Vic sighed.

'You daft bastard,' the driver said.

'None of your damn business.' Vic sat back and closed his eyes.

The whole stripper thing left Vic with conflicting emotions. It was like porn; despite knowing it was a cruel and misogynist industry, where most of the participants were coked up, he was still addicted to it. How could he not enjoy watching a naked twenty-year-old cavorting? But what confused him more was how often had he been given the chance to take a stripper home? Never, that was how often. He was still struggling to come to terms with it as he told Mia about it all.

'So, let me get this right,' Mia said. 'You had an offer of sex with a twenty-one year old stripper and you turned it down?'

Vic nodded.

'Are you mad?'

Vic shrugged.

'I bet you regret it now, don't you?'

Vic gave another shrug

'Well, don't you?'

'No, I don't.'

'Okay, stop messing around—you slept with her, didn't you?'

'No, I went home, alone.'

'I don't believe you.'

'It shocked me, too, but it would have been meaningless sex.'

'I thought that's what you were after.'

'I thought so, too, but no, I think I want to have meaningful meaningless sex.

'Is that even a thing?'

'It is now.'

'Good luck in finding it.'

'Are you finding it? How's it going with that Internet bloke?'

Mia looked at the floor and then her phone. 'I don't know what's happened to him.'

'Why? I thought you were going to meet up.'

'I was but he's disappeared. Remember I told you we'd had that intense conversation?'

'Yes.'

'Well, that was the last time I heard from him. He's not even reading my messages.'

'Strange. Perhaps he's dead.'

'Don't say that. It's more likely his wife found out.'

'I knew it.'

'Knew what.'

'That he was married. It makes perfect sense, now.'

'What does?'

'This whole thing.'

Mia sighed. 'Enlighten me.'

'Sex with his wife gets boring. He gets her to experiment to put the sparkle back in. The trouble is, she's not into it or, maybe, it doesn't feel right with her. It's hard to role-play when you know someone so well; they tend to giggle.'

'Talking from your own experience?'

Vic smiled. 'Anyway, it's much better to be dominated by a stranger. So, he goes looking, and finds you.'

'How come you're such an expert?'

'I've been giving it a lot of thought, ever since we had that monogamy conversation, when you started with Andy.'

'Fucking hell—Vic Bead: the relationship advisor.'

'That could be the title for my new show.'

'Come on, let's hear your theory.'

'As we said, we think everyone is normal but actually we're all fucked up. I'll tell you a secret—you tell anyone and I'm in big trouble.'

'Tell me.'

'Remember I asked who's the most normal person you know? Who did you say?'

'Ash, probably.'

'The man who uses hookers.'

'You're joking.'

'It's true.'

'How do you know?'

'He told me, late one night, after half a bottle of whiskey.'

'Why did he tell you?'

'He felt guilty and needed to share. It's not a regular thing but, when he goes on business trips, he participates in some extracurricular business.'

'I thought Ash and Lily were the perfect couple.'

'That's what they look like. Along with all the other happy couples who share their brilliant lives on Facebook. But it's all a scam. Humans are not designed to be monogamous. We get to a stage in a relationship where we love the person but don't fancy them. We yearn for something else. Why? Because marriage was designed when life expectancy was around forty. Look at us: me, you, Ash, Andy, Tina, we're all around forty. We're passed the marriage sell-by-date. And we're not the only ones. Take a look at Mumsnet. Every other discussion is about a loveless marriage.'

'What the fuck are you doing on Mumsnet?'

'Research—it's the only reason I'm on Tinder and Instagram.'

'Yeah, right.'

'Anyway, the Mumsneterati would kill me for saying this.'

'The who?'

'The Mumsneterati, the radical wing of the website—mums

with guns.'

Mia smiled.

'They wouldn't want to hear this, but Ash is saving his marriage by going to hookers.'

'You baffle me with your logic sometimes, Vic.'

'Hear me out. Lily doesn't want to have sex with him. But he still wants sex. He has three options: leave the woman he loves; have an illicit affair; or pay for sex. He chose the latter and I tend to think he did the right thing. We all need sex and we all need love, it doesn't mean we have to get them from the same person. Sex with a hooker is meaningless. It's just sex—it fulfils his desire. If he had an affair, he'd be investing emotions; here he's just spending money. But you know what's really weird?'

'That he goes to prostitutes isn't weird enough?'

'No—well, yes, but he could go to any type of woman. In their twenties, in their sixties, Black, Asian. Who does he choose? He chooses women who look like Lily. Your guy, Geraint, is similar but, instead of paying, he wants kinky sex. He figures there's less chance of getting involved emotionally. I bet you look like his wife.'

'And what about you?'

'Oh, I'm no different. I'm chasing a dream, the perfect sex, and where's it getting me?'

'You've ended up with a twenty-one year old who wants a sugar daddy on one hand, and a complete and utter nutter on the other.'

'Quite,' said Vic. They sat in silence for a moment. 'I wouldn't be in the least bit surprised if Lily is having an affair.'

'She'd never do that.'

'Wouldn't she? She must have a sex drive, she just doesn't fancy Ash. Same with Geraint's wife, it's not the kinky stuff she doesn't like, it's the bloke inside the gimp mask. Neither of them would want to break up the happy home—they're both in love with Dear Hubby—but they're bored. An hour with the milkman, once a week, and everyone's happy.'

'Especially the milkman.'

'But you're the same. Why don't you leave Stan? You say the

sex is almost non-existent, but you love him and you like being with him, so you stay together. He's your security but you need excitement, so you have Andy and Harry and Geraint.'

'Okay, but how do you explain couples who stay together for 60-odd years?'

'Who knows? Were they truly happy or did they stay together for the sake of the children, or to keep up appearances? We don't know because no one tells the truth. Can you imagine going on the local news, on the occasion of your sixtieth anniversary, and telling the world that the secret of your success was the dogging and the wife-swapping parties?'

'You're a cynic, Vic.'

'Or a realist. But don't worry, we're the lucky ones. We know this. It's the rest of society I feel sorry for.'

'None of this explains why Geraint has disappeared.'

'Because you were about to turn his fantasies into realities.'

'Isn't that what he wanted?'

'Yes and no. He didn't know what he wanted. He bottled it. You were asking him to jump out of a plane and he didn't trust his parachute. He's probably started the whole thing again with someone else. He'll never go through with it.'

'Poor man,' Mia said.

'Poor you,' Vic replied. 'Shit, look at the time. Elis finished computer club five minutes ago.'

'Hey, Elis, what do you want for your tea?' Vic didn't often give Elis a choice but he felt he owed it to him, after forgetting to pick him up. He looked at his son and wondered what was happening to the boy's brain. The iPad was playing a PewDiePie video, the TV was blasting out a cartoon and, on the phone, was a music vid.

'Elis, tea?'

'Don't mind.'

Vic took a breath. 'Toad in the hole?'

Elis put the iPad down and turned off the music. 'I can't eat sausages, I'm vegetarian.'

'Very funny, Elis.'

'No, Dad, really. I'm not eating meat anymore.'

'Since when?'

'Since Nat showed me that horrible video.'

'What horrible video?'

'About how they make meat.'

'So, you're giving up, just like that? No bacon, no sausages, no chicken nuggets, no McDonalds, no roast dinner at Granny's? Have you really thought about this?'

'Yes. Look—' Elis handed Vic the phone.

'What the…? Nat showed you this?'

'Yep. It's gross, isn't it?'

'It's disgusting.'

'Are you going to be a veggie, too, Dad?'

Vic chucked the phone onto the settee and put his arm around Elis. 'El, not all farms are like that. And, anyway, I've been a veggie longer than your mother.'

'But you eat meat.'

'That's because there are two types of vegetarian, practising and non-practising. I'm a non-practising one.'

'What's that?'

'I know eating meat is morally wrong but I love meat too much to change, so I'm a vegetarian up here—' Vic tapped his temple.

'That's a cop-out.'

Vic's whole argument had been unravelled by four words from the mouth of a ten year old. 'In a way, yes, I agree but I think we should try to get rid of human suffering before worrying about animals.'

'Maybe, if we were less cruel to animals, we'd be less cruel to people.'

Those words took Vic back to his third or fourth date with Kylie. He'd taken her to his favourite pub and recommended the lamb and mint pie and she'd dropped her V-bomb. They'd kind of argued and now, with his mother's looks and gestures, Elis had recreated the conversation they'd had, perfectly. Sometimes, it was difficult to love someone who reminded you so much of someone you hated.

'Cheese and potato pie, then? Or have you given up dairy too?'

'I could never give up cheese, or ice cream—be real.'

Vic attacked the potatoes with the peeler. 'Another vegetarian in the house, bloody hell,' he muttered. 'Please don't let him ask for veggie sausages. They are the devil's work.'

He wondered if he could make veggie food so bland it would drive Elis back to meat. But no, that would mean Elis would be enjoying veggie food at his mother's and he'd refuse to eat with him. With a sigh, he dropped another potato into the saucepan.

'Can I have my phone, please Elis?' he yelled.

'Here— Do you need help, Dad?'

'No, I'm fine. You watch your, whatever you…'

Elis was gone.

Vic scrolled through his numbers and pressed Call.

'Hi, Vic, what's up? Elis okay?'

'Hi, Kylie, yeah he's fine, but…'

'What?'

'He's just told me he's a vegetarian now.'

'Oh, I know. Isn't it great? Our little boy is growing up.'

'Is that what it is? Right, fine. Why didn't you think to tell me? I've got a freezer full of turkey twizzlers.'

'We thought it would be best coming from him.'

Vic clenched his fists as he stared into the pan of potatoes. He took a deep breath.

'Vic?'

'And what were you thinking, showing him that film? It's disgusting. Not fit for ten year olds.'

'It's a bit gory but we felt it was educational.'

'Educational? It's enough to give anyone nightmares. If I showed him horror films, you'd hit the bloody roof.'

'This is different.'

'How?'

'Horror film's are gratuitous; this is real life, Vic. This is what

226

is happening out there.'

'Jesus, let the poor boy have a childhood.'

'We thought it was a chance for Elis to make up his own mind. That was one of *our* principles, if you remember, Vic.'

'Fine but we also agreed not to expose him to the horrors of the world.'

'He was listening to The Smiths' 'Meat is Murder', with Nat. They were talking about what that meant and Nat thought—'

'Nat thought? It's not her place to think. She's not his mother. Where were you?'

'In work.'

'Leaving her alone with our child, brainwashing him with horror videos.'

'A little over dramatic, don't you think?'

'No, I don't, Kylie. Imagine if my girlfriend decided to take him to church.'

'Like, you'd let that happen.'

'Exactly. I wouldn't allow it. That's my point. You shouldn't have allowed Nat to expose our son to that video.'

'Oh, grow up, Vic.'

Vic listened to the dead line, swore, slammed the potato pan onto the hob and lit the stove.

June 2017

Most of the tables in the café were filled with people discussing business or students writing essays. Mia and Vic were squeezed in a corner where the student next to them was talking loudly into a mobile phone about a sexual encounter he'd had with a boy called Jeff.

'That bloody video, at his age.' Vic shook his head. 'I can live with him being a vegetarian but showing him that...'

'Terrible,' Mia nodded,

'Nat's got a lot to answer for.'

'I'm going to put that on your gravestone.'

'Sorry, it just pissed me off, that's all.'

Mia's phone buzzed. She looked at the screen and turned it over.

'Geraint?'

'No. He's gone. Just a distant memory.'

'That's a shame. Anyone else on the horizon?'

'Just a load of boys telling me how manly they are.'

'Ha, you'd eat them alive.'

'They should be so lucky. And you? Any luck with Tiffany?'

'Nope, that went exactly the way you predicted. The flood became a trickle, became a drought. Not had a message from her in ages.'

'And Tina?'

'Nothing. Thank god.'

'So, you're all alone?'

'Looks that way.'

'How does it feel?'

'Haven't really thought about it until you mentioned it. And now, I think I'll go home and cry.'

'Shut up, Vic.'

'I need a wee,' Vic said.

As soon as he was gone, Mia turned her phone over.

> *Hey beautiful, how's life. What say you dress up smart and I take you somewhere special for your birthday.*

'Ha,' Mia said.

'What's up?' asked Vic as he settled back on to his seat.

'You were quick.'

'Was I? I washed my hands and everything.' Vic made a show of wiping his hands on his jeans.

'Look at this—' said Mia, turning her phone screen towards Vic

'Andy!'

'Remember what I said about him being dead?'

'I do.'

'See what I mean?. A dead person can't rematerialise and expect me to drop everything and go out for dinner with him. Prick.'

'Please tell me you're going to ignore it.'

Mia didn't reply.

'I'm amazed he remembered your birthday, mind.'

'It's a simple ploy from the playboy rule book,' Mia said. 'Remember the little things, like birthdays; help them on with their coats; be good in bed; and then they'll forgive you when you shag anything else that moves.'

'Tell him to stick it.'

Sitting at the wheel of her car Mia read her message again She composed her reply.

> *You don't speak to me for weeks and then you invite me out for my birthday. Is that how you treat all your women?*
> *I thought it would be nice. I still like you, Mia.*
> *Okay, but one night only, and no funny business. Okay?*

Three days later, Vic was tidying the flat. His phone buzzed— his agent.

'Hi, Marie, not been to bed yet?'

'Very amusing, Victor. Listen, exciting news—I've got you a

meeting with Tammi English and Rick Ardon, the creative directors at TERA Productions.'

'Who?'

'Get with it, Victor. TERA are the next big thing. They have so much in the pipeline, right now, they're calling it a tunnel.'

'Right, great.'

'Exactly. Anyways, they're launching a topical news show.'

'Another one?'

'This is going to blow all the others out of the water. It's going to be edgy, controversial, divisive.'

'Don't all those mean the same thing?'

'It doesn't matter, Victor. What's important is they want *you* to send them a page or two of topical jokes.'

'I don't do topical jokes.'

'You do now. By Friday.'

'That's tomorrow.'

'It's topical, Victor. Clear your desk and get writing. This could be big. We're talking Channel Four.'

Vic was meant to be doing his taxes but he was only too happy for that to wait. He made a cup of tea and sat down with his computer.

'Right, what's in the news?

'What's funny about bombs, inflation, and sex abuse?' Vic wondered.

'Just write what's in the news,' he said to himself.

He made another cup of tea and dunked a biscuit, popping it into his mouth just before it collapsed. He flicked from website to website, looking for inspiration. He wrote lists, played with words, made a third cup of tea. Maybe a shower would help, or a trip to YouPorn. Or both.

Twenty minutes later, clean and relieved, he stared at his screen. It was like a thief had broken into his brain and stolen all his ideas. He'd take his iPad to a café—surely a change of scenery would get the cogs moving.

Vic blew on his coffee. watched the barista at work, watched the people pass by in the rain, and sighed. The two newspapers he'd brought with him were bereft of news, his brain bereft of ideas. The hour flew by, the change of location made no difference, and it was time to get Elis from school.

'Hi, Elis, you okay?'

'Where's the car, Dad?'

'We're walking.'

Elis pulled a face.

'Sorry, have I stolen valuable gaming time?'

Elis grunted.

'But I thought ice cream on the way home?'

'Cool.'

Elis had a sixth sense. His superpower wasn't seeing dead people, it was delaying his bedtime for as long as possible when he knew his father had work to do.

Following a battle of wills, Elis finally got the hint.

Vic poured a glass of wine and, feeling peckish, went into the kitchen to get a Mars Bar. Back at his desk, he picked up his old fountain pen. He'd bought one for Elis, for big school, and they'd been writing in ink for the first time in El's life. Vic had forgotten how good it felt. Perhaps writing with pen and paper would inspire him.

Facebook was open on the screen in front of him.

> To find your rapper name, put 'young' before the last thing you bought.

Ha, Vic thought, *that makes me Young Interdental Sticks. Not exactly street.*

He leaned forward and began to write, enjoying the sensation of the nib scratching out the words. He glanced across at the chocolate bar; it looked small. *No wonder people use them on that site Mia had shown him*, Vic thought.

He laughed and wrote, *I thought my dick had grown until I realised Mars Bars have got smaller.* Not topical but quite amusing. His wine was left untouched. He filled one page, two, three.

'Dad, can I have some water?'

'What are you still doing up?'

'I only went to bed ten minutes ago.'

Vic checked his watch. He felt like he'd been writing for hours but it had only been twenty-five minutes. He filled a cup for his son, shooed him back to bed and read his notes.

With a smile, Vic picked up his glass and downed the wine in one.

Mia looked at herself in the mirror again before rechecking her watch. She was just about to curse him for being late when the doorbell rang. She buzzed him up and went back to the mirror one last time. Had she over done it with the make up?

'Wow,' Andy said, looking at Mia, 'you look amazing.'

'You said dress smart.'

Andy planted a kiss on her cheek and tried to unzip her dress.

'I said, no funny business and, anyway, I thought you said we had reservations.'

'They'll hold them.'

Mia pushed him away. 'Where are we going?' she said, pulling on her coat.

'Wait and see.'

'Look at you, being all mysterious.' Mia ushered him out of the flat.

Andy grinned and held the taxi door open. 'Your carriage.'

Light rain dotted the windscreen on the way into town. Andy's hand felt warm in Mia's hand; it wasn't like him to hold hands.

The taxi dropped them in an old street near to the centre of town.

'Andy, I can't walk in these.'

'Don't worry, we're here,' Andy said.

'Where?'

Andy guided Mia towards the door of a ramshackle building. 'What are you doing?' Mia said as a door opened.

'Come on,' Andy said. 'Don't be scared.'

Andy led her in. 'Secret cocktail bar, best cocktails in town.'

A *maître d'* bowed and motioned to take Mia's coat. He led

them through the hubbub to their table. Mia looked at the menu and tapped her feet along to the jazz the live band were playing.

'It's lovely,' Mia said.

'Glad you like it. It's not your birthday every day.'

'It's not my birthday.'

'You know what I mean.'

'Look at these cocktails. I've never heard of half of them,' Mia said.

'Oh, these guys are real mixologists. They can do anything.'

'I haven't got a clue what to order.'

'Well, you like gin? Let's ask the waiter what they can do for you.'

Mia stared at her drink. Gin, pomegranate liquor, pomegranate seeds, orange peel, dry ice and something the waiter had said that she hadn't recognised. She took a photo.

'This looks amazing,' Mia said. She took a sip. 'It tastes great, too. How did you find out about this place?'

'I read about it in the local paper.' Andy smiled. 'I thought you'd like it.' He picked up the menu. 'What are you going to have next?'

'Hang on, I've barely started this one. Are you trying to get me drunk?' Mia popped an olive into her mouth. She was beginning to wish she'd eaten before she'd come out.

'Listen, I've been thinking—' Andy took Mia's hand— 'I think we should get married.'

'What?' She coughed, half choking on the olive.

'I think we should get married. You should leave Stan and marry me. I know I've been a dickhead but that's the past.'

'Are you proposing to me?' She was waiting for the bazinga.

'Yes. Marry me, Mia.'

Mia took a gulp of her drink. 'You're crazy.'

'Look, I know this is a bit of a surprise but imagine, you and me, a lovely wedding at a quaint country house somewhere, a honeymoon in the Caribbean. We could get a cute little place together, maybe a cat.'

'A cat?'

'You don't have to answer today, think about it, but I mean this. Let's order another drink,' Andy said looking at the menu. 'How about a mango margarita?'

'Um, fine. Order for me. I need the toilet.'

Leaning against the cool tiled wall of the Ladies, Mia found Vic's number. 'Fuck, fuck, come on, Vic, answer your bloody phone. Oh, thank God—Vic, you're not going to believe this, Andy just asked me to marry him.'

'What? No way. What did you say?'

'I didn't say anything.'

'What are you going to say?'

'I don't know. It doesn't feel real, like it was spur of the moment There wasn't even a ring.'

'No ring? Classy. Where are you? It's all echoey.'

'Oh, we're at some amazing, secret cocktail place. I'm in the loos.'

'Right, I hope you're not…'

'No, of course not.' She straightened her dress in the mirror. 'What am I going to do?'

'Is there a window?'

'What?'

'To escape through.'

'Vic, be serious.'

'Do you *want* to marry him?'

'I don't know. I've never thought about it. It would mean giving up Stan, living together. I don't know. Look, I'd better go. Have you got time for a coffee tomorrow?'

'Yeah, usual place?'

'Great, see you.'

'Don't forget to wash your hands.'

'What's that place like?' Vic said, as he ordered the coffees.

'It's amazing. Live jazz, attentive staff, quirky cocktails—it's like being in the 1920s. You should definitely go.'

'Ha, yes, on my own, that'll be fun.'

'Take Ash.' Mia picked up her coffee and looked around for a table. 'You two would make a lovely couple.'

'Don't you start. So, come on then. Did he go on one knee? Did the band play a special song?'

'Not exactly.' Mia looked out of the window. 'I told you, it was more spur of the moment.'

'Well, that can be romantic.'

'His exact words were, 'I think we should get married.''

'Ah,' Vic nodded.

''I think we should' isn't a proposal, it's what you say if you fancy a bag of chips on the way home, or if someone needs to see a doctor.' Mia picked up her coffee cup.

'Do you think he meant it?'

Mia sighed and stared at the ceiling. 'I think he meant it then, in those five minutes. Does he mean it now? God knows.'

'So, what're you going to do?'

Mia shrugged. 'He's probably panicking now. Thinking what the hell did I say that for.'

'You don't know that.'

The coffee machine hissed and spluttered. Three men in orange overalls came into the coffee shop.

Mia sighed again. 'I just don't know. Anyway, enough of Andy. You told me you had exciting news.'

'Oh yeah. I've got to write topical jokes for some production company that my agent says is the next big thing. They're putting together a topical news show.'

'That doesn't sound like your thing.'

'I know but… Now, be honest,' he said, reading out some of the lines he'd worked on the previous night.

'They're good.' Mia said.

'I've already sent them, so we'll see. Right, back to your problem. Why don't you tell Andy you'll give him an answer once he's given you a proper proposal? That way you give him a chance to back out, or see if he means it.'

'Oh, I don't know,' Mia said.

Vic's phone rang. 'It's my agent,' Vic said. 'I need to take it,' he added, as he made his way towards the exit

'Hi, Victor,'

'Hi, Marie.'

'You'll never guess what—TERA want to see you.'

'Don't sound so surprised.'

'Not surprised, Victor, excited. This could be big.'

'Do you feel it in your vodka?'

'Very amusing. Anyway, they want you to come in on Monday, 2 p.m. Can you make it?'

'Where?'

'Basingstoke.'

'Basingstoke?'

'It's in Hampshire.'

'Oh, the glamour. Let me see if Kylie can take Elis. I'll call you back.'

The road to Basingstoke. It had a ring to it. Was this the step up he'd been dreaming of? All those shitty gigs in shitty places, the late nights in service stations, driving home, or lonely nights in Holiday Inns in Huddersfield—were they about to pay off?

'Calm down,' he said to himself. It could go horribly wrong. 'Don't get your hopes up.' But they'd liked his stuff, they wanted to see him. He was in with a chance. He saw a magpie. Just one. One for sorrow. He frantically looked around for the second one. He couldn't see only one on today of all days. There it was, up in the branches; two for joy. He got Mia on the hands free.

'Hey, Mia, Happy Birthday.'

'Cheers.'

'Doing anything special?'

'Stan's taking me out for a meal, probably a Chinese.'

'Cool, want anything from Basingstoke?'

'A stick of rock please. Good luck. I'll keep my fingers crossed.'

As he pulled up outside Unit 17 on an anonymous industrial

estate, Vic wondered if Hollywood was as disappointing. He sat in the reception, half looking at the file of material he'd brought with him, half taking in the photos of famous faces dotted around the room.

One of the doors opened and an impossibly tall man ushered two well-known comics out. Vic gave them a quick wave. Both nodded back. They'd been beamed up into the limelight just as Vic was starting on the circuit. Was that what he was up against? If so, he may as well get back in his car and drive back home now.

'Vic?' the tall man said.

'Yes.'

'We'll be with you in a few minutes, okay?'

Vic nodded, tapping his feet to an imaginary tune. He closed his eyes, tried to slow his breathing; he could hear the two comics laughing and joking outside, he could smell their cigarette smoke. He glanced towards the exit and wonder if he should simply leave; save himself the humiliation. No, too late. The door opened and the tall man came back into the reception, smiling.

Vic noticed a small urine stain on the man's trousers and immediately felt a little better.

'I'm Rick,' the tall man said as he shook Vic's hand; Rick's hand was slightly damp. 'Come on in.'

He led Vic into a small conference room. There was a massive screen attached to the wall and, sitting at a desk, a serious-faced woman looking through a pile of papers.

Rick nodded towards the woman. 'This is Tammi.'

'Pleased to meet you.' Vic said.

Tammi looked up and nodded.

Rick signalled that Vic should sit down.

'We loved your stuff,' said Tammi.

'Yes,' Rick agreed. 'Absolutely, exactly what we're looking for. The perfect tone and voice for the show.'

'Right,' Vic said. He sat up straighter.

'Right,' Tammi said, smiling for the first time. 'Very funny.'

She looked back down at the papers. 'We're so glad we found you. Very good craft. Tight writing, edgy. But the thing is…'

Vic slumped back in his chair.

'You as a person, well, you're not really going to appeal to our target audience. We're looking for someone young, dynamic, edgy, and, well, to be frank, you simply don't fit that mould.'

Have I driven here to be told I'm past it? Vic thought.

'Also,' Rick said, 'we're looking for more women, people from the minorities, you know, less blokey types.'

Apart from the two blokey blokes smoking outside, Vic thought. 'Yes, I see,' he said.

'We've got Jessie Hulme lined up. Do you know her? She's very good.'

Vic nodded. 'Yes, I've seen her live act.'

'So, we're looking at you as more of a writer on the show, rather than the onscreen talent,' Tammi said. 'The power behind the scenes, as it were.'

'Right,' Vic said.

'We'll tell you more about the format,' said Rick, as he made his way towards a whiteboard.

The meeting lasted another twenty minutes. When Tammi led him out to the car park and shook his hand, Vic noticed the two jokers still laughing outside. They nodded again as he went past. Tammi joined them and lit her own cigarette.

It was a grey day in Basingstoke. Vic's windscreen wipers thumped a depressing tune. For a moment, he'd let himself believe. He'd dreamed of sitting on that panel, cracking his own jokes, making his own name. He'd imagined being recognised in the street, signing autographs for fans. He'd allowed himself a dream and it'd been shattered before he'd even woken up.

His phone rang. He hit the hands-free button.

'Hi, Marie.'

'Well done, Victor. Look at you, TV star in the making.'

'Hardly,' Vic said.

'They want you, Victor. They loved you.'

'Ha, they've just spent thirty minutes telling me I'm too old.'

'They just spent ten minutes telling me they love your material and loved you.'

Vic indicated and overtook a lorry.

'Look, Victor, I hate to say this but you're not going to be the next big thing. You're fantastically talented, when you put your mind to it, but the new talent they want are twenty-somethings, not forty-somethings, unless you've got tits, you're gay or black. You know how it is, Victor.'

Great, another person telling him me I'm past it, Vic thought.

'But this is like the second prize, and it's a glittering one. 'Writer on a hit TV show' gets you up the bill in the clubs. Remember the stripper gigs? With 'writer on hit TV show' on your CV, you can wave those goodbye and say hello to corporate.'

'Same bloody audience, just in suits.'

'Double the money, Victor. And think about it, talent only appears on three, four or, possibly, five, shows in a run. Writers are needed for all of it.'

The windscreen wipers swooshed.

'And, once you've got your foot in the door, other doors will open. I've just sent you an email with their offer. Pull over, have a look at it and then call me back, okay? And Victor, cheer up. It's great news.'

Vic indicated and pulled into the services. The rain was heavier and he sat listening to it on the car roof. When it eased, he walked through the puddles to the main building. Sitting down with a coffee, he toyed with his phone. The email was in there. The offer. The offer that told him he was too old and ugly for TV. He tapped his fingers on the table, poured too much sugar into his coffee, took a swig, and opened the email. He stared at the screen. He read the email again. The coffee mug shook as he took a sip.

'Bloody hell.' He sat back. 'It looks like I'm going to be a writer,' he said.

'Happy Birthday,' Stan said and held out a bunch of flowers.

Mia took the them and kissed him on the cheek.

'You look amazing,' he said.

'Don't sound so surprised. Where are you taking me?'

'It's a surprise. Come on, the taxi's waiting.'

'Don't tell me, the new McDonald's?'

'Give me some credit,' Stan said.

Mia glanced out the window as the taxi weaved a familiar path through the rain. She bit at the skin around her little fingernail. They pulled up in a deserted street.

Act surprised, Mia thought. 'Stan, I can't walk far in these,' she said.

'It's okay, we're here.'

'Here? Stop messing about.'

Stan rang the doorbell. Mia recognised the *maître d'*. She gave him what she hoped was a pleading smile.

'May I take your coat, madam?' he said and, as she handed it to him, he winked.

Oh god, he probably thinks I'm an escort.

Same table, same band, same waiter.

Stan looked at the menu. 'I guess they don't do Carling,' he said with a smile.

'It looks amazing. How did you find this place?'

'I read about it in the local paper, thought it'd be perfect for your birthday.'

'Thanks,' Mia said. 'It is.'

The waiter looked at Mia but didn't say anything.

'Do you have anything with gin and pomegranate?' Mia asked.

'I'll see what I can do,' replied the waiter with a wry smile.

They were on their third cocktail when Stan looked at her. 'Happy Birthday, beautiful,' he said and raised his glass. 'You know, I've been thinking. I don't always show it, but you make me so happy.'

Mia held her breath. He wasn't going to, was he?

'Would you like to move in with me?'

Mia let out her breath.

'Wow,' she said. 'Um, I don't know. Can I think about it?'

'Take all the time you need,' Stan said. 'Now, shall we get out of here? I'm starving. Curry or Chinese?'

'Either,' she said. 'Just give me a minute. I need the loo.'

Once again, leaning against the cool tiled wall of the Ladies, Mia called Vic's number. 'Fuck, Vic, answer the phone.'

'Yo.'

'Vic, you're not going to believe this.'

'Are you in a toilet again?'

'Not any toilet, the *same* toilet.'

'What? I hope you're not...'

'No, I'm here with Stan and—'

'Stan took you to the same place? Did people recognise you?'

'Yes, of course they bloody did, and... Vic, stop laughing.'

'They probably think you're an upper-class escort.'

'Oh, very amusing.'

'It's just priceless,' said Vic. 'Don't tell me—he asked you to marry him?'

'He asked me to move in with him. Vic stop, I didn't phone you to be laughed at.'

'What are you going to do?'

'I don't know. What a mess.'

'Happy Birthday.'

'Fuck off.'

Because he'd subjected Elis to an extra night at Kylie's, Vic was preparing one of his son's favourite meals. Bacon, egg and chips—the dinner of champions. Okay, there'd be no bacon for veggie boy, but vegetarian bacon wasn't too bad.

'Poached or fried, Elis?'

'Fried please and, Dad...'

'What?'

'Could I have some of your bacon?'

'You can't eat bacon, you're a vegetarian.'

'I know, but I think I've become a non-practicing veggie.'

'That's a cop-out.'

'It's just... well, I like bacon and sausages and McDonald's.'

Veggie sausages are horrible.'

'Does your mum and Nat know?'

Elis looked down at the floor and shook his head. 'I thought it could be our secret.'

'Are you sure? Once you've eaten something, you can't uneat it.'

'I can poo it out,' he giggled.

'You can but your brain and body will know. Look, think about it while I cook the eggs. I want you to be sure.'

Vic returned his attention to the stove and did an imaginary ner-ner, ner-nerner to Nat. Childish? Yes. Satisfying? Completely. He wasn't a meat eating evangelist. In fact, the more he'd thought about it, the more he respected Elis's decision, but this felt like a mini victory.

He slid an egg onto Elis's plate. 'So?'

Elis nodded.

'Okay, but only a little bit. It's been a few weeks since you last had any meat, so you need to start slowly.'

Elis tackled the bacon with enthusiasm.

'And I know you said you wanted to keep it secret but we have to tell your mother.'

'No, Dad. Why?'

'Well, one, if you get ill, she needs to know what you've been putting in your tummy. And two, she'll bloody kill me if she finds out I've been secretly feeding you meat.'

Elis stared at the floor. 'Can... can you tell them?' Elis's bottom lip quivered.

'It's okay, Elis, it's no big deal. I'll call your mum later. I'll tell them we've decided to buy only ethically sourced meat.'

'What's that?'

'It's where farmers are nice to their animals and you don't get conditions like in that film.'

'Thanks, Dad. Oh and, Dad, can I have a bit more bacon, please? I've been eating meat in school for three weeks, now.'

'What?'

'I've been swapping my cheese sandwiches for ham ones.'

'You scoundrel.'

*

Vic and Elis did the washing-up together and, while Elis went to get his homework, Vic picked up his phone. He took a deep breath and rehearsed his lines.

'Hi, Vic, what's up? Elis okay?'

'Yeah, he's fine. It's just, um, at dinner time he asked for bacon.'

'You didn't give him any, did you?'

'I did; he'd made his own mind up. That, as I recall, is one of our principles.'

'And you accuse me of brain washing.'

Vic massaged his forehead. 'Kylie, I didn't brainwash him.'

'Yeah, right.'

'I just thought I should tell you. Do you want to speak to him?'

'Yes.'

'Elis, it's your mum.' Elis looked worried. 'It's okay, I've told her,' Vic mouthed.

Vic handed the phone to his son.

'No, Mum, I asked for it... I've been eating it in school anyway... Dad said I should tell you in case I'm poorly.'

Vic signalled to Elis to give him the phone back.

'See? I'm not a meat eating monster.'

'Okay, I'm sorry. But what the hell were you doing eating bacon in front of him?'

'I'm not going to change my lifestyle and become a vegetarian because your girlfriend wants my son to be one. And how about a 'thanks Vic' for being a responsible parent, for making sure he's made the right decision, for—'

'Shut up, Vic.'

'Kylie, I need to ask you something.'

'What?' snapped Kylie.

Vic took another deep breath and blurted. 'Is everything okay between Elis and Nat?'

Vic could hear the theme tune to *The Archers* in the background.

'Of course it is, why?'

'It's just Elis sounded scared of her, that's all.'

'Don't be ridiculous, he's not scared of her. He just knows how much his decision to become a vegetarian meant to her. She was so proud of her boy.'

'Her boy?'

'You know what I mean.'

'Right. Can you make sure she's come to terms with it *before* you collect Elis on Thursday? I don't want him scared again and, remember, he's not *her boy*, so it has nothing to do with her.'

'Yes,' Kylie sighed. 'I'll think of a way to tell her.'

Dust danced on the sunbeams streaming through the pub windows. Ash walked in and put his umbrella down just as Vic was about to order.

'Is it raining?' Vic asked.

'No, I'm using the brolly against the heat,' Ash said, shaking the umbrella.

'Pint or a softy?'

'What the hell, it's Friday. A cheeky lunchtime pint won't do any harm.'

'Two Guinness then, please, Rosie,' Vic said.

'Working tonight?' Ash asked.

Vic nodded. 'Two gigs, then one tomorrow.'

'And how's the writing going?'

'It's tough but, yeah, it's good. How are you?'

'Same old. It's Ash's taxi service again this weekend.'

Vic smiled.

'Have you thought anymore about meeting up with Kylie to have a tête-à-tête?'

'It never seems to be the right time. I was just about to and then this whole vegetarian thing blew up,' said Vic as he watched Rosie top up their pints.

'Here you are, boys.'

'Thanks, Rosie,' said Vic.

'What veggie thing?' asked Ash, taking a swig of beer and wiping his lips.

'Oh, Elis became a vegetarian for a while. Nat showed him some horror vid.'

'Probably the one doing the rounds at Molly's school. Not fit for a ten year old, though.'

'That's what I said. Anyway, I don't think now's the right time for a serious discussion.'

'That, my friend, is where you're wrong. This is the perfect time. Strike while the iron is at its coldest. You said you've got a ninety percent chance of winning the court case, right?

'That's what the guy Chris put me in touch with said.'

'Right, so her lawyer must be advising her she's only got a twenty to thirty percent chance of winning. So, call her, sort it out directly with her. You help her save face *and* you look like the good guy.'

Vic took a mouthful of beer. 'Maybe.'

'Vic, do it.' Ash looked at his watch. 'I'd better get back to work.'

They said their goodbyes and Vic ordered another pint. Ash was right, he should just do it. But he needed an angle, something foolproof. What would evoke a memory, in Kylie, that would break through the force field she'd activated? He thought about the two of them, reliving memories stored in the dusty corners of his mind. Vic smiled, he had it.

'Penny for them?'

Vic opened his eyes and saw Rosie standing there.

'What?'

'You're thinking happy thoughts.'

'Good shot, Rosie, good shot.' Rosie went away shaking her head and Vic texted Kylie. It had to be worth the price of a soy milk latte.

Mia had spent the whole week thinking about Andy and Stan. She could almost feel her hair turning grey. She lay back in the bath. Did she want to move in with Stan? Stan the man who always left the toilet seat up, and the kitchen cupboards open;

the man who he hardly spent enough time in the shower to get wet, let alone wash his parts or give her time to text Andy. The man who left the bathroom as soon as he got out of the shower, leaving sopping footprints across the carpet, and left mugs and plates anywhere and everywhere. He was well-behaved at her place but, if they moved in together, how long until he started treating the place like his sty? She'd always claimed she hadn't moved in with Stan because of Sid but, deep down, she knew that was just a nice, convenient excuse. She'd been there, seen it and done it with Sid's dad. She needed her independence.

But then Mia thought about Stan's hugs. How he made her feel safe. The way he'd cook for her and make her laugh so naturally. Why had he thrown a spanner in the works? What would happen if she said no? Would they have to split up? Would they be able to go back to where they were and pretend it had never happened?

And Andy? What was he up to? Loveable rogue. If she were married to him, at least she'd know where he was most of the time. But she couldn't keep him on a lead. He'd have to go for walkies sometimes. She'd be checking his phone, his pockets, his search history. It would give her a nervous breakdown every time he said he was going out with his 'friends'. Was there a switch to turn off her suspicions? And was his spur of the moment proposal serious? She hadn't seen him for weeks and then— boom! If she said yes, would he find excuses to keep putting the marriage off? If she said no, then what? Back to the status quo, or end of relationship? She'd done okay without him for the last few weeks. Then there was Sid. He knew Stan, they got along okay. But how would he react if his mother declared she was binning her long-term partner to marry a complete stranger?

She took a mouthful of wine and looked at her phone. It was time to ask the great relationship guru himself. She texted Vic.

The coffee shop was full of weekend shoppers, each one looking stressed.

'How was the gig last night?' Mia asked, as they looked for a table.

'Gigs, I had two. They were good.' Vic pointed to a family getting up to go and they made their move.

'Moving up in the world?'

'Kinda,' Vic said as he settled into his seat. 'And you? Have you made a decision?'

Mia slumped onto a chair and groaned. 'I've no idea, Vic. What do you think I should do?'

Vic took a mouthful of coffee and scratched his chin. 'Do you want me to be honest?'

Mia nodded.

'And you won't be upset with me if I am?'

Mia shook her head.

'If you move in with Stan, he'll drive you mad. You'll either split up after three months or you'll murder him.'

'Will you come and visit me in prison?'

'I'll bring a file in a cake.'

'He could change.'

'He could but he won't.'

'So, I should marry Andy?'

'I'm not saying that. The problem is, I just don't believe him, Mia. He's painting this picture of an utopian existence but can he deliver?'

'He might.'

'He won't, Mia. It will always be tomorrow, next month, next year. I'm afraid Andy's future never comes.'

'You just don't like him.'

'There is that but I told you I was going to be honest and I am trying to be objective. For me, he's—what did you call it, 'future faking'?'

Mia nodded.

'He's trying to trap you in a make-believe world and, by the time you realise, one hundred years will have passed and you'll be dust.'

'So, you're saying I should turn them both down, yes?'

Vic nodded.

'But then both relationships will finish.'

'Not necessarily.'

'That's how it happens in the movies.'

'This ain't the movies, Mia. But say that does happen, would it really be so bad?'

'Yes, Vic. I don't want to end up alone.'

'You won't, there's plenty of—'

'Don't you dare say 'more fish in the sea'.'

'I was going to say, 'there's plenty of time'.'

Mia stared out of the window. 'How about you? Anything on the horizon?'

'No, not even looking.'

'What happened to kid in the sweet shop?'

'I think he got diabetes. Or perhaps he just grew up.'

Walking down the high street, Mia felt better. She still didn't know what to do but talking about it had helped. All Vic had done was confirm what she already knew. It didn't make the decision easier but at least... at least what?

As she browsed the aisles in Next, Vic's words swam in her brain. *Would it be so bad?* she wondered. Start again. Find someone new who made her knees go weak and her head spin. Someone who, when they uttered the romantic line, 'will you move in with me?', made her scream, 'Yes, yes', and made her stomach feel like she'd gone down a hill too quickly. Would that be so bad?

But was there any such thing as a clean slate, or just a dusty, chalky one you could barely write on? Should she settle for what she had? Settle? What a horrible word. Did she want to settle? When she was a teenager and she'd daydreamed about her future, she'd never thought of the words, 'I do... I suppose'.

Why on earth would anyone think this would be a good idea?

Kylie sat opposite him, staring out of the window, her arms crossed across her chest. Vic took a deep breath.

'Do you remember what you said to me the moment Elis was

conceived?'

'What's this about?'

'Just bear with me a minute,' Vic said. 'Do you remember?'

Kylie stared at her feet and mumbled. 'I said, good shot.'

'That's right. Good shot. Even before we knew we'd made a little human. That was one of the happiest nights of my life. Singing karaoke at home, like we were in front of ten thousand people, laughing at my attempts to bake you a birthday cake, making lo—'

'Okay, I remember.' She picked up the menu.

'It's one of my happiest memories but, every time I think about you these days, my brow furrows and I feel my body tense. That's not good for you, me, or Elis, is it, Kyles?' Vic hadn't used that nickname for ages.

Kylie stopped looking at the menu. 'Do you remember when I threw up in your mum's garden?'

'Ah, the famous Diamond White night.'

'That stuff was lethal. I've never drunk it since.'

'Nor me.'

They stared at each other across the table.

'Don't you want those memories to be happy memories, without hating the other person in them?'

Kylie gave a quick nod.

'That's why I asked you here. To get together and talk and see if we can sort this out, without lawyers and without the animosity that seems to be part of our conversations these days. I accept that we're no longer husband and wife, and that we might never be friends, but we can at least try to be friendly.'

'It would help if you weren't so unreasonable all the time.'

Vic's jaw clenched. 'I'm not...' He took a deep breath. 'Be fair, I've given on a few things. I've agreed to let Nat pick him up from mine and from school. I agreed to you guys going on holiday. I love the school you chose.'

'I know but...'

'I just think it should be me and you who make the big decisions.

'But Nat's such a big part of his life.'

'For now, but who's to say you two will be together five years from now?'

'We will.'

'I hope you are but you never know and what if, god forbid, something happens to you? I think I should have sole responsibility. Is that really unreasonable?'

Kylie set the sugar pot straight on the table and played with the stem of her glass. 'You're right,' she said. She adjusted the sugar pot again and looked up. 'You're right,' she repeated. 'Nat pushed too hard on this. It's just that she loves Elis and wants to feel like she's part of the family, a legal part, not simply my partner.'

'I understand,' Vic said. 'And I'm happy with her playing a role, she's a good influence on Elis. But...'

'I know.'

Both of them looked out of the window and stared at the cars waiting at the traffic lights.

'So, what now?' Vic asked.

Kylie was tearing a napkin to pieces. She brushed up the debris and, realising she had no place to put it, placed it in a neat pile next to her orange juice. 'I'll talk to Nat. It won't be easy.'

'Thanks. And, Kyles, we should do this once a month—just a coffee and a chat about Elis. It's got to be better than frosty texts and sulky phone calls.'

Kylie sighed. 'I suppose. Oh, I don't know, Vic. Let me talk to Nat first.'

July 2017

Mia had a mouthful of coffee and took a deep breath. A smell of burning cheese wafted across the cafe.

'What a summer,' Vic said.

Mia watched the rain fall for a second before turning to face Vic. She took another deep breath.

'I've been offered a new job,' she said.

'Brilliant.' Vic took a bite of his brownie. 'What is it?'

'Head of department.'

'Wow, well done. I didn't know you were looking.'

'I wasn't but my friend, Cathy, told me to apply for a vacancy at her school. I did and I got it.'

'Cathy? She works in Bath, doesn't she?'

Mia nodded.

'So, you're moving to Bath?'

'I haven't accepted it yet.'

'When do you need to decide by?'

'Before the end of term, so just a few days, really.'

'I see.'

They both watched a woman struggle with her brolly in the wind

'She'll never win that battle,' said Vic.

'No, waste of time.'

'It's a nice city, Bath.'

Mia nodded. 'Expensive, though.'

'True… What about Sid?'

'He'd come with me. Do his A-levels at the same school. He's cool about it.'

'And Stan and Andy?'

'They'd stay here. That's what makes it so appealing.' Mia drained her coffee. 'I mean, professionally it's a step up, a challenge, but I am ready for it. Then, personally, it's a clean slate, isn't it? Like you said, how bad can it be?'

'You'd get rid of them both?'

Mia nodded. 'New start.'

'So do it.'

'You know what's stopping me?'

'No'

'It's you.'

'Me?'

'Yes. This—coffees, chats. Wouldn't you miss me?'

'Of course I would but we'd survive. We could have Skype coffees and chats. When does the job start?'

'September but I'd need to get up there before that, you know, to find a place to live and…'

'Busy summer, then?'

'Very.'

'Do it! It's exactly what you need. You'll be so busy in that new job, you'll forget about all of us back here and hey, Bath is on the way to Basingstoke, so you won't get rid of me.'

Mia reached for her phone did something on it and smiled.

'There, done.'

'What?'

'One resignation letter sent, one acceptance letter sent.'

'That was quick.'

'I wrote them five days ago.'

'Wow, congratulations, Ms Head of Department.'

The rain was belting down outside and Vic and Elis were cwtched up on the sofa watching *The Lego Batman* movie. In Vic's mind, this is what summer holidays should be like. Hot chocolate, wet rain and daft movies. He'd just had a text from Ash saying he was on the holiday from hell. Two days into a two-week driving tour around the Lake District, with a fifteen-year-old, a ten-year-old, his wife and her mother. Vic hadn't had the heart to remind him it had been Ash's idea. Tomorrow, Kylie and Nat were taking Elis off to Gran Canaria for a week, and then to Kylie's parents for a week. For Vic, two weeks to himself; time to write, time to relax, time to visit Mia in

Bath. Perfect.

'Dad?'

'Yes, Elis?'

'Remember last year, you suggested the science museum for my birthday?'

'Yes. We never did get there.'

'Can we go this year?'

'I don't see why not. I'll need to check with your mother. She might have plans.'

'If she has, can we go another time?'

'Of course. Let's see what she says, shall we? I'll call her now.' He paused the film and scrolled through his recent calls to find Kylie's number.

'Hiya, Vic, how are you?'

'Hi, Kyles, I'm good. Just wondering, have you made any plans for Elis's birthday?'

'No, I was going to ask you about that.'

'Well, he's just asked me if he can have his birthday treat at the science museum.'

'Sounds like a great idea. Want to sort it out?'

'Sure, when would be good for you?'

'Sunday the thirteenth?'

'Brilliant,' Vic said. 'I'll book it while you're away.'

'Okay. I'll send the invites out when I get back, if you like.'

'Or I can do it if you send me a list of addresses.'

'Thanks, Vic.'

'No problem.'

Vic put the phone down. 'Thanks Ash,' he said under his breath.

'All systems go, Elis.' He pressed the Play button and Lego Batman sprang back into action.

August 2017

Vic parked the car in a leafy street. He stretched on the pavement and loosened his damp shirt stuck to his back. He checked the number of the house and rang the doorbell. As he waited, a cat jumped down from the garden wall and purred at his legs.

'Vic,' exclaimed Mia as she hugged him. 'Come on in.'

The cat was already one step ahead.

'Yours?' Vic said.

'Mrs Roberts's.'

Mia knocked the downstairs door and Vic caught a glimpse of a handsome woman letting her cat in. He followed Mia up the stairs.

'So, this is it,' said Mia, pointing at each door in turn: toilet, bathroom, bedroom, bedroom, living room, kitchen. 'Have a nosey. I'll put the kettle on.'

Mia's stuff was strewn around the place. The flat was okay but the furniture was grey and shabby, there were no pictures on the walls and, despite the warm summer's day, it was chilly. *She's only been in a few days*, Vic reminded himself. *She'll make it feel like home.*

'Lovely,' said Vic, as he entered the kitchen. 'Neighbours okay?'

'Mrs Roberts, downstairs—friendly, fifty-something, a real gossip. Nice couple next door.' Mia pointed left— 'And empty that side.' She put the coffees on the table.

'Perfect.' Vic took a sip of his coffee.

'It's small but it'll do until I've found my feet.'

'And your place?'

'Renting it out. One of my colleagues pounced as soon as she found out I was leaving.'

'Not Andy?'

'No, not Andy.' Mia reached up to a cupboard, retrieved a packet of biscuits and arranged them on a plate.

'A plate, there's posh.' Vic said. 'You've changed since you've moved to Bath.'

'Shut up, Vic.' Mia gave a weak smile.

'Much around here?'

'The location's great. I've got shops just down the road, including an offie and a pub, and the school's a ten-minute walk.'

'It's so quiet,' Vic said.

'I know. At night I can hear myself think.'

'From your tone, I'm guessing that's not good.'

'It's tough, Vic. I'm trying to go cold turkey but there's temptation everywhere. I do things and think, 'Andy would enjoy that', or 'I must tell Stan'. There feels like there's a huge gap in my life.'

'It'll get easier, I promise.'

'How long's it been for you now?'

'Must be three months and look, I'm still alive.'

'So, there's hope for me. How's Basingstoke?'

'Going pretty well. An excellent writing team. It's amazing to see how other people can take your idea and run with it. And, even more amazing, to see how the on-screen talent can make those ideas appear like their own spontaneous words.'

'I would have thought they'd want to use their own material,' Mia said, popping some biscuit in her mouth.

'They do, sometimes, but most of the stuff that makes the edit is the scripted stuff. Jessie Hulme is brilliant She brings ideas to the table. The rest of them, not so much.'

'That's a pity.'

'I guess it's hard work, coming up with new stuff every week, plus they know they'll be fed lines by us that'll make them look good.

'True.'

'Anyway, if they were all like Jessie, I'd be out of a job. I'll take you to a recording, when I'm more established.'

'That'd be great Vic. That's the second time you've mentioned this Jessie woman. Any news?'

'No, nothing doing. She's lovely but so different from me. We'd never be compatible.'

'When has that ever stopped you?'

Vic shrugged.

'What's happened? What have you done with the real Vic?'

'Getting older, wiser maybe.'

'Vic, what if we never meet someone compatible?'

'We will, Mia. It'll happen, don't worry. Hey, are you coming to Elis's party on Sunday?'

'I can't. Sid's coming here for the first time.'

'He'll love it.'

'I hope so.'

As Vic drove home, he couldn't help but worry. The place hadn't looked like a home and Mia had looked gaunt. He hoped she was eating properly and not drinking too much. Had this been his fault? His stupid advice—How bad could it be? he'd said. Well, as far as he could tell, it had looked awful.

'It's so cool here,' Kylie said, watching the kids as they tried out various activities.

'Right up Elis's street,' Nat said.

'Why didn't we think of this place before?' Kylie added.

Vic smiled to himself. They didn't need to know.

'Mum, come and look at this.'

Kylie glanced at Nat.

'Go on,' Nat said. 'We won't kill each other.'

Nat and Vic stood in silence, watching Elis show his mother how some great feat of science worked.

'It's like magic,' they heard him say.

'Is that a Blues top?' Vic pointed to the Nat's collar jutting up from under her jumper.

'Sure is.'

'You a fan?'

'Too right I am. Cut me, and I bleed disappointment.'

'What do you think of our chances this year?'

'Not a hope in the world.'

'Need investment, don't we?' Vic nodded. 'Shame Elis is a

footie nut, not a rugby fan.'

'I know, there's only so much pretending I can do. I mean, what *is* the point of football?

'I've no idea,' said Vic, laughing.

'What are you two laughing at?' Kylie said.

'Rugby,' they said together.

September 2017

'Elis. You can't go looking like that.'

'Dad, stop fussing.'

'Just stand still so I can do this properly for you,' said Vic as he fumbled with Elis's tie. 'This is hopeless.'

Vic removed his son's tie, put it round his own neck, tied the knot and put it back on his son. 'There, perfect. Tonight, I'll teach you how to do it. Now, let me take a photo for your mum.'

'I thought she was coming over.'

'She is but you might mess yourself up before she gets here.'

Elis pulled a silly face and Vic took the photo.

'Don't you dare put that on Facebook,' Elis said.

'Yes, boss.'

The doorbell rang.

'Go and let your mother in.'

Vic smiled as he heard Kylie in the hallway. 'Oh my, look at my little boy.'

'He looks good in uniform,' Vic said, handing Kylie a tissue. He smiled and put his hand on her shoulder.

'Come on, Elis, stand with your mum, so I can take a photo.'

'It's just a day in school,' Elis said.

Vic snapped one and then another.

'He's almost as tall as you, now.'

'Here, let me take one of you two.' Kylie reached for the phone.

Vic stood behind his son.

'Two handsome men,' Kylie said.

The doorbell rang again.

'Dylan,' Elis said, relief in his voice.

'Have a good day and don't forget to phone me tonight,' said Kylie, giving her son a kiss.

Elis groaned and immediately wiped the kiss off his face with his sleeve.'

Vic straightened Elis's tie one last time. 'Have a good day.'

The door slammed. 'All grown up,' Vic said.

'All grown up,' Kylie agreed. She put her head on Vic's shoulder.

'Coffee?'

Kylie looked at her watch. 'Quick one.'

Vic poured two cups from the cafetiere.

'How's the writing going?'

'Great. We've nearly finished season one but they've got me working on another project. The drive to Basingstoke once a week is a bind but I can do most of it right here.'

'I knew you'd make it.'

'Where's Nat?'

'Fuck, I was meant to send her photos. Quick, send me the ones you took.'

'So, where is she? Sent…'

'I told her not to come,' Kylie said, fiddling with her phone. 'This was our moment.'

'Thanks,' Vic said. 'How is she?'

'They're doing the procedure in the next few days.'

'Exciting. Fingers crossed.'

'Thanks,' said Kylie, draining her mug. 'Right, I'd better get to work.'

'Have a good day. I'll make sure he calls you when he gets home.'

'I'd appreciate that, thanks.'

Kylie smiled as she left.

Vic loved that smile.

Elis had settled into secondary school in no time at all. The first two weeks flew by. He became an expert at tying his tie and even learnt to tie it the cool way, so only the thin part of the tie was visible.

'What subjects have you got today, then?' Vic asked.

Elis was sitting at the kitchen table, pulling books out of his bag and replacing them with others.

Vic picked up a French exercise book and smiled. 'Francais?'

'*Non hier, ajourd hui*, um, double maths.'

'Yuck.'

'No, maths is great. I love it. And Mrs Williams is brilliant. She asks me all the tough questions.'

'That's because she knows you'll get them right.'

'I know.'

'Don't forget, I'm going to work today and I'm calling in on Mia on my way back.'

'You've told me, like eight times already, Dad.'

'Right, so, I'll pick you up from your mum's around eight. Make sure you do your homework with Nat.

'I always do my homework.' Elis checked the timetable on his phone. 'Urgh. We've also got double drama.'

'Now that's more like it. I used to love drama.'

'It's so lame. The thick kids love drama.'

'That's me told.'

'Oh, Dad, look.' Elis held out a letter addressed to the parents or guardians.

'What this?'

'A letter.'

'Thank you, Einstein,' said Vic as he opened the envelope. 'Parents' evening? Already? You only started two weeks ago. What do they have to say?'

Elis shrugged.

The doorbell rang and Elis let himself out.

Vic tidied up the books left strewn around the place, grabbed his car keys, and set off for Basingstoke.

As soon as he was on the motorway Vic asked Siri to phone Kylie.

'Hiya, Kyles,'

'Hiya, how are you?'

'I'm good. Nat okay?'

'She's glowing.'

'Congratulations again. Listen, Elis has just given me a letter saying there's a parents' evening tomorrow. Well, more a parents' afternoon; three till five.'

'Crap, I can't make it. Why don't they give us more notice?'

'Well, I've got a suspicion Elis has had the letter in his bag a while,' said Vic as he manoeuvred around a lorry. 'Why they need a chat after only two weeks is beyond me. If you can't make it, does Nat want to come?'

'She's got a doctor's appointment, I think.'

'Okay, well, let me know if anything changes. I'll call you to let you know what they say. See you later.'

As soon as Vic rang the doorbell, the cat jumped down from the windowsill and weaved between his legs, purring. 'You again,' he said.

Mia opened the door and Vic was relieved to see she had a little colour in her cheeks. She led him upstairs and put the kettle on.

'Wow, you've really got this place looking good,' said Vic as he walked around the apartment. 'It really feels like a home, now.'

'How was your day?' Mia asked, handing Vic a coffee.

'Yeah, good. I had a meeting with the top two, today. They've offered me two new shows.'

'That's amazing. Any chance of screen time?'

'Do you know what? I don't think I want it anymore. I've watched the onscreen talent. It's such a fuss; the make-up, wardrobe, the nerves, the competitiveness. I'm more than happy in the writer's room, banking a regular pay cheque. And I'm getting new gigs, too. My agent was right. 'TV writer' looks good on my CV.'

'You deserve it.'

'Oh and my agent bought the rights of Vicbead.org from the crazy woman. So now I have a proper website.'

'Congratulations,' said Mia, holding her mug up and clinking it against Vic's.

'Only downside is that—you know that floppy-haired comic that everyone raves about?'

Mia nodded.

'Well, he's using my material in his new stand-up show.'

'Bastard. Can you sue?'

'My agent said she'll have a word but, apparently, it happens a lot. There's no way to prove it's mine.'

'That's not fair.'

'I'll survive. Hey, those are nice—did you put them up?' asked Vic, pointing to three pictures of Sid mounted on the wall above the television; one when he was a baby, one when he was eight, and one when he was a teenager.

'Well, sort of. Joe helped me.'

'Joe? Who's Joe?'

'A guy I met in a café by my school. We got chatting.'

'And he came to your flat to help you hang pictures?'

'Yes.'

'Does he help with anything else?'

'Not yet.'

'How are your knees?'

'My knees?'

'Any weakness?'

'Just a little.'

'Congratulations, Mia, you nearly lasted one whole month.'

'Do I get a medal?'

Vic looked at his watch. 'I better go, I've got to pick up Elis tonight. Nat has a hospital appointment early tomorrow.'

'Oh, right, is it…?'

'Not my place to say but the signs are good.'

This time, Vic drove home with a whistle on his lips. Mia had done what Mia did. She was going to be just fine.

Vic looked around the school hall. There were smart kids in uniforms showing lost-looking parents to various classrooms. Vic had to go to room 17, Maths, room 12, English, and room 9, form-teacher. He decided to start with Ms Williams, Elis's favourite.

A young girl came up to him. 'Which room are you looking for?'

'Room 17.'

'Ah, maths,' the girl said and led the way. 'There's someone in there. Just wait here and go in when they come out.'

'Thanks.'

He stood outside the classroom feeling like a naughty school boy. The door opened. Vic nodded to the parents as they left the room and headed in, but he stopped in the doorway as he caught sight of the maths teacher. Now he understood why Elis liked Mrs Williams so much.

'Cariad,' he said.

'Hi, Vic, what are you doing here?'

'I was just about to ask you the same thing.'

'Well, I teach here.'

'My son's in your class. Elis Bead.'

'Of course, you're Elis's dad. Bead. I should have put two and two together.'

'You're the maths teacher.'

'And you're a comedian.'

'So, what brings you here?'

'I did placement here and they offered me a job.'

'Wow, congratulations. Why didn't you tell me?'

'Probably because you never let me get a word in edgeways.'

Vic looked down. 'Sorry. So, how's Elis doing?'

'He's doing great, really settled in well. Bright as a button. Bit cheeky but I now know where he gets that from.'

'And how are you doing?'

'So far, it's all good.'

'Elis seems to think you're the best teacher in the world.'

Cariad blushed. 'Well, that's very kind of him,' she said.

The English and the form teacher both spoke highly of Elis and so, by the time he picked Elis up from the after-school club, Vic was glowing with pride.

'How about a visit to the ice cream place?'

'Great.'

Vic gave Elis a ten-pound note. 'You order the ice creams and I'll text your mother.' His phone buzzed within seconds.

'Bloody hell, that was quick,' he said.

But it wasn't Kylie.

'So, why now?' Vic said, as he leant against the headboard.

'Why now what?'

'Or maybe, why not before?'

'Vic, what are you babbling on about?'

'I was just wondering why you changed your mind. You didn't want to know me before, left me on the roof of a multi-storey, and now, well…' Vic spread his arms.

'Things change, Mr Bead. Neither of us were ready back then,' Cariad said.

'Ready for what?'

'Ready for this. You were like a cat waiting for a feed. I was studying, working part-time, struggling with the divorce and the kids and I definitely didn't need a cat to take care of as well.'

'I see.'

'But, when I saw you're the other day, something was different. You looked ready.'

'Ready? How?'

'You looked happy.'

'And you thought you'd try to ruin that?'

Cariad thumped him, kissed him and then pulled him under the sheets for round two.

But with Caraid, Vic didn't mind.